Dear Reader:

I have one big fear that has haunted me my entire life: fire. I have always been wary of campfires, barbecues, and sparklers on the Fourth of July. Even fires in fireplaces make me nervous (I still have to take a deep breath before I turn on the gas fireplace at my parents' house, and that's controlled by a switch!). For some reason, despite all evidence to the contrary, I have this nagging fear that my house is going to catch on fire, so I am overly careful when I burn candles, I check to make sure I turned the oven off several times before I go to bed, and I keep a fire extinguisher nearby whenever I'm in the kitchen. I've even been known to come home from work midday just to make sure I unplugged my automatic shut-off iron. I understand that it's really irrational, but that's the thing about fear—you can't turn it off, even when you know it's silly.

This is why writing Sadie's latest mystery was so much fun for me. The opening scene of *Wildfire,* where the old Silver Peak school-house burns to the ground, is pretty much my worst nightmare. This made it kind of fun to have Sadie investigate the old fire, especially since, in this story, the answer has real, modern-day consequences. It was the kind of mystery where I could understand the motivation to find answers. As Sadie comes closer to finding out the solution, I felt (just slightly) less worried about my own fears. In any case, I hope the story is as much fun for you to read as it was for me to write!

Best wishes,
Elizabeth Adams
writing as Carole Jefferson

Mysteries of Silver Peak

A Mountain of Mystery
Nobody's Safe
Silver Surprise
Wildfire

MYSTERIES
of SILVER PEAK

Wildfire

CAROLE JEFFERSON

Guideposts
New York

Mysteries of Silver Peak is a trademark of Guideposts.

Published by Guideposts Books & Inspirational Media
110 William Street
New York, NY 10038
Guideposts.org

Acknowledgments

Every attempt has been made to credit the sources of copyrighted material used in this book. If any such acknowledgment has been inadvertently omitted or miscredited, receipt of such information would be appreciated.

Scripture quotations are taken from *The Holy Bible, New International Version*. Copyright © 1973, 1978, 1984, 2011 by Biblica, Inc. Used by permission of Zondervan. All rights reserved worldwide. www.zondervan.com

Cover and interior design by Müllerhaus
Cover art by Greg Copeland represented by Deborah Wolfe, Ltd.
Typeset by Aptara, Inc.

Printed and bound in the United States of America
10 9 8 7 6 5 4 3 2

Prologue

HE COULDN'T BELIEVE WHAT HE WAS SEEING. IT HAD STARTED with just a spark, just one little flame, and now, the whole place was engulfed. Flames licked at the side walls and charred the front doors. Tongues of fire raced up the bell tower, leaping high into the night sky. The roof was almost entirely lit up now. He heard a low rumbling, and then a deafening boom as something inside the schoolhouse exploded, sending flames shooting out of the blown-out windows.

The lights in one of the houses across the road flicked on, and he stepped back farther into the shadows. He should go, get far away from here before anyone saw him, but he couldn't quite pull away from the spectacle. He had never seen anything like it—the unbearable heat, coming off in waves; the ethereal glow the flames cast on the trees and the houses across the way; the sound, like a roaring lion, like a locomotive. The very air shimmered. It was horrible, and it was somehow strangely, shockingly beautiful.

From somewhere down the road, he heard sirens. He needed to get out of there. He moved off, stepping into the cover of the trees. It was just a short distance through the woods that bordered the old property. Just a few minutes, and then he'd be gone, with nothing to tie him to any of this. Still, he hesitated, casting one last look back at the burning schoolhouse, taking it all in. And then he turned and disappeared into the woods.

No one must ever find out what he'd done.

1

SADIE SPEERS TURNED UP HER COLLAR AGAINST THE COLD SPRING rain and closed the car door.

"Come on, Hank."

Her golden retriever, who had stopped to sniff a pinecone, bounded after her, racing toward the house. Sadie moved a bit slower, picking her way carefully across the soggy yard toward the front door. Her work boots were caked with mud from Milo Henderson's horse farm, and she tried to keep her balance as another gust of wind blew.

For April, it sure felt like winter. The forecasters had called for rain mixed with sleet tonight, and it looked like they were right about that. It had been sunny and in the high sixties over the weekend, but that was life in Colorado, she supposed. You never knew what the weather was going to do.

Hank was pawing at the door when Sadie reached it, and she unlocked the door and stepped inside gratefully. Now that she'd checked on the horses and taken Hank for a walk, all she wanted to do was take a hot shower and settle in with a good book for the evening. She pulled off her boots and peeled off her wet coat and hung it in the closet by the door. Claribel had been here today, and the whole house smelled like the lemon and fresh pine soaps the housekeeper used. Sadie inhaled deeply, and then walked into the vaulted living room, eyeing the tall stone fireplace. It was the perfect night for a fire. First she would—

She jumped. Her cell phone was ringing. Where did she—oh yes. She rushed back to the coat closet and pulled it out of the pocket of her jacket. It was Virginia Radcliff calling.

"Hello?" Sadie said.

Sadie had always liked Virginia, a teacher at the high school who had taken over Sadie's history classes when Sadie retired. They'd been friendly through the years, and when Virginia asked Sadie if she'd be interested in helping her with a presentation for the big spring fund-raiser at the high school, Sadie had been glad to help. As part of a gala event that would raise money to update the school's library, Sadie and Virginia would give a short multimedia presentation on the history of Silver Peak's first schoolhouse, a historic one-room structure that dated back to the early days of the mining town's boom years. Though the schoolhouse had burned down in 1965, when Sadie was still a child, it was a key piece of Silver Peak's history, and their presentation at the fund-raiser next week would be one of several that traced the history of education in their beloved small town. Sadie had spent many happy hours at the Historical Society and library researching the old schoolhouse and had found some neat old photos and accounts of its early days.

"Sadie?" Virginia's voice sounded a bit muffled, like she was speaking into a headset, but Sadie could still hear the excitement in her voice, as well as some soft music playing in the background.

"Virginia. How are you? Where are you? What's going on?"

"I'm in my car. Let me—" There was a shrill noise, and then Virginia was back on the line. "There, is that better? I adjusted the headset."

"Much better."

"Oh good. Sadie, you'll never believe what I found."

"Oh?" In their research into the old schoolhouse, they had uncovered some old rumors and suspicions about the schoolhouse fire. Though the blaze was determined to be an accident, the result of dated and shoddy electrical work, Virginia had come across some old newspaper articles that suggested that things might not have been so simple. Virginia had become fascinated by the idea that the fire had been set on purpose, and had spent much of the past few weeks digging through old town records, looking for clues to see if she could find any truth to the rumors. Sadie had been interested to see her conclusions, but she had been left doing the bulk of the work on the history of the schoolhouse itself. Sadie didn't mind—history was her passion, and as a former high school teacher, she could think of few subjects more fascinating.

"It's true," Virginia continued. "The fire was definitely not an accident. I know who—"

The reception cut out, as it often did on these twisty mountain roads.

"Virginia?"

There was some static, and then Virginia was back on the line. "—anyway, I'll tell you more when I get there. I should be there in just a few minutes."

"You're coming here?"

"Is that okay? I'm sorry, I shouldn't have assumed. I just thought—"

Sadie was used to the bad cell reception out here, but still felt herself growing frustrated.

"No, no, that's great," Sadie said. "Of course you're welcome. I just wanted to make sure I was hearing you right. I'm home, and I'm anxious to hear what you found."

"It's unbelievable, Sadie. All this time, it was right there, and no one thought to look for it." As she spoke, Virginia's voice lost the excitement Sadie had heard earlier, and something like hesitation entered.

"Is everything okay?"

"Yeah, it's fine, it's just—"

Sadie couldn't tell if the line cut out again or if Virginia had just hesitated again.

"This car has been behind me the whole way. It's weird."

Sadie knew seeing the same car behind you for miles was usually nothing to worry about on these old mountain roads. They were generally limited to one lane in either direction, and there weren't a lot of places to turn off. But Virginia knew that too.

"Where are you?"

"I was working in my classroom at the school, and when I figured out who set the fire, I came straight to the car and set off for your house. I'm close now, out on Country Rock Road." Sadie heard the hum of Virginia's windshield wipers swishing across the smooth glass. She was surprised to hear that Virginia had been at her classroom at the school this late. She had a husband and two small boys at home. "Something about this car behind me is weird. It's far enough back that I can't really see it, but it slows down when I slow and has made every turn I've made."

Again, under most circumstances, this wouldn't seem strange at all. Of course, the car behind her would slow down whenever Virginia did—she was no doubt braking for the curves in the road and stop signs, and other drivers would need to brake for the same reasons. But if Virginia was nervous, Sadie had reason to be as well.

"Maybe you should pull over and see if they pass," Sadie suggested.

"Good idea. Hang on." Virginia said, and Sadie heard the click of her blinker. "That's weird."

"What?"

"The other car slowed way down. It's—okay, now it's pulling over too."

Sadie's heart started racing. Was someone really following Virginia to her house? Why?

"What kind of car is it?"

"I can't really tell. It's far enough back that it just looks like a sedan of some kind, in some dark color. I don't recognize it, but it just kind of looks like any other car."

"Where on Country Rock Road are you?"

"I just passed Mickelson's Garage. Now I'm just before that big curve."

"You're close then." She wasn't more than a couple miles from Sadie's ranch house. "Why don't you get back on the road and come here, and we'll see if the car follows you."

Sadie didn't know what she would do if the car did follow Virginia to her house, but they'd cross that bridge when they got there.

"Okay, I'm pulling out now." Again, Sadie heard the click of the blinker, and then the quiet hum of the car moving.

"Is the other car coming too?"

"It's hard to tell…" Virginia's voice trailed off. "Oh yes, now it's pulling out into the road again too…" The line went fuzzy. "—this is really weird."

The line cut out again, and Sadie held her breath.

Static again, and then "—getting closer to me. I don't know what it's doing. I can't—" The line cut out again, and Sadie wanted to throw her phone across the room, but then Virginia came back on. "—about the fire. Here, Sadie, write this down. I tracked down the old police ch—" Sadie scrambled to get a pen and paper, but just as she began writing, the line cut out again. *Old police what?* "—The Wilc—" Sadie copied it down even as Virginia's voice disappeared again. "5100—"

The line went dead again, but this time it came back quickly, and she heard Virginia yell, "He's coming at me!"

And then, all she heard was the screech of tires and metal scraping against metal.

"Virginia!?" Sadie yelled into the phone, but the only answer was a loud *thud* and the sound of glass shattering.

"Virginia! Are you okay?" Sadie shouted again, but there was only silence, and then the line went dead.

2

MOMENTS LATER, SADIE CALLED VIRGINIA'S NUMBER, AND WAITED
as it rang. She couldn't get the sound of what she'd heard out of her
head. The squeal of rubber on pavement, the grating of metal on
metal, the shattering of glass—it sounded bad. Very bad. "Come
on, Virginia," she said, but her heart sank with every ring. Why
wasn't she picking up?

Sadie had a very bad feeling she knew why. It sure sounded
like Virginia had been in an accident. Still, she ended the call and
tried again.

When Virginia didn't pick up the third time, Sadie hung up
and called 911 instead.

"Nine-one-one, what's your emergency?" The woman at the
other end of the line was calm, and her voice was soothing.

"I was just on the phone with my friend, and she was driving
to my house," Sadie said breathlessly. "A car had been following
her. I think it ran her off the road. I heard a crash, and—"

"Do you know where your friend was located at the time of
the crash?"

Sadie told the woman where her house was and gave them the
approximate location of the crash, based on what Virginia had

told her. Sadie tried not to think about the steep ravine that sloped down away from the side of the big curve on Country Rock Road. There was no reason to assume—

"Please hurry. I think it might—" Sadie took a deep breath. It wouldn't help anyone if she got hysterical. "It sounded like it might have been bad."

"We've already got police and EMS on the way." The woman's voice was calm, but there was something solid about it too, like she was used to being in control. "Can you tell me anything more about what you heard?"

Sadie recapped the basics of the conversation, from the way the car had followed Virginia to the fact that she had been on her way to Sadie's house to reveal the identity of the person who had set a fire more than fifty years ago. Sadie heard the woman typing as she talked, and then the woman asked for Sadie's information and confirmed that the ambulance was arriving on the scene of the crash as they spoke. Indeed, off in the distance, Sadie could hear the high-pitched whine of a siren piercing the night.

"I should go then," Sadie said, looking toward the door. "I'm headed to the scene now, but if anyone needs me, this is my cell—"

"Ma'am, I know they'll appreciate the offer, but it's best to stay away from the area so the paramedics can work without interruption," the woman said.

"But if they have any questions—"

"I have your contact information already entered into the system. If they have any questions about what happened, the paramedics and the police know where to find you," she said calmly, and again, Sadie could tell that she was used to being listened to. "You did the right thing by calling for help immediately. The best thing you can do right now is to stay out of the way and keep the roads clear."

Sadie weighed this. Virginia must be so scared. Wouldn't a familiar face at the scene comfort her friend?

But was this woman right? Would Sadie be in the way? She would never forgive herself if she prevented the professional rescuers from helping Virginia as quickly as possible.

"All right then," Sadie said reluctantly. "Will someone be able to give me an update on what they find?"

"Are you a relative?"

"No," Sadie said slowly. Goodness. She hadn't even thought about how Virginia's husband, David, and their two sons would find out. Someone would need to tell them that Virginia had been in an accident.

"The authorities will notify her family if there is anything to report," the dispatcher said. "You should expect to get any updates from them." There was more typing. "I'm sure they will be thankful that you were there for her and that you called for help so quickly," she added kindly. "Thank you for calling nine-one-one."

Sadie hung up the phone and looked around her house blankly. She still wanted to go out to the site of the crash, but she remembered the dispatcher's warning to let the experts do their jobs.

So that was it, then. All she could do was wait for news.

Almost immediately, she realized how silly that was. Of course that wasn't all she could do. She could pray. That was actually the most important thing she could do.

Slowly, Sadie lowered herself into the overstuffed couch and closed her eyes. Hank hopped up next to her, and she stroked his head gently as she brought Virginia's care before the Lord.

"Lord, I know that You care about Virginia more than any of the rest of us do, and You know exactly what she needs right now. Please help her. Give the police and EMTs the skills they need to help her and to heal her in any way she needs. And please be with her family as they hear the news."

And yet, even as she prayed, Sadie still wished there was something more she could do, some way to make sure Virginia was okay. For now, though, it seemed all she could do was wait.

Sadie looked at the phone in her hands. She was still keyed up, antsy. There was no way she'd be able to go to sleep. She could call Roz, her best friend, and she knew Roz would pray with her and help calm her down. But suddenly, she longed to talk to Edwin, her boyfriend—although the word always sounded silly to her at their age—more than anything. She dialed his number and waited while it rang.

"Well, hi there," Edwin said tenderly. Just hearing his voice was comforting, and Sadie felt her shoulders, which she hadn't realized had become tight, relax. "How's everything going?"

Sadie quickly filled him in on what had happened, and he listened carefully.

"My goodness," he said, and Sadie could hear the concern in his voice. "I hope she's okay."

"So do I," Sadie said. "And I wish I knew who was driving the car that was following her."

"I'm sure the police will look into that," Edwin said, and though Sadie knew he was right, she couldn't help but wish there was something more she could do to help. She thought about the conversation she'd had with Virginia, about the answers she'd finally uncovered about the old schoolhouse fire. She couldn't have… There was no way anyone could have known… Even if they did, it had been so long ago…

"Sadie?" Edwin's voice cut into her reverie. "What's going on?"

Sadie sighed. "Sorry, I was just thinking."

"About?"

"About how strange the timing was. How Virginia had just figured out who set the old fire, and was on her way to tell me, and how someone followed her and, from what I heard, probably knocked her off the road…"

"Sadie." Edwin's voice was calm, but firm. "You don't really think someone was trying to stop her from sharing what she'd learned, do you?"

"It sounds crazy, doesn't it?"

"A little." Edwin's voice was warm, but the words still stung a little. "I mean, even if the fire *wasn't* an accident, and even if she had just discovered who set the fire, the statute of limitations on that crime expired decades ago. What could anyone possibly have to gain by keeping that from coming out now? Never mind the impracticalities of knowing what she'd found out, what she was on her way to do, and purposely running her off the road."

Sadie knew that Edwin, a former circuit court judge, knew what he was talking about. But his calm, rational manner of looking at the facts still rankled sometimes. She *knew* it sounded crazy. But she also knew that just before the accident, Virginia had been trying to tell her things she'd uncovered in her search. It was worth considering, anyway. She wasn't saying that whoever set the old fire had caused Virginia's accident to keep the truth from coming out. She was just saying it was quite a coincidence, and worth thinking about.

"I'm sure the police will be looking into every angle," Edwin said. "And in the meantime, we can be praying for Virginia, and the whole family."

Sadie knew he was right, and as they continued to talk, she felt herself relaxing. She didn't know what had happened to Virginia, but she knew her friend was in God's hands, and for now, that was enough.

Sadie had returned from her morning walk with Hank the next day and was getting ready to go to her antique shop when the doorbell rang. She'd slept poorly, worried about Virginia, and had gotten up earlier than usual to make an extra-strong pot of coffee and spend time in the Word before heading in to the shop. Now, hearing the doorbell ring, she took a quick sip of her coffee, set the mug down on the counter, and opened the front door. Hank followed her to the door, and she shooed him back as she swung it open.

"Good morning, Sadie. Sorry to bother you so early." Sheriff Mac Slattery tipped his hat and gestured behind him to Kyle Kenmore—Officer Kenmore, Sadie reminded herself. Kyle had been a student in her Introduction to Business class when he had been in high school, and it was hard to now remember that he was a police officer and not a squirrely senior itching for the lunch bell. It was a hazard of the occupation, she guessed. Students always stayed children in a teacher's mind.

Generally, a visit from the sheriff this early in the day would fill her with dread, but Sadie was glad to see them now, hopeful they would bring news of Virginia.

"That's quite all right. Please, come in." The rain had stopped overnight, but there was a chilly bite in the air, and Sadie gestured for them to enter. They stepped inside gratefully and wiped their feet on the mat just inside the door. "Would either of you like some coffee?"

"Not for me, thank you," Sheriff Slattery said, running his hair through his gray hair. Officer Kenmore also declined, but Sadie grabbed her coffee mug and then led them into the living room and gestured for them to sit on the couch. She settled into one of the brown leather chairs. The big windows on the wall let in the muted morning sunlight.

"We're told you placed a nine-one-one call reporting an accident last night," the sheriff said without preamble.

"That's right. I was on the phone with Virginia Radcliff, and while we were talking, I heard what sounded like skidding tires and breaking glass, and then the line went dead." Sadie took a sip of her coffee. "Did they find her?" She wasn't sure if she really wanted to hear the answer.

Sheriff Slattery nodded slowly. Sadie had worked with him in the past, and she knew him well enough to recognize the hesitation in his eyes. Her heart started pounding.

"I'm afraid there was an accident. It happened right near where you reported it, just past Mickelson's Garage. Her car went through the guardrail and into the ravine along that big curve."

"Oh no." Sadie set her mug down on the coffee table. "Is it... is she okay?"

"She's alive." The sheriff nodded, and Sadie felt a sense of relief flow through her. "She's badly bruised, though, and she's in a coma."

"Oh dear." Sadie's heart sank. How could this have happened?

"The doctors are hopeful. They got her into surgery right away, and her condition is stable. Because she received care so quickly, chances are good she'll recover completely. Your call might have very well saved her life."

That was something at least, but...poor Virginia. Sadie couldn't quite believe it.

"We're looking into the cause of the accident, and for obvious reasons, Virginia can't help us at the moment," Officer Kenmore said. He was young, no older than his late twenties, and had a boyish face, which made it even harder for Sadie to remember that he was grown up now, even though Sadie knew he now had a wife and two young daughters at home.

"We were hoping you might be able to help us," Sheriff Slattery said. Sadie nodded eagerly. She wanted to help however she could.

"We're very interested in something you said to the nine-one-one dispatcher last night, Mrs. Speers," Officer Kenmore said.

"Sadie, please," she said, and Kyle's cheeks flushed. Apparently he was having a hard time making the adjustment from student to peer as well.

"Sadie." Office Kenmore cleared his throat. "You mentioned in the call that a car had been following your friend. Can you tell us anything more about that?"

Sadie nodded, eager to share what she knew and what had occurred to her last night. "Virginia and I had been working on a project about the old schoolhouse fire for the big fund-raiser at the high school next week." Both police officers stared at her blankly. Kyle had grown up in Silver Peak, so he no doubt had heard about the infamous fire, but Sheriff Slattery had only moved here from Denver a few years ago, and might not know of it.

"It was a big fire at the old schoolhouse back in 1965. Burned it clean to the ground," Sadie said.

"I'm aware of the fire," Officer Kenmore said, and gave the sheriff a look that said he'd explain later. Sheriff Slattery nodded skeptically. They obviously didn't see the connection yet, so Sadie kept going.

"Virginia was working in her classroom last night on our presentation. She had gotten really interested in some evidence that suggested the fire hadn't been an accident like everyone thinks it was. Apparently there's been some speculation over the years that someone set the fire on purpose, and last night she called to tell me she had figured out that it was arson after all and that she knew who had set it. She was coming here to tell me who did it, but on the way she noticed a car was following her. It had apparently been following her since she left the school."

"Did she recognize the car?" The sheriff had his pen poised over a pad of paper but had yet to write down anything.

Sadie shook her head. "She didn't, and it was dark out, so all she could see was that it was a sedan of some sort. She pulled over to let it go by, and it stayed behind her. That's when she started to get really scared. She knew it was following her for sure. And we didn't say this straight out, but I wondered if it might have been someone who didn't want the truth about the fire to come out."

There was a pause. Sheriff Slattery seemed to be trying to think of how to respond.

"Could she tell anything about the driver of the car?" Officer Kenmore finally asked. He adjusted his position, moving one of Sadie's pillows out from behind his back.

"Not that she told me." Sadie thought back, trying to remember any detail she could think of. "Did she…" She didn't know how to word this. "Was the other driver involved in the accident?"

The two policemen looked at each other, and then Sheriff Slattery spoke. "We have reason to believe there was another car involved in the crash."

Based on what she'd heard last night, Sadie agreed, but that wasn't really what she meant. "Did the other car go off the road as well?"

Officer Kenmore shook his head. "But there is evidence it might have been the cause of the accident. Right now we're looking at it as a hit-and-run." He looked at the sheriff and cleared his throat. "As you might imagine, we're very interested in finding out who was driving the other car."

"Of course. I hope you find the other driver as well," Sadie said.

"Did Virginia say anything else about the car that was following her?" the sheriff asked.

Sadie replayed the conversation with Virginia in her mind and realized she'd forgotten to tell them one very important piece of information. "You know, just before the crash, she told me to write a few things down. Hold on, let me go get my paper." She pushed herself up and walked into the kitchen, where she'd left the paper by the charger for the cordless phone. Hank was sitting in front of his food dish, waiting patiently for her to fill it up.

"I'll feed you soon, Hank," she said, but he still gave her a plaintive look as she stepped back into the living room.

"Here's what she told me to write down just before the line went dead," Sadie said, holding out the piece of paper.

Sheriff Slattery looked down at the paper. "'old police ch.' 'The Wilc.' '5100.' Do you have any idea what any of that means?"

Sadie shook her head. "I don't really know. The line was spotty and it kept cutting out, so there was more, but this was all I caught. But I did wonder if maybe the last bit was part of the license plate number of the other car."

Sheriff Slattery nodded and copied the numbers down onto his notepad. "Could be. If it's a Colorado plate, it would be 510-O, since the format is three numbers followed by three letters, but that would be an easy mistake to make looking at a plate from some distance." He looked down at the numbers for a moment. "Is there anything else you can think of that might be important?"

Sadie considered, thinking back to the previous night, to how the car had been following Virginia since she left the high school. She knew Edwin hadn't been impressed by her theory, but it was still a possibility, she thought. "I think it's possible that whoever was following Virginia was interested in the old fire," Sadie said. She saw the police glance at each other again, and Sheriff Slattery shook his head slightly.

"Anything about the car?"

Sadie felt herself growing exasperated. "She didn't say anything more about the car. But she did say that she had finally just figured out who had set the old fire. She was on her way to tell me who it was. Surely that could be significant."

"It might be," the sheriff said quickly, giving her a smile she was sure was meant to placate her.

"It might be at least worth looking into," Sadie insisted.

"I can promise you we'll be exploring every angle as we look for the culprit," Sheriff Slattery said. "And if you think of anything else Virginia said that might be important, please do let us know."

With that, he slipped his notebook and pen into his pocket and stood, and Officer Kenmore also rose from his seat.

Sadie tried to be gracious as she walked them to the door. They were just doing their jobs, trying to follow the most likely leads. She could see how, to them, it might seem crazy that a fifty-year-old fire might have had something to do with Virginia's accident last night. And Sadie didn't know if the two events were connected. But Sadie still felt dismissed and disregarded. She was the one who had been on the phone with Virginia, who had heard the excitement in her voice as Virginia announced that she'd found the answer, and heard the fear in her voice as she realized the car was right behind her.

Sadie promised to call if she had any updates, and closed the door softly behind the policemen. She knew they hadn't given her suggestion about the fire much credence, and they wouldn't be spending much time investigating that channel.

But Sadie had a feeling there was something to it. Whoever had been following Virginia could have known what she'd uncovered. She hadn't exactly been quiet about her investigation—Sadie knew she'd been asking around town and had even talked to some of the people involved in the original investigation. Someone must have learned what she'd been doing and been scared of what she'd find out. Someone might have been watching her and known she'd just discovered their long-buried secret. And if Sadie was right, if this was a possibility, that person must have been desperate enough to have knocked Virginia's car off the road to make sure that the long-buried secret never got out.

It seemed far-fetched, she knew. But it also made sense. If Sadie was right, someone had gone to very great lengths—seriously hurting her friend—to make sure no one knew what Virginia had learned. Sadie thought about Virginia, lying comatose in a hospital bed. *How could someone do that?* If only she knew who Virginia thought had set the fire…

Sadie leaned against the door and felt a surge of adrenaline rush through her. If she knew what name Virginia had been about to tell her, Sadie suspected she might have a very good idea who might have run her off the road.

And, Sadie thought as she straightened up, if the police weren't going to find out who might have wanted to keep Virginia quiet so badly, maybe Sadie would do it herself.

3

AFTER SADIE HAD GOTTEN READY FOR THE DAY, SHE CLIMBED into her car and started out toward town, mulling over her meeting with the policemen. The morning was clear and cold. Sadie slowed as she approached the big curve in the road, and even though she knew it would be there, she still sucked in her breath when she saw the break in the guardrail. Sadie hadn't intended to, but she slowed her car and pulled over to the side of the road.

There it was, plain as day. Two sets of tire tracks. One swerved and stopped a few feet from the guardrail, and the other...

Sadie stepped out of her car and walked toward the side of the road. The other tire tracks went right through the guardrail and over the edge of the ravine. Sadie moved closer, and she saw light winking on broken glass.

Goodness. The drop-off was steep and wooded, and Sadie could barely see the car from the road. She couldn't explain why, but she suddenly felt the desire to see the car. She looked around, and then, without really understanding why, climbed through the break in the guardrail and started to climb down into the ravine.

She held on to cottonwood branches as she picked her way down the wet dirt of the hill. And there, braced against a tree trunk about twenty feet below the road, was Virginia's white Ford Focus. The hood was crushed, crumpled like a tin can, and the windshield and all the windows were shattered. The air bag had been deployed, and now hung lifeless, draped over the steering wheel. Broken glass littered the ground.

It was hard to believe anyone could have survived this accident. And this far below the road, no one would have seen the car. She shuddered. *Lord, thank You for saving Virginia's life,* she prayed. *Please heal her, completely and quickly.* Sadie took a deep breath, shook her head, and then started to turn back up the hill. *And please help us to find whoever did this to her,* she added.

A thousand thoughts swirled through her head. It was a good reminder to be thankful for every moment the Lord gave us, she mused, but that idea collided with the thought that someone had done this on purpose, and that she should check in on Virginia's family to see how she could help them. Sadie reached for the thin trunk of a poplar, but something caught her eye. There, on the left side of the car, just over the rear wheel well, was a stripe of maroon paint.

Had the car that had hit Virginia been maroon? Or had the stripe been there before? Sadie stepped forward and leaned in close, checking to see if the strip of paint held any more clues, but she couldn't find anything. Still, it was something. She would be on the lookout for a maroon car. Rationally, Sadie knew searching for the right maroon car was still a needle-in-a-haystack operation, but as she picked her way up the ravine again, she felt a sense of triumph. She had something to go on, and that was more than she'd had a few minutes ago. She thought about calling the sheriff to let him know what she'd found, but surely they would have seen the same thing themselves.

Sadie said another prayer for Virginia as she buckled herself back into her Chevy Tahoe. She knew the police were searching for the car that caused the accident, but after seeing how bad the accident really was, how clear it was that someone had run Virginia's car off the road, Sadie was even more determined to look into it on her own as well.

She pulled back onto the road slowly, and as she drove the short distance to her antique shop, she tried to come up with a list of all the maroon cars she could think of. Jane Remington, who ran the Silver Peak Bed-and-Breakfast, drove a small reddish car, she thought. Roscoe Putnam, her best friend Roz's husband, had a deep-red pickup truck. Jeanne Sweeting, the pastor's wife, had a maroon-colored minivan. But she just couldn't imagine any of those people running Virginia off the road. The color of the car was a good start, but it was not going to be enough to find the culprit.

Sadie sighed as she unlocked the glass front door of the Antique Mine a few minutes later. No matter what was happening in her life, she always enjoyed stepping inside her antique shop. She took a deep breath, inhaling the slightly musty smell of history and possibility. She'd never get tired of that smell.

She walked past a mahogany Stickley sideboard, its clean, straight lines balanced nicely by the ivory lace table runner and the pink and white porcelain pitcher and basin set on top. Beyond that was an original red Radio Flyer wagon, dirty but intact, piled with a collection of Madame Alexander dolls from the 1950s. Sadie didn't really understand the appeal of antique dolls, but she knew collectors prized them highly, and she did a fair trade in them. Sadie admired the way the collection of Depression glass lined up against the midcentury kitchen hutch caught the early morning light as she slipped behind the front desk, tucked her purse into the bottom drawer, and peeled off her coat.

She ran through her morning routine—hanging up her coat, turning on the lights, setting up the till. She turned on some Loretta Lynn, and, satisfied that everything was ready, she settled in behind the mahogany desk that served as her front counter. She still had a few minutes before the shop officially opened, and she tried to think of how she could figure out how many people drove maroon sedans in Silver Peak. Did the DMV track things like that? Sadie wasn't sure, but she would try to find out. Still, she felt sure the police would be looking into that; what she wanted to do was try to find out who Virginia thought was behind the fire.

Sadie sighed. She had no real idea how to do that. Most of the work Sadie had done on their project had focused on the early years of the schoolhouse. First set up as a drafty timber cabin in 1883, she knew that it evolved into a more permanent wooden building as the years progressed, and though it was abandoned for educational purposes in 1934, when the new elementary school was constructed over on Madison, plumbing and electricity were added to the old schoolhouse in 1945, when the building was opened as a tourist attraction. But Virginia had done most of the work on the later years of the schoolhouse, and she was the one who had been so focused on the fire itself. Sadie had no idea what sort of side research she'd done. How would Sadie figure out what Virginia had uncovered?

She supposed the first thing to do would be to talk to Virginia's husband, David, and see if Virginia had left any records of her search, or better yet, if she had revealed anything about her investigation to him. But Sadie hesitated to bug him just yet. His wife had just been in a life-threatening accident. Surely he would be wrapped up in caring for her; it felt insensitive to ask if Virginia had left behind any records right now.

But it couldn't hurt to give him a call and see if there was anything Sadie could do to help, she realized. In fact, she desperately wanted to do anything she could to help Virginia's family in this rough time, but she had no idea what they needed. Maybe she would just give him a quick call and see if she could offer support, and if she had a chance to ask him about Virginia's records, great.

Sadie pulled out her cell phone. She didn't know David's cell phone number, but she had Virginia's home number, and she called that now.

She held her breath as the line rang, but no one picked up. Sadie left a message asking if they needed help and offering to be of service however she could, and then she hung up.

Sadie sat back in her desk chair. She hoped David would call back soon. In the meantime, she needed to find another way to figure out what Virginia had been looking into. Sadie supposed the first thing she should do would be was to try to retrace Virginia's steps.

Sadie thought back to a few weeks ago, when Virginia had been working on their project and gotten so excited about the fire. What was it that had set her off on that course?

Sadie wasn't sure, but she thought she remembered Virginia saying she'd come across some old newspaper articles about the fire, and that they had contained hints that the fire was not an accident. It looked like a trip to the library was in order.

Just then, Julie Pearson came in the front door of the shop and greeted Sadie. Tall and athletic, Julie always had a cheerful smile, and she knew almost as much about antiques as Sadie herself. Sadie was grateful to have found such a capable assistant for her shop.

"Hey there, Sadie. How's everything this morning?" Julie said as she threaded her way around antiques toward the desk.

"Oh, just fine." Sadie gave her a weak smile. "I'm grateful, I suppose."

"Amen to that." Julie took off her coat and hung it in the back room. "I read on *The Chatterbox* about that car that went off the road over by your place last night. They're saying it was pretty bad."

Sadie wasn't surprised to find out that news of the accident had been spread on the local-news site. The site was written anonymously and often veered from news into gossip, and this was exactly the sort of story that would take off there.

"That's what I've been thinking about this morning as well." Sadie filled Julie in on the phone call last night, the visit from the sheriff this morning, and her theory that the crash had to do with what Virginia had uncovered about who set the old schoolhouse fire.

"Goodness." Julie seemed stunned. "Well, if I know you, I'm going to guess you're not about to sit here and sell antiques all day while whoever hurt your friend is still out there. I'm happy to watch the shop if you have errands you need to do."

Sadie smiled gratefully. Julie knew her too well. "I was thinking I might run over to the library for a while this morning if you don't mind watching the shop."

"Of course I don't mind." Julie had already pulled a dust cloth from the back room and was gently running it over a display of old phonographs in the rear of the store. "I can handle things here for a while."

"Thank you." Once again, Sadie was grateful that God had brought her such a reliable and capable employee in Julie. Sadie knew the shop was in good hands while she was out. "I'm expecting a shipment of old quilts from an estate sale in Amish country this afternoon, so I'll try to be back in time to sign for that."

"Take your time. I'll be here."

Sadie thanked her again, and then she slipped on her jacket, grabbed her purse, and headed for the door. The air had warmed up, erasing the bitter bite from the morning, and the sky had cleared, and brilliant sunlight filtered down over the heart of Silver Peak, casting the brick buildings of downtown in a beautiful orange glow. Window boxes in front of the shops and restaurants sprouted with daffodils and lilies. Sadie loved living in Silver Peak in all seasons, but spring, when the world felt alive and imbued with the promise of new things to come, had to be her favorite season.

Sadie strolled past Arbuckle's Coffee, and waved at Luz Vidal, and Mark DiMatteo, just unlocking the door of Sophia's, and Debbie Sunshine behind the counter at Bless Our Souls jewelry shop. As she started across First Avenue, her phone rang, and she dug it out of her purse and smiled when she saw it was Edwin calling.

"Hi there," she said, putting the phone up to her ear. Edwin was her boyfriend, though it always made her feel like a teenager to use that word, and her heart gave a little thrill whenever he called to check in.

"I wanted to see how you're doing this morning." Edwin spoke quickly, and she could hear the sounds of his office on his end of the line.

"Tired." Sadie sighed. "But okay, overall. The police came by this morning to see what I could tell them about the accident, so at least I know they're looking into it."

"I'm glad to hear it," Edwin said. "I'll check in with Mac today and see if I can find out anything more about what's going on with their investigation."

Edwin was the mayor of Silver Peak, and that usually meant he heard news about things in town before most anyone else—and it also meant he was one the few people who could get away with asking the sheriff for what was probably confidential information. Whether the sheriff would provide that information was another story. But the mayor calling to ask wasn't as audacious as, say, a retired teacher turned antique shop owner.

"That would be great," Sadie said. "And please let me know if you hear any news on how Virginia is doing."

"I sure will. And I'm glad you're doing all right." There was a noise on his end of the line, like someone knocking on his door. "I have to go, Sadie. But will you let me take you out to dinner tonight?"

"That sounds wonderful." That was one thing Sadie loved about Edwin—he was such a gentleman.

"Perfect. I'll pick you up around six thirty?"

"I'll be ready." Sadie hung up just as she got to the doors of the Silver Peak Library. Sadie stepped inside, awed, as usual, by the soaring main room, which rose three stories. The building itself was an old brick structure, but it had been redone inside in a distinctly modern style, with light woodwork and airy large windows and bright lighting. It wasn't how Sadie would have imagined a library, but she had to admit it was striking and efficient, and she knew the style appealed to the younger folks in town. If it got the next generation interested in spending time in the library, Sadie could live with a few chrome finishes.

Sadie waved to Kimama, the head librarian, who was checking out a line of schoolchildren, and headed to the reference room on the second floor, where Sadie knew the old newspaper records were kept. The room had tall white walls and was hung with historic newspaper photos of Silver Peak, some going back to its earliest mining days. Sadie looked around the deserted room and tried to figure out where to start. These days, all newspapers and magazines that came in were digitized, which made the records much easier to access and search, but Sadie suspected that if she was looking for newspaper articles that came out in 1965, she'd need to use the old microfiche machines. Sadie had used them before, and she moved to the small room where the machines were kept and quickly located the film for editions of the *Silver Peak Sentinel* from 1965. The fire had taken place on May 5, 1965, but she took cards for April through July, just in case, and she settled down in front of the machine, fit the first card into the machine, and turned the machine on. The familiar hum was comforting, and Sadie began looking through the old issues of the paper.

Sadie knew many people found research like this tedious, but Sadie was a historian, and she loved reading old newspapers. They gave you such an interesting picture of what life was like in a certain time and place. Her eye caught on a front page story about how plans had been approved for the new Town Hall building, and another about the then-governor's political fund-raising. She tried to not let herself get distracted, but she did let her eyes dwell on the old advertisements. Here was one for a performance of Tosca at the Silver Peak Opera House; Sadie's father had loved Tosca. And here was another, a full-page ad for a new western-wear store called McLaren's that had closed when Sadie was in high school. Sadie had bought a pair of boots there with her babysitting money before her junior year.

As much fun as the old papers were, Sadie didn't see anything related to the schoolhouse fire until she came across a small piece on May 6, 1965, the morning after the fire. HISTORIC SCHOOL-HOUSE BURNS; NO INJURIES REPORTED, the headline read.

Sadie read the article. It was a short piece, no doubt written quickly in the hours before the paper went to press and before they had had time to gather much real information:

Fire crews responded to a call placed at 11:30 PM, Wednesday night, reporting a fire at Silver Peak's historic first schoolhouse. According to Fire Chief Melvin Loffredo, when fire trucks arrived at the scene, the entire structure was in flames. They were able to prevent the fire from spreading to the nearby Harriman State Park, a heavily forested area, but the schoolhouse itself could not be saved. The cause of the fire has not yet been determined.

It was straightforward, Sadie thought as she reread the piece carefully, looking for clues that Virginia might have picked up on. But Sadie couldn't see anything that indicated the fire had been set on purpose. She scrolled to the next day's paper.

This was more like it. On the front page of the May 7 paper was a photo of the burned-out shell of the schoolhouse. Sadie had seen the picture reproduced in some of the reference books she'd used on her project. SCHOOLHOUSE FIRE UNDER INVESTIGA-TION, the headline read. Sadie scrolled down and read carefully.

Police and fire crews continue to investigate the cause of the fire that destroyed the historic Silver Peak Schoolhouse Wednesday night. The Silver Peak Fire Department responded to a call placed by Joe Curr at 11:28 PM on Wednesday. Curr, who lives across the road from the historic site, was woken when his dogs started barking. "I looked out my window to see what was going on, and there was this huge wall of flame," Curr said.

When fire trucks arrived at the scene, the whole structure was engulfed, and though they were not able to save the building, they prevented the fire from spreading. "There's hundreds of acres of old-growth forest right there. This thing could have been really bad if it had gotten out of control," said Fire Chief Melvin Loffredo.

While the official cause of the fire is still under investigation, many residents of Silver Peak have theories as to what started the blaze. Several witnesses reported seeing a vagrant in town in the preceding days. Reports as to the man's physical description vary, but several witnesses mentioned his shaggy beard and unkempt hair. "He was one of those hippies," says Judith Marley, a school-teacher in Silver Peak who had interactions with the man in recent days. "His clothes were filthy, and he looked like that horrible Jerry Garcia," said Marley. "He has to be the one responsible."

Other witnesses reported seeing a group of boys from the local high school in the vicinity of the fire Monday night, though no names have been released.

The schoolhouse, owned and maintained by the Silver Peak Unified School District, was insured, but District Superintendent Samuel Bradley is not sure yet how and if the schoolhouse will be rebuilt. "We're still reeling from this sad turn of events and haven't yet had a chance to determine our next steps," says Bradley.

The police are not ready to start drawing any conclusions about the cause of the fire. "We are investigating every possibility," says Sheriff Robert Greene. "But I will tell you one thing. If someone did this on purpose, we will find them."

Sadie read the piece again, slowly, trying to make sense of every detail. Then, she reached into her purse and pulled out a journal with a distressed leather cover, as well as a pen, and started making a list.

Vagrant/hippie? Ask Judith Marley.

Sadie knew Judith; Judith was more than a decade older than Sadie, but their paths had overlapped throughout the years. Judith was always well put-together and proper, and though Sadie would probably never be either of those things, she admired Judith for them. Maybe Sadie could ask Judith about this vagrant who had been seen in town before the fire. Had Virginia already spoken to Judith, or even the vagrant?

Sadie also wrote down the other names in the article: Joe Curr, who had reported the fire; Melvin Loffredo, fire chief; Samuel Bradley, school superintendent; Robert Greene, sheriff. Joe Curr had been a friend of Sadie's father's, and she knew he had passed away years ago. The only other man Sadie knew was Samuel Bradley. The former school superintendent still lived in Silver Peak, and was a fixture in town. He was an avid supporter of the arts, and he was part of a crowd that showed up at the fanciest gatherings and donated vast sums of money to keep the town's arts and cultural events running. Centennial Park, down by the river on the west end of town, had been built after he donated the money to turn an old slag heap into a public park. Sadie didn't exactly run in the same circles as Bradley, but he had a reputation as a kind and generous man. Had Virginia tried to talk to him to see what he remembered from that night? Maybe Sadie could try to do that, as well as track down some of the others mentioned in this article.

Sadie tapped her pen against the desk. Then there was that matter of the group of unnamed high school boys. Could they have had something to do with the fire? Sadie knew teenage boys could be impulsive and reckless. It wasn't hard to imagine a prank gone wrong or a careless action resulting in the blaze. But how could she find out more? She added *high school boys?* to her list.

Sadie scrolled to the next day's edition of the paper and saw that the fire was still front-page news. This time, there was a large photo of the blackened school bell that had hung in the small bell tower, surrounded by ashes and burned timbers.

All that's left of the schoolhouse is the silver school bell, brought over from England by Walter and Marion Jones and donated to the schoolhouse in 1896, read the caption.

Sadie knew the school bell well. She'd read about it in her research about the schoolhouse, of course, but she'd also seen it regularly. The historic bell was on display, encased in thick glass, along with a handful of other artifacts, outside the principal's office at Silver Peak High School. If Sadie remembered correctly, it sat between the trophy the first state championship basketball team had won in the 1970s and a medal of recognition from the State of Colorado for outstanding standardized test scores from 1984. Sadie doubted many of the students had ever taken the time to read the small placard that accompanied the bell, but Sadie had, many times, and she knew that it was valuable both for its historic worth, as the only part of the schoolhouse to survive the blaze, and for the sheer amount of expensive silver used to mold it. Sadie and Virginia had been planning to feature a photograph of the bell in her presentation next week.

Goodness. The presentation. It seemed very unlikely Virginia would be able to help give the presentation now. Was it too late for Sadie to get out of it? Surely people would understand, what with the accident, and no one could expect Sadie to do it alone. Sadie shook her head. She would worry about that later.

Sadie turned back to the article at hand. The piece beneath the photo of the bell was shorter than the previous day's reporting, and covered much of the same territory, but the concluding few paragraphs were what interested Sadie the most:

"The burn pattern of the blaze is definitely suspicious," says Fire Chief Melvin Loffredo. "I cannot comment beyond that, but we will be looking into the matter further."

While questions still swirl about the circumstances surrounding the blaze, Police Chief Robert Greene has officially determined the fire to be the result of faulty electrical wiring and closed the police investigation. "This was a tragic accident, but at this point we'd all just like to move on," says Greene. Residents of Silver Peak are ready to do just that.

Sadie tried to make sense of what she'd read. The burn pattern was suspicious? What did that mean? And if there were still questions about the burn pattern, why had the police closed the case so quickly?

The article raised a lot of questions, that was for sure. This had to have been the piece that piqued Virginia's interest in what had really happened the night of the fire. Now all Sadie needed to do was figure out what Virginia had discovered since then and why it had angered someone enough to land her in the hospital.

She let out a sigh. Easier said than done.

Sadie added *burn pattern?* to her list of things to look into and then studied the list:

Vagrant/hippie? Ask Judith Marley.

Joe Curr reported the fire.

Melvin Loffredo, fire chief

Samuel Bradley, school superintendent

Robert Greene, sheriff

High school boys

Burn pattern?

It didn't seem too promising, she had to admit. But it did give her a few people to talk to. She'd no doubt do better once she got access to whatever else Virginia had found. She hoped David would call her back shortly.

"How's it going up here?" Sadie turned and saw Kimama coming into the room. "Sorry, I wanted to say hi earlier, but I had a first-grade class to deal with."

"That's quite all right. Getting books into the hands of children is more important than anything I'm working on."

"What *are* you working on?" Kimama came further into the room. Her long brown hair was threaded with streaks of silver, and she was dressed, as always, impeccably, in navy blue pants with a sharp crease and a loose white button-down shirt. Turquoise rings studded several fingers. Kimama was a dear friend and had helped Sadie on several research projects in the past, and was very good at coming up with creative ideas for finding information.

"Have you heard about the old schoolhouse fire back in the sixties?" Sadie wasn't sure of Kimama's exact age, but she was pretty sure she was too young to remember it firsthand.

Kimama nodded. "Sure. That bell at the high school is from that, right?"

"That's right. I'm trying to find out about the fire, I guess."

"You guess?"

"Well, Virginia Radcliff was looking into the old fire. I guess I'm really trying to figure out what she found."

Kimama's face changed to one of concern. "Oh, I heard about her accident. It's horrible, isn't it? Do you know if she's okay?"

Sadie shook her head. "I don't really know all that much. I called her husband to see if there was anything they needed, but I haven't heard back, and I'm sure he has so much going on right now that I don't know when I will."

"If you do find out any way to help, please let me know."

"Will do." Sadie sighed. "In the meantime, I'm trying to track down whatever it was that she found when she was researching the old schoolhouse fire."

"I think I may be able to help you there. Turns out Virginia was in here last week looking through these same records," Kimama said, gesturing at the microfiche terminal Sadie was seated in front of.

"I thought she must have been looking at these old articles," Sadie said. "Do you know if she found anything?"

"I know that when I came in to check on her, she had that same frustrated look on your face you have right now." Kimama smiled. "And when she told me what she was looking for, I suggested she look through the old police records at the sheriff's office."

"I suppose that's probably my next step." Sadie knew she was legally allowed to access the files through the Colorado Open Records Act and the Colorado Criminal Justice Records Act, but she also knew that the sheriff's office was notoriously reticent about giving out information from their files. She was also upset that she had to retrace Virginia's steps in the first place. If Virginia hadn't been hurt, all of the information Sadie sought would already be available.

"It would be a good place to start, anyway," Kimama said. "It might not turn up anything, since they generally only have to show you things like arrest records, indictments, parole sentencing, that kind of thing, which might not be relevant in this case. But you never know. It's worth looking into."

"It certainly is. Thanks for your help."

Kimama gave her a wide smile. "That's my job."

"And you're very good at it." Sadie thanked her again and quickly printed out the articles she had been examining, and then headed downstairs. Anthony Parker, the assistant librarian, was reshelving a cart of books when Sadie passed by, and Sadie gave him a wave as she headed out.

Main Street was bathed in golden sunlight, and though there was still a chilly breeze, it was turning out to be a glorious day. Still, Sadie couldn't stop herself from hurrying toward the sheriff's office, just a few blocks off Main Street on Jefferson. A few minutes later, she approached the building, a two-story brick structure, and stepped inside.

Sadie crossed the polished hardwood floor and approached the counter at the front of the lobby. Behind the glass wall beyond the desk, Sadie could see people moving around, talking, using computers. Sadie had worked with the sheriff enough to know that his office was at the back of the building, with large windows that looked out over the mountains.

Janet Parks looked up from her computer and gave Sadie a tight smile. "Hello, Sadie."

"Hi, Janet." Every time Sadie saw Janet, she marveled at how little she'd changed since high school. She still had the same bobbed hair, the same oversize glasses, the same intense gaze. Janet had graduated at the top of their class, and had always been fastidious with details and unyielding in how she did things, which was part of what made her so good at the front desk of the Silver Peak sheriff's department. "I'd like to place a request to gain access to some old police records, please."

"Sure thing. Just fill out these forms." Janet opened a desk drawer, pulled out a sheaf of papers, and set them on the counter. "You know what you're looking for, right?"

Sadie looked down at the thick packet dubiously. It was covered with tiny black lines and boxes to fill out. The answer was no, but Sadie knew better than to say that. "I'm interested in information about a case from 1965. Would you have those records here?"

"I'm not sure. We'll have to do an official records search. It could take up to three weeks." Janet smiled at Sadie pleasantly.

"Three weeks?" Sadie didn't have three weeks. She needed to find out what was in those records as soon as possible. Sadie tried to figure out how to persuade Janet to bend the rules a bit—no small task for this faithful gatekeeper. "Is there anything I could do to get the information sooner?"

Janet shook her head. "There's a good chance it won't take that long, but we do have to follow protocol."

Sadie had expected as much. She decided to try a different tactic.

"You know, I think there's a chance this particular police file was accessed fairly recently, by Virginia Radcliff. Do you happen to know if the file was located when she requested it?"

A flicker of recognition passed across Janet's face. "I'll still need you to fill out the form, Sadie." She pushed the packet across the counter with her fingertips.

Sadie sighed, took a ballpoint pen out of the cup on the counter, and dutifully began filling out as many of the squares as she could. Janet turned to her computer and started typing something while Sadie did her best to complete the forms, and when she finished, she set down the pen and handed the packet to Janet.

Janet scanned the papers. "You're looking for the file Virginia Radcliff accessed?"

Sadie nodded.

"All right. Come with me." Janet set the packet down in a tray on her desk, then stood and gestured for Sadie to follow her. Sadie felt a wide smile spread across her face. "It's down in the archive room."

Sadie followed Janet through the glass door to the back of the station and down a long hallway, and then through a door marked Private. "It took me a while to dig it up when Virginia asked for it, but I know right where it is now."

Sadie was thrilled to hear it, both because it would save her time and also because it meant she was on the right track after all. Virginia had been here, and Sadie felt sure she must have found something. Sadie followed her down a cement staircase and into a lower level, and then down another hallway to a room with a blue metal door. She opened the door, flicked on the lights, and gestured around the room, which looked about the size of Sadie's whole house. There were rows of beige metal filing cabinets lined up throughout the space. The hanging fluorescent lights hummed and popped as they warmed up.

"I think the file you're looking for is here..." Janet turned into an aisle between two rows of cabinets and stopped in front of a cabinet halfway down. She pulled open a drawer and reached in, flipping through a couple of thick manila files until she landed on the right one. She pulled it out and shut the drawer.

"You'll need to stay in the reading room with this," Janet said, leading Sadie to a small, windowless room just off the archive room. It had a table, a plastic chair, and a dangling fluorescent light. "Bring the file back up to me when you're finished."

And just like that, the ever-efficient Janet was on her way back up to the front desk, and Sadie was alone with the file in the small reading room. Sadie lowered herself into the chair and opened the file.

It only took a few moments to find what she was looking for, and she couldn't believe what she saw.

4

———

SADIE LOOKED AT THE FIRST PAGE OF THE POLICE FILE ABOUT THE old schoolhouse fire and tried to make sense of what she was reading. It was a thin sheet of paper mostly taken up with typewritten paragraphs signed by Sheriff Robert Greene. It was a summary of the case, Sadie saw, and it ended with the conclusion she'd read earlier, that the fire had been declared an accident. But what was surprising was a handwritten note, dated five days after the official report, scrawled at the bottom of the page.

After consultations with the fire chief and key witnesses, I disagree with the conclusion that the fire was an accident, read the note, which was signed by a—Sadie squinted to make out the name—an officer Jim Sharlett.

Well. That was interesting. Sadie hadn't read too many police reports in her life, but she had to assume they didn't always include dissenting opinions from the sheriff's subordinates. Virginia must have seen this file, and this bit had no doubt only encouraged her to keep reading.

Sadie turned the page and saw that the next page was notes taken at the scene of the fire. Officer Sharlett had noted the time and date of the fire, the location, and how long it had taken the fire department to put out the flames. He'd also included notes they'd found while surveying the scene—the charred school bell, the proximity to the woods, the distance from the houses across the street. He also indicated a number of unusual things they'd found after surveying the property, including a number of Victory cigarette butts around the property and a pair of tortoiseshell glasses.

Sadie added glasses and cigarette butts to her ever-growing list of things to look into. She wasn't sure how they would be useful, but she'd have to keep reading.

What followed in the file were mostly notes written by officers after they interviewed different suspects in the case. Sadie first read the notes from an interview that had taken place on May 6 between an Officer Sharlett and an Orville Montgomery, who, according to this sheet, was a maintenance worker for the district. It appeared Orville was responsible for keeping up the historic site, but when he was interviewed, he was vague about his whereabouts on the night of the fire. The notes in the report also indicated that Orville was known to smoke Victory cigarettes. The clear implication was that Orville might have set the fire with one of his cigarettes, and his reticence to say where he had been that night certainly put him under suspicion. Sadie flipped to the next page—what in the world?

There had to be more…and yet, Sadie flipped through the rest of the folder and didn't see any other notes about Orville. Why hadn't the police followed up with him?

But when Sadie looked again at the date Orville had been interviewed, the answer was obvious. The very next day, Sheriff Greene had declared the fire officially an accident, and the investigation had ceased. Sadie found this suspicious, to say the least.

Sadie took out her notebook and added the name *Orville Montgomery* to the list, and then she looked at the next interview in the folder.

This one had taken place the same day as the interview with Orville, also by Officer Sharlett. He had apparently spoken to Joe Curr on the day after the fire. Sadie knew from the newspaper articles that Joe, her father's friend, had been the neighbor who had called in to report the fire. When Officer Sharlett interviewed him, he gave the same story as he had in the newspaper—he had woken to see the flames shooting out and called the fire department. He also reported seeing a group of teenage boys headed into the woods that night before he went to bed. He'd noticed them, he said, because he'd known there had been a rash of petty thefts and disturbances around town recently, and he had been nervous when he'd seen them near his house. Sadie had read about them in the newspaper, but saw that here, in the interview with the police, Joe Curr had named the boys: Martin Goring, Justin Orr, Michael Leonard, and Tully Stewart.

Sadie quickly wrote down the names, and then flipped the page and realized she was in luck. The next interview the officer had done was with the boys. Sadie read the interviews quickly. All four boys had been interviewed separately, and all had denied having anything to do with the fire. Michael Leonard admitted they'd gone into the woods to drink a fifth of whiskey they'd gotten their hands on, but other than that, none of them had revealed anything that stood out to Sadie as important. Still, she wrote down their names and continued reading.

The next interview was with Samuel Bradley, the then-superintendent of the schools. The other interviews hadn't been long, but the notes for this one were only a few sentences long: *Bradley says that many people have keys to the property, and it was insured but will need to check how much. Was at home with wife the night of the fire; wife substantiates.*

The remainder of the file was filled with photographs, sketches, and diagrams, but nothing else. None of the interviews had been followed up on, because, presumably, the case had been closed when an official determination had been made as to the cause of the fire.

But that was strange, Sadie thought. Had no one looked into whose glasses were found at the site, or whether one of the cigarettes had contributed to the fire? How had electrical work been determined as the cause of the fire? There was no indication in the file. The day after the interviews, the case had simply been closed.

It was suspicious, all right. She could understand why, once Virginia had seen this file, she had been consumed with finding out what really happened that night. There were so many questions raised, and no adequate answers supplied. The determination of electrical fire seemed to come out of nowhere, and Officer Sharlett's notes on the first page of the file made it clear to Sadie that she wasn't the only one unsatisfied with the answer as to what had really happened that night.

Sadie looked around for a photocopier, but unsurprisingly, there wasn't one in this room. Sadie didn't want to press her luck by asking upstairs, so she took out her smartphone and took photos of the pages of the file. They weren't perfect, but they would do, and when she blew them up, she could see the writing well enough.

Sadie stuck her phone and her notebook back in her purse and picked up the police file. As she carried the file back up the stairs,

Sadie thought about what she'd read. When she reflected on how the clues didn't add up to the conclusion reached, she realized she felt the same curiosity and frustration Virginia must have felt. Sadie walked out of the police station more determined than ever to find out what had really happened on the night of the schoolhouse fire.

5

SADIE STOPPED IN AT THE MARKET TO GRAB A SANDWICH FOR lunch. She stood at the small display case, trying to decide between the Wild West Chicken Salad and Buffalo Bill's Ham and Cheese. The cheese on that one had some sort of spicy peppers in it, and it was always delicious—but then again, so was the chicken salad.

"The ham is particularly good today, if I do say so myself," Lou Price said, coming out from the swinging door that led to the small kitchen area carrying a tray of premade salads. "We're trying a new source for the ham, a local farmer, and it's delicious." He started arranging the salads behind the glass case.

"In that case, I'll try the ham and cheese," Sadie said, laughing. There was something funny about seeing this big man known for his butchering skills arranging delicate salads behind the case.

"Coming right up." Lou grabbed a sandwich and wrapped it up in white butcher paper, then gestured for Sadie to follow him to the register. "How is everything going, Sadie?" Lou said as he punched in her order.

"Just fine." Sadie smiled, but she was distracted, eyeing the treats in the pastry case. Lou's wife, Maggie, was a very fine pastry chef, and her croissants were flaky and buttery, her scones light and satisfying. Sadie had such a hard time passing up one of her treats, but in the end willpower won out—this time.

Lou announced her total and Sadie handed him the money, then she waved and headed out onto the sidewalk and started back toward her shop. When she stepped in the door, she waved to Julie, who was busy helping a customer sort through a bin of vintage lace table runners, and she settled in at the desk and unwrapped her sandwich. While she ate, she studied her notes about the fire.

She had quite a list of names to look into. There were also the glasses, the cigarette butts, and the burn pattern to investigate.

Vagrant/hippie? Ask Judith Marley.

Joe Curr reported the fire.

Melvin Loffredo, fire chief

Samuel Bradley, school superintendent

Robert Greene, sheriff

High school boys: Martin Goring, Justin Orr, Michael Leonard,
and Tully Stewart

Burn pattern?

Orville Montgomery, maintenance worker, smoked Victory
cigarettes, unaccounted for night of fire.

Jim Sharlett, officer who disagreed with conclusions

Tortoiseshell glasses

Sadie tapped her pen against the counter. Where to even start? She supposed she should start tracking down the people listed in the article and police file, especially Officer Sharlett, who had disagreed with the final conclusions. Though maybe she should start with Sherriff Greene, who made those final conclusions, to see if she could figure out why he made such a seemingly hasty decision.

Sadie looked up when the front door of the shop opened. A delivery man was wheeling in a large box. Sadie clapped her hands and scooted off her chair toward the door. The man held out his machine for her signature, and then set the box in the space in front of the desk. Sadie inspected the box carefully, but it looked like it had survived the journey intact, so she thanked him and waved as he headed back toward the door. Carefully, Sadie started to peel away the tape. She had box cutters in the drawer at the counter, but she worried about accidentally nicking the delicate quilt fabric, so she worked, slowly and methodically, peeling away the layers of packing tape.

Once she had the box opened, Sadie took a pair of white cotton gloves out of the desk drawer and slipped them on. When touching old fabrics, you could never be too careful, and the oils from your hands could easily stain an old quilt. Finally, she turned to the quilts. Sadie always loved opening up new shipments. Even though she had thoroughly researched the quilts that were in this box, studied their patterns and construction, and analyzed photos at the online auction site, it was always different to see the real thing. It was like opening a birthday present she knew she was going to love. Gently, she folded back the flaps of the cardboard box.

On top was a Sunshine and Shadow quilt, done in reds, blues, and yellows. She pulled it out gently and spread it out as best she could. The cotton fabric was woven in simple designs, but the way the tiny squares radiated out from the center in concentric diamond shapes was stunning. The stitches were tiny but regular, and it was clear they were hand-done. She gently ran her hand over the fabric and imagined dozens of Amish women hunched over quilting hoops, working diligently on this. The idea made her smile. There was a small stain on one red square up in the top corner, but otherwise it was immaculate, and well taken care of. Sadie folded up the quilt gently and set it on a mahogany bureau near the desk. She reached into the box and pulled out the next quilt in the bunch just as Julie led her customer to the desk.

"That's beautiful," the woman said, gesturing at the crazy quilt done in purples, blues, and greens. Sadie didn't recognize the woman, but she was dressed smartly and carried what looked like an expensive purse. Julie nodded and stepped behind the counter to ring up the table runner the woman had selected. "I just love the jewel tones, and the pattern is so interesting."

"Crazy quilts were very popular in Victorian times," Sadie said, running her hand over the different textures of the pieces. Unlike a more traditional quilt, which was usually constructed following a strict pattern of repeating squares, this one was made up of scraps of different sizes and shapes from a wide variety of fabrics pieced together in what looked like a haphazard way, but the effect was actually very ordered and quite stunning. Here, there was a rich eggplant-colored velvet triangle stitched up with an emerald green silk paisley rectangle and a mauve corduroy, and the color combination and shapes, while unexpected, came together beautifully.

Julie announced the total for the lace runner, and the woman handed over a credit card without looking up from the quilt. Sadie stifled a smile. She'd selected a piece of fine hand-knotted Belgian lace in an open rose pattern, and it was one of the more rare pieces in the bunch, but the customer didn't flinch at the price.

"I thought you were getting a shipment of Amish quilts," Julie said, wrapping the delicate lace runner in tissue paper before placing it into the bag. "That doesn't look like something I'd imagine Amish women making."

Sadie laughed out loud. The riot of colors, the uneven design, the rich and varied fabrics—no, this was nothing like the neat, even, orderly designs produced by Amish and Mennonite quilters. Sadie actually preferred the more regular patterns and careful hand-stitching of traditional quilts, but she had to admire the bold, brash way this quilter had taken disparate leftover scraps and made something unique and beautiful.

"No, this quilt is definitely not Amish. This shipment came from the estate of a collector who lived in Pennsylvania Amish country, so she had many Amish-made pieces, but she collected from all over."

"Well, she had excellent taste," the woman said. "May I take a closer look?"

Sadie carefully handed her the quilt, and she spread it out on the desk, admiring the different patterns and textures. "This is truly lovely. How much are you asking?"

Sadie looked at Julie, who shrugged. Sadie hadn't had time to think about pricing yet, so she named a figure that was a nice markup from what she'd paid for the quilt. The woman nodded, and continued to examine the piece.

"I'll take it," she said, sighing. "It's too beautiful to pass up."

Sadie shot another glance at Julie, who smiled and reached for the woman's credit card again. While Julie rang up the sale, Sadie carefully folded the quilt in tissue paper and gently settled the bundle into a paper shopping bag.

"This store is absolutely charming. I'll definitely be back." She tucked her credit card back in her purse, reached for the bag, and thanked them both, and then headed toward the front door.

"Nice work," Sadie said, nodding at the woman as she walked away from the store.

"You too," Julie said. She lifted up onto her toes and peered into the large box. "Let's see what else you've got in there."

A few minutes later, they'd unpacked a stunning Lone Star quilt done in muted browns, a red and white Flying Geese pattern, and a delicate appliquéd Sunburst quilt done in pastels. Each was in fine condition, just as promised.

"Looks like a good haul," Julie said, nodding approvingly. Sadie was pleased. They were fine quilts, and they would fetch fair prices from the right customers. She folded them gently and carried the stack toward the back of the store. She would price and tag them later. For now, she needed some caffeine and a treat. The sandwich she'd wolfed down had sated her hunger, but left her drowsy and ready for something sweet, and the scent of brewing coffee that drifted over through the open doorway from Arbuckle's next door was too much to resist.

"I'm going to pop over to Arbuckle's," Sadie said, gesturing to the opening in the wall that led to the neighboring coffee shop. "Want anything?"

"No, thank you." Julie smiled. That was probably how she kept her figure so trim, but Sadie thought a few extra miles on one of her walks in the hills around her home were worth the extra calories.

"I'll be back in a few minutes," Sadie said, and stepped over to the coffee shop.

Arbuckle's was hopping, Sadie noted, and most of the tables and comfy overstuffed chairs were occupied. Sadie looked around and smiled when she noticed her grandson, Theo, at one of the small round tables. He was sitting across from…was that Elena Garza? Sadie recognized the pretty dark-haired daughter of Ramon and Gloria Garza, who ran Los Pollitos, her favorite Mexican restaurant. Elena was popular and pretty, and Sadie was surprised but pleased to see Theo sitting across from her. But then she noticed what looked like an open textbook between them, and it started to make more sense. Sadie had heard Theo was doing some math tutoring. Still, she was glad to see him out with a pretty girl, even if he was just helping her with math. Sadie waved, but Theo didn't see her, so she shrugged and got into the line at the counter.

Luz Vidal was making a series of what looked like complicated espresso drinks for a group of teenage girls, and while Sadie waited, she looked back at Theo. He was saying something to Elena, pointing to something in the open math book, but his cheeks were pink, and he laughed nervously. His feet were shifting under the table. Sadie wasn't sure but…Elena said something, and Theo laughed again, only it almost looked like he was in pain, except there was a huge smile on his face.

Huh. It looked like Theo had a crush on Elena. It made sense, Sadie realized. He was seventeen, after all, and she was pretty and popular. It was just that Sadie had never seen Theo with a crush on a girl. It was sweet and endearing watching him interact with her, but it also opened up a whole world of scary possibilities in her grandmother's mind. She tried not to let her brain race ahead to shotgun weddings and great-grandchildren. After all, they were only working on math homework together.

"What can I get you, Sadie?" Luz Vidal smiled at Sadie, the tan skin around her eyes crinkling. Sadie looked forward and realized she hadn't even noticed when the gaggle of girls ahead of her had moved off.

"Just a large coffee, please," Sadie said, and Luz nodded and turned to the coffee machine.

Theo was now leaning in, explaining something to Elena, but he was focused on Elena instead of at the page. The look in his eyes—well, despite her fears, it warmed her grandmother's heart to see the naked emotion on his face. He was a bit awkward about it, but he cared about this girl. Sadie tried to read Elena's body language, but her back was to Sadie. Of course Elena liked him back, though. Theo was handsome and smart and funny, and he was a kind soul to boot. What girl could resist that?

"Can I get you anything else?" Luz set the steaming paper cup of coffee on the polished wood counter and smiled at Sadie. Sadie knew she should say no, but that chocolate croissant in the pastry case was calling her name.

"I'll take that chocolate croissant as well," Sadie said, pointing at the flaky pastry.

"Excellent choice." Luz used a square of wax paper to reach into the pastry case and pull out a treat, and she slid it into a small paper bag and handed that to Sadie. Sadie paid, and then turned to carry it back to her store, but she cast one last glance back at Theo. Now he was laughing as Elena said something, but his laugh came out higher-pitched than it should. The poor guy was nervous. Sadie knew that he had nothing to be nervous about, that any girl would be lucky to be with Theo. Sadie smiled, turned, and headed back through the passway into her store.

But still, Sadie thought she might casually try to give Theo a couple of pointers about interacting with girls next time she got a chance. It couldn't hurt to help him out a bit.

That evening as she drove home, Sadie saw a tow truck from Mickelson's Garage at the side of the road right next to where Virginia's car had gone off the road. She supposed they were working on getting the car back up the ravine. Sadie said a prayer for Virginia as she passed. Maybe Edwin would have some good news when he picked her up in—goodness. Sadie glanced at the clock on her dashboard. She only had an hour until Edwin was supposed to come pick her up. Still, she took the curves of the old mountain road carefully. She'd been driving these roads her whole life, but last night, she'd been reminded that you can't be too careful.

Sadie had just finished putting on a coat of tinted lip balm when her doorbell rang. Right on time.

"Is Los Pollitos okay with you?" Edwin asked as he pulled his car out of her driveway. It was a European model, with buttery soft leather seats and individualized temperature gauges. You could hardly hear the engine in this thing, even though Edwin had the classical piano music turned down softly. Sadie loved riding in his car, but it was highly impractical for winters in the Rockies. She would stick with her trusty Tahoe.

"Do dogs like country music?"

Edwin laughed. "I have no idea." He shook his head. "But I'm guessing I should take that as a yes?"

"Indeed." Sadie was laughing. "Los Pollitos sounds perfect. I haven't had Mexican food in a while."

Sadie and Edwin chattered easily as they made the short drive into town. Edwin told her about a project to improve flood control measures around Silver Peak that he'd been working on at City Hall today, and Sadie told him about trying to determine pricing for the new shipment of quilts she'd received. Soon they were walking in the front door of Los Pollitos. Gloria Garza greeted them warmly and ushered them to a table in the corner. She set down chips and salsa as they looked over the menu, and then took their orders.

Sadie looked around the restaurant as they waited for their dinners to arrive. About half of the tables in the small restaurant were full, and Sadie smiled when she saw that Elena Garza, daughter of the owners, Ramon and Gloria, was working on homework at a table in the corner. Well, it seemed like she was supposed to be working on homework. It actually looked like she was texting on her cell phone. That might explain the need for tutoring, she thought, and smiled as she remembered seeing Theo so concentrated on the young beauty. Elena had always seemed nice; she would be thrilled if Theo ended up with her.

"Elena." Ramon Garza's head appeared in the window that led to the kitchen, and Elena dropped her phone immediately and turned back to her schoolbooks. Ramon mumbled something under his breath and shook his head, and Elena focused on the paper in front of her. Sadie watched Elena a few minutes more. Sadie acutely remembered the frustrations of having a teenage daughter, but Ramon's reaction seemed to be a bit stronger than Sadie would have expected. Elena had her head buried in her books, but Sadie looked back at Ramon, and he was still watching his daughter, mumbling under his breath. It seemed odd—Sadie had only ever known Ramon to be jolly and upbeat. Was this just typical frustration between a father and his daughter?

"What are you thinking about?" Edwin asked, and Sadie turned away from the Garzas and back to the handsome man in front of her. He looked especially nice in the button-down shirt and sweater vest he was wearing tonight, and the blue in the shirt really brought out the intense color of his eyes.

"Just people-watching." She took a chip and popped it in her mouth. She loved this place. The warm terra-cotta floor and colorful art on the walls made the place feel festive, even on the dreariest of days.

"I like being here with you," Edwin said. They chatted about their days for a few minutes, and then Edwin turned to her, his face serious.

"So what's this I hear about your going through old police records?" Edwin said.

Sadie took a chip from the basket between them and dipped it into the bowl of salsa. "Goodness. You really do know everything that goes on around town, don't you?" Sadie laughed. She knew she shouldn't be surprised; in a town this size, it was hard to keep secrets, especially from the mayor. She put the chip in her mouth and chewed.

"Don't forget, I pay their salaries down at the station." He winked, and Sadie knew he wasn't malicious, but it still felt strange to know that someone had not only noticed what she had been up to today, but also mentioned it to Edwin.

"I suspected Virginia had seen something in the old police file that had led her to figure out who started the old schoolhouse fire, and I was trying to think what it was," Sadie said, wiping her fingertips on the paper napkin in her lap.

"So you're trying to retrace her steps?" Edwin said, taking a sip of his water. "Are you sure that's a good idea?"

"As I mentioned last night, I suspect that what happened to her last night was linked to what she'd just uncovered," Sadie explained. "And I want to know who was responsible for her accident, so it seems that figuring out what she knew is a good way to get there."

Edwin took a chip and nodded. "I guess that's what I'm getting at. If your theory *is* right, whatever she knew landed her in the hospital last night." He broke the chip into two pieces, but he was focused on Sadie. "I worry about your retracing her steps. If you're right that the accident was related to whatever she found out, you could be in danger if someone thinks you are looking into it too."

Sadie stuffed a chip into her mouth to give herself time before answering. She appreciated his concern, she really did.

"I'll be careful," she said, and he nodded, but he didn't look convinced.

"I'd really prefer you left this to the police to sort out," Edwin said.

Another chip went in. Sadie knew Edwin was simply taking care of her, and usually she loved that about him. But what did he expect her to do, sit back and ignore what she knew while whoever had landed her friend in the hospital walked around free? He knew her better than that. Still, she didn't want to quarrel with Edwin; this was supposed to be a nice evening out.

"I'll cooperate with the police in any way I can," Sadie said. It wasn't a real answer, and they both knew it, but Edwin nodded resolutely.

"Besides, like I said last night, it doesn't really matter what she found out, unfortunately," Edwin continued. "The statute of limitations for that old fire is long past, so even if she had concrete evidence that someone set it on purpose, no judge worth his salt would hear the case."

Sadie knew Edwin was no doubt right, but that wasn't the point. Sadie was trying to find out what Virginia had uncovered in case Sadie was right about that being why someone had knocked her car off the road, not because she expected to take the old case to trial. As much as she loved his calm, reserved professionalism, sometimes Edwin took things too literally. She decided to change the topic, and thankfully, Gloria Garza set down two steaming plates of enchiladas in front of them just then.

Sadie took the opportunity to distract him from this line of thinking. "Do you remember the old schoolhouse fire at all?" she asked.

"Sure," Edwin said, and nodded as he cut into his enchilada. "We were in what, seventh grade?"

Sadie nodded. She and Edwin had both grown up in Silver Peak and had gone to school together, though they hadn't begun dating until high school.

"I remember my parents talking about it one night at dinner. I was fascinated by the idea of a building burning down, and the next day on my way home from school I went by the site to see it."

"You did?" Sadie's cheese enchiladas sent up a puff of steam when she cut into them, so she scooped up a bite of rice and beans while she waited for them to cool. "What did you think?"

"I was a twelve-year-old boy. I thought it was great." He shrugged. "I loved seeing the burned-out shell of the school, and that bell, the only thing left intact." He set down his fork and took a sip of water. "I didn't realize then how dangerous fires were or how bad it was for the school district. I just wished I'd been there to see it burn."

Sadie shook her head. Sadie didn't have brothers, and she had only had one daughter herself. The mind of a junior-high boy was one thing she'd never understand as long as she lived. Though she supposed there was some small comfort in the fact that Edwin had turned out just fine.

"Do you remember what your parents said about the fire?" Sadie asked.

Edwin tilted his head and chewed while he thought. "All I really remember about it was that my mom kept talking about some homeless man who'd been seen all over town. She was convinced he was responsible for the fire, and she was afraid of what he might do next, so she forbade me to go out around town on my own."

"And yet you went to the burn site anyway."

He shrugged. "Like I said, I was twelve. I wasn't always a judge. And don't try to tell me you never disobeyed your parents. I know you better than that."

Sadie smiled. She'd been a pretty obedient child and had honestly valued her parents' opinions, but there had been a few times she'd done exactly what she wanted regardless of what they thought. She supposed everyone did.

"Well, there was the time I declared I would never wear another dress to school and they couldn't make me."

The corners of Edwin's mouth turned up, and she told him about the fight that had ensued after her declaration. But as she talked, she watched Ramon, who came out from the kitchen to say something quietly to Elena. Elena first rolled her eyes, but then, when Ramon took her arm and said something under his breath and glanced toward Gloria, she nodded and stood up and followed him into the kitchen.

It was none of her business, Sadie knew. Probably just some small family drama they didn't want playing out in front of customers. But something about it seemed strange. And if Sadie wasn't wrong, there was some sort of tension between Gloria and Ramon as well. She hadn't seen any interaction between them all evening, and they were usually so full of jokes and relaxed. In fact, the entire Garza family seemed on edge tonight.

Sadie shook her head and reminded herself not to let her imagination get away from her. Every family had its off days. This was no doubt just a small family issue that was none of her business.

Sadie didn't think anything else of it until Edwin had paid and they were walking back to his car. Then, as they stepped out of the restaurant, she noticed Ramon Garza's car. It was a Mercury Sable, and it was covered in dirt. And it was maroon. And, she noticed, there was a long, jagged scratch along the front left side of the car.

It didn't mean anything, Sadie told herself. Ramon's certainly wasn't the only maroon car in Silver Peak. But that scratch—

It could have come from anything, Sadie thought. There was no reason to assume he had anything to do with Virginia's accident. But along with the strange behavior she'd witnessed in the restaurant...Sadie didn't want to assume anything. But something didn't sit right. She wondered how she could find out more about what Ramon Garza had been up to last night.

As Edwin drove her back home, she tried to keep her voice light and her mind on what Edwin was saying. She didn't want him to know she was thinking about Ramon and planning to investigate the crash further. He wouldn't like it, but he worried too much. For now, what he didn't know wouldn't hurt him.

Edwin walked her to her door and gave her a hug and a kiss on the cheek. Sadie thanked him for dinner and for a nice night, and promised to give him a call in the morning, and then, as he climbed back into his car, Sadie pushed open her front door.

And she froze. There was an envelope on her entryway floor. Someone had obviously shoved it under her door while she'd been out. Slowly, hesitantly, she bent down and picked it up. It was a plain business-size envelope, and there was no writing on the outside, no marking of any kind. She lifted the flap, pulled out a single typewritten sheet, and read it quickly: STAY OUT OF THE SCHOOLHOUSE FIRE OR YOU'LL BE SORRY.

6

It took Sadie quite a while to get to sleep Thursday night, as she mulled over the note she'd found under her door and its implications. Someone knew she was looking into whatever Virginia had found out. That someone had likely been responsible for causing Virginia's car to go off the road. This person knew where Sadie lived, and had known that she wasn't home last night. Edwin had been right—she needed to be careful.

But as she lay awake in bed, she thought about how she also now knew that Virginia had been right. Someone knew more about the schoolhouse fire than they had admitted. And, given the lengths they had gone to to keep their secret safe, this person likely had a lot to lose if anyone found out the truth.

Instead of scaring Sadie away from finding out more, the note only made her more certain that discovering who set the schoolhouse fire would lead her to who knocked her friend off the road. As she finally started to drift off to sleep, Sadie vowed that she would do whatever it took to get to the bottom of this mystery.

Friday morning, Sadie groaned when her alarm went off. She needed several more hours of sleep to make up for her fitful night, but there was no time to lie in bed this morning. She had a few stops she wanted to make before she headed in to the shop.

Sadie started a pot of coffee while she dressed, and she'd had several cups and felt almost human by the time she'd walked Hank, finished her devotions, and headed out the door. Sadie made her way to Silver Peak Hospital, and when she asked at the desk, was directed to a room on the fourth floor.

The lights in Virginia's room were low, and Virginia looked small underneath the thin hospital blanket. Sadie set the bunch of wildflowers she'd picked from her yard down on the windowsill and sat gently in the chair next to her bed. The room was filled with flowers and balloons, but aside from Virginia and Sadie it was empty. Virginia's husband, David, must be at home, no doubt getting the boys ready for school. She still hadn't heard back from him, and though a small part of her had hoped to be able to talk to him about Virginia's files here, mostly Sadie felt bad for all he must be juggling right now. Sadie should bring by a meal or find another way to help the young family out.

Virginia's breathing was low and even, her chest rising and falling steadily. Two days ago, this woman had been vibrant and full of life, and now, here she was, trapped in a coma, strapped to a hospital bed. Seeing Virginia here, Sadie was reminded, once again, that someone had done this to her on purpose. Someone had a secret they wanted to protect, apparently at any cost. But Sadie wouldn't let them get away with it. She would find out what it was and who had done this to her friend.

Sadie bowed her head and spent the next twenty minutes praying for Virginia and her family, and then, reluctantly, she stood to leave. She had to get going. She turned back and took one last glance at her friend, then sighed. Virginia hadn't even known she'd been there.

Instead of heading straight to her store, Sadie drove to the police station and asked at the front desk for Sherriff Slattery. A few minutes later, she was led back to his office. He looked up from his computer screen and nodded when he saw Sadie. He gestured for her to take a seat in the visitor's chair next to his desk and took a sip from a paper cup of Arbuckle's coffee.

"What's going on, Sadie?"

Sadie reached into her purse and pulled out the note that had been shoved under her door. Sadie had debated about telling Sheriff Slattery about the threat, since in all likelihood it would get back to Edwin if she did, but in the end she had decided that it might be the impetus the police needed to investigate the link between the fire and the crash.

"I found this shoved under my door last night." Sadie smoothed out the paper on his desk. "I thought you might want to see it."

The sheriff's eyes flicked back to his computer for just a second, then he gently brushed her hands away, pulled a pair of rubber gloves out of a box in a desk drawer, and picked up the paper.

"Who has touched this?" the Sheriff said, examining the paper carefully.

"Since I found it, just me," Sadie said. He nodded. It was too late now, but Sadie realized she shouldn't have handled the note with her bare hands. They would no doubt test for fingerprints. She only hoped she hadn't messed up whatever prints had been left on the note before she got to it.

"You said you found this inside your house?" Sheriff Slattery asked. He took a magnifying glass out of a drawer and studied it further. Sadie had no idea what he was looking for, but she hoped he would find a clue that would point to whoever wrote it.

"It was shoved under my door," Sadie said. "I wanted you to see it because I think it makes clear the connection between the old fire and what happened to Virginia."

Sheriff Slattery didn't say anything, just nodded, and continued studying the paper. Finally, he laid down the paper, sat back, and looked at Sadie.

"What time was this?"

"I left the house around six thirty, and got home just before eight thirty, so it was some time in that window," Sadie said.

He looked at his computer screen, then back at the note. "I'll have this dusted for fingerprints," he said. Sadie waited for him to go on, to acknowledge the connection that was so obvious to her, but he didn't. His eyes were resting on his screen. Sadie looked around his office, taking in the big picture window that looked out over the wooded hills, the impeccably neat desk, and the pictures of his four grandchildren on skis perched at the top of a snowy slope. And she looked at what was apparently so interesting on his computer. Sadie saw that screen held what looked to be an image from a video of some sort. The camera had been placed high up, and the video showed a street at night. Sadie could see cars parked by the side of the street, as well as branches from a tree at the top of the screen, but the foreground showed a figure huddled in front of a pay phone.

"We'll let you know if we find anything," he said, and Sadie realized she was being dismissed. Just like that? Well—Sadie started to push herself up—maybe they had all they needed. She hadn't expected them to send a security detail to follow her around, but given the nature of the note, she would have thought—

The door opened, and Officer Kenmore poked his head into the office.

"Have you seen it yet?" Kyle asked, stepping inside. And then he noticed Sadie, and shook his head. "Sorry, I didn't realize you had a visitor," he said, and stepped backward.

"It's okay. We're just wrapping up," Sheriff Slattery said, and again, Sadie understood that she was being asked to leave. She reached down to pick up her purse, but Officer Kenmore stopped her.

"We should have her take a look," Officer Kenmore said, gesturing at Sadie. "She's involved in this, and she knows everyone in this town."

Sadie's heart surged with appreciation for her former student. She had no idea if she could help, but not being underestimated meant a lot. And she truly did know many more people in town than the sheriff, who had only moved to Silver Peak a few years ago.

Sheriff Slattery sighed and seemed to be thinking for a moment. Sadie focused on the computer screen, trying to make sense of the image. Where had this been taken? Why the strange angle? Finally, Sheriff Slattery seemed to make a decision, and he used the cursor to start the video over. He zoomed out, and Sadie saw that the original image was actually a much wider shot of what she now recognized as Main Street. She could just make out the bottom of her shop's front window at the top edge of the screen.

Sadie held her breath as she saw cars driving by on the street but not much else. It was raining and it was dark out, and the street was quiet. Then, from the bottom left corner of the screen, a figure appeared, hurrying down the sidewalk. It was wearing a wide-brimmed hat and a raincoat, and you couldn't see the face. He—there was nothing that overtly indicated the figure was a man, but for some reason Sadie assumed it was—moved quickly to the pay phone and pushed a few buttons. There was no sound on the video, but it looked like his mouth was moving, like he was talking, and then, just a few seconds later, he hung up the phone and scurried away, his face still hidden in shadow.

"What is this?" Sadie asked as the clip came to an end. Sheriff Slattery backed the video up and stopped it on a shot of the man stopping at the phone booth.

"This is security footage from a camera outside of Silver Peak Bank," Sheriff Slattery said. "Taken just about eight twenty on Wednesday night." Sadie immediately recognized the significance of that time; that was just minutes after Virginia's accident. "Yours wasn't the only phone call to nine-one-one reporting the accident, Sadie. Another call came in to nine-one-one just minutes after yours, and we traced the call to this pay phone. We believe this security footage shows the call being placed, but the caller didn't identify himself on the line, and we're very interested in finding out who placed that call."

"Goodness." The police had been busy, that was for sure. She hadn't realized. "How would this man have known about the accident?"

"That's what we're trying to figure out," the sheriff said. "Do you have any idea who this might be?"

"He may have simply been driving by and seen it happen, and headed for the first phone he could find," Officer Kenmore said. Sheriff Slattery shot him a look, but he didn't notice. "But we would really like to know what he saw."

Sadie focused on the man on the screen. It was so dark, and the video quality was so grainy, that with the hat on, you really couldn't tell much of anything about who it was.

Sadie shook her head. "I'm sorry, I really can't say. Is there a tape of the phone call? Can you tell anything about him by his voice?"

"We haven't been able to trace the voice," the sheriff said.

She continued to stare at the video still, but finally she shook her head. "I'm sorry, but I'll let you know if I think of anything."

"We'd appreciate that. And we'll let you know if we find out anything about the note."

Sadie stood to go, thanked both officers, and headed back out to the street. Today had dawned a bit warmer than yesterday, and the sun was a brilliant robin's-egg blue dotted with cottony clouds. It was time to get the shop ready to open, so Sadie drove the few blocks and parked her car in front of her shop. As she climbed out of the car, her eyes traveled over to the far side of the street and rested on a pay phone in front of the bank. She thought about the video of the man using the phone, and shook her head. There had to be a way to figure out who he was. Then, she turned and walked to the door of her shop. But the lights inside were on, and the door was unlocked.

"Hello?" Sadie called out, and smiled when she saw Julie walk out of the back room. She was wearing a light blue sweater and boots with dark, fitted jeans, and she looked fresh and young.

"You're in early today," Sadie said, peeling off her light spring jacket. The rich smell of freshly ground coffee beans was wafting over from Arbuckle's. Sadie would definitely be stopping in for a cup sooner rather than later.

Julie laughed. "No, I'm not. It's already a few minutes past ten! I was starting to get worried about you." Julie slid behind the counter and started sorting the bills for the register.

"It can't be—" But Sadie looked at the antique pendulum clock that currently hung behind the counter and realized Julie was right. Her errands this morning had gone longer than she had realized, and she still had more stops to make today.

"I'm so sorry. I didn't realize how late it was," Sadie said, but Julie waved her concerns away.

"That's what I'm here for. I'm happy to be here when you have other things to do." Julie slid the drawer into the old-fashioned register, and a bell rang as the drawer went into place.

Sadie looked around the shop. Everything looked neat and ready for business. The glassware was dusted, and the jewelry sparkled in the display case. Even the Lone Star quilt she'd unpacked yesterday was draped beautifully over an iron bedstead. All that was missing was the customers, and on a beautiful day like today, Sadie had no doubt they'd be in soon.

"Well, if you have everything under control, I think I'll run out to do a few more errands."

"Sounds great. I'll hold down the fort," Julie said.

"Thank you," Sadie said, and picked up her purse and jacket again. A few moments later, she had a cup of coffee in hand and was walking down Main Street toward Madison Avenue, where the Silver Peak Fire Station was. A moment later, she was standing in front of the large red garage door of the redbrick building. That must be where the fire trucks went in and out. A smaller, human-scale door was to the right of the garage, and Sadie went there and knocked gently. When no one answered, she knocked again, and then, a few moments later, tried pushing open the door. It swung open and led to a long hallway. To the left was a door to the garage, and straight ahead was a staircase that led up to the second floor.

"Hello?" Sadie called out. Her voice seemed to echo in the cavernous space, but a moment later, a head appeared at the top of the stairs.

"Hi there, Sadie. Did you need something?"

Sadie smiled to see Tyson Williams at the top of the stairs. Tyson had deep bronze skin and soulful eyes, and she knew he was something of a heartthrob among the single ladies in town.

"I was hoping I could talk to someone about a fire," Sadie said.

Tyson laughed. "Well, then you've come to the right place. Would you like to come in?"

He gestured for Sadie to come up the stairs, and Sadie nodded and started up the cement steps. As she passed, she peeked in the open door to the garage area and saw two trucks, as well as racks of equipment and rows of yellow protective gear for the men hanging from hooks.

At the top of the stairs, he led her past a small exercise room and a row of lockers, and then past what looked like a row of small rooms with bunks, and into a large and bright lounge area. There was a full kitchen with handsome maple cabinets, a dining table, and a flat-screen television, as well as a seating area with comfortable couches and chairs. A few men were parked in front of the TV watching some cable news program, and they waved as Tyson led Sadie by and gestured to one of the couches.

"This is really nice," Sadie said, sitting back against the plush cushions of the overstuffed couch.

"Fortunately, most of the calls we get aren't serious emergencies, so we spend a fair amount of time in here," Tyson said, shrugging. "It's comfortable, especially on long shifts."

Sadie nodded. She was glad the men could spend a few minutes relaxing between emergencies. Anyone willing to rush into a burning building to save a life earned himself a few minutes of cable TV news in his downtime, in her mind. She set her coffee cup on the low wooden table in front of the couch.

"So what can I help you with?" Tyson asked.

Sadie thought about how to phrase her questions. "I'm looking into an old fire, and I found a few discrepancies in the report of how it started. I wondered if you might be able to help me make sense of it," Sadie said.

"I can certainly try." Tyson gave her a warm smile.

"Are you familiar with the old schoolhouse fire from 1965?" Sadie asked.

He shook his head. "Sorry, I wasn't born yet," he said, and Sadie laughed.

"No, clearly not. I was just a child myself." She smiled when Tyson smacked his forehead. It was endearing, and he was warm and genuine. She briefly wondered whether her daughter, Alice, would be mad if she tried to arrange a way to set them up. "It's just that a lot of locals have heard about it over the years."

He shook his head. "Sorry, I only moved to the area a few years ago, and I haven't heard of it."

"That's okay," Sadie said, and reached into her purse and pulled out her phone. She pulled out the photos she'd taken of the police report about the fire and zoomed in on the section of notes from the fire chief, Melvin Loffredo.

"I was wondering if you could help me make sense of this," Sadie said.

He took the phone from her hands and looked at the screen.

"Okay, this is interesting. The fire chief found several points of origin for the fire."

"How could he tell? Isn't the evidence all burned up in a big fire like this?"

"That's what a lot of people think, but actually there's usually a fair bit of evidence left behind after a fire, and we can often trace a fire's origin by looking at how it burned and working backward. Usually the first thing we try to do is determine the origin point." He used two fingers to enlarge the image on her screen. "Fire burns up in a V pattern, so often we can look at charred walls and trace the source back down to the point of the V. In an electrical fire, for instance, the V often points to a faulty outlet, and you know that's the source of the blaze."

Sadie's ears perked up. "And that's not what you see here?"

"That's not what the report indicates. They traced this fire to several origin points, which would be very unusual if we were just dealing with some faulty wiring. And in this case, the origin points all seemed to burn in a very narrow V shape."

"What does that mean?" Sadie asked.

"That's an indication that the fire started hotter than normal and burned much more quickly than it should have. That generally indicates the presence of an accelerant."

"An accelerant?"

"Like gasoline, or kerosene. Something to get it going faster."

"Goodness." That sure made it sound like someone had lit this fire on purpose.

Tyson was squinting at the screen, and he used his finger to scroll down. "Yep, and it looks like they found evidence of the floor being burned too, so definitely gas of some sort was used." He saw Sadie's confused look and explained. "A fire burns up, right? So usually the floor beneath a fire is not completely burned. Unless an accelerant was used, in which case the fire will have burned down into the floor, often in a pattern that follows the line of the gas."

Sadie tried to process all of this. "So what you're saying is, the evidence shows this fire was set on purpose. Somebody poured gas on the floor and lit it in a few places."

"That's sure what it looks like to me, based on this report."

Sadie nodded. Virginia had been right.

"Can you think of any reason this fire would have been declared officially the result of bad electrical wiring?"

Tyson laughed. "Not unless someone was trying to cover something up. If this report is to be trusted, the result is pretty clear."

This left Sadie with the obvious conclusion: someone had been trying to cover up the real cause of the fire. But who? And why? And who had purposely started the fire, and for what reason? Sadie had more questions now than when she'd come in.

"Thank you so much for your help." Sadie reached for her coffee and started to stand.

"My pleasure. We don't see too many old-fashioned straight-up burn cases like that these days."

Sadie paused. "What do you mean?" She lowered herself back down.

"Oh, just that there's so much fire prevention equipment these days that it's rare for a fire to burn unchecked like that." He must have seen the confused look on Sadie's face, because he laughed.

"Don't get me wrong, it's a good thing. It saves lives, and it keeps fires from burning out of control more often than not. You just don't see free burns like this very much these days."

"So you're saying that a fire like this wouldn't happen today?"

"Not necessarily. But every public building these days is built with fire sprinklers and fire access stairs and fire-resistant materials and such. The new library was built with a state-of-the-art system. And schools especially—this wouldn't have happened at a school these days. You should see the setup they have down at the high school. They've got sprinklers, of course, but we just put in a high-tech system in the main office that can tell you where in the building a fire is when an alarm goes off. They can trace it to the exact classroom within seconds, and if it's bad enough, usually by then the fire sprinklers will have gone off in that room and doused it anyway. If a kid lights a match in the bathroom, the front office knows about it."

Sadie was glad to hear it; she couldn't think of many buildings more worthy of a high-quality fire prevention system than a school.

"A system like that isn't standard, then, in public buildings?"

"It depends. But fire codes have advanced so much that just about any building these days is safer than one built a century ago."

That did make Sadie feel better, though as she stood to go, she felt like she was leaving with so many more questions than she'd come in with.

"Thank you so much for your help. I really appreciate it."

"Glad to help. Come on back if you have any more questions."

Sadie waved to the other firemen and headed back down the stairs. As she walked back to the shop, she thought through all she had learned that morning. The schoolhouse fire had almost certainly been set intentionally, with gasoline or some other flammable liquid used to start it. Someone had seen the report that indicated that and declared the fire an accident anyway, which probably meant someone had a distinct reason to cover it up. On the night of Virginia's accident, someone had known about the car accident and called 911 to report it, but no one knew who it had been or how they had found out about the crash. All they knew was that the call had been placed by a man in a wide-brimmed hat.

Come to think of it, Edwin had a hat like that. She'd seen him wear it dozens of times, usually to protect his head from the rain. Was there any way...but then, he would have said something to Sadie, wouldn't he?

Sadie shook her head. Lots of men in town wore hats in the rain. She couldn't just go around suspecting everyone she thought of.

Sadie stepped back inside her shop and smiled when she heard Johnny Cash playing over the sound system. She loved his smooth, mellow voice. She waved to Julie, who was rearranging a collection of Depression-era glass bowls, and set her things in the back room, then went to see if a customer looking at a sterling silver tea set needed help. The woman assured Sadie she was just looking, so Sadie decided to use the time to finish pricing the quilts that had come in yesterday. She pulled the box to the back room and slipped on her gloves. Then she pulled out the Flying Geese quilt and spread it out as best she could, running her hands over the delicate fabric.

There was a small brown spot on a white square in the upper right corner, and the fabric was faded in a few places, but it was pretty close to pristine. The quilting stitches were small and even, and the design was intricate. This had obviously been made by someone who knew what she was doing, but the tiny imperfections in the stitching—a slightly longer stitch here, a line that veered off just a bit—showed that this had indeed been quilted by hand. Next Sadie checked the binding, and though it was worn around the corners, it was intact. She didn't want to damage the fabric to check the batting, but it felt heavy and solid, like cotton, not like the synthetic fillers that had been introduced in recent decades. She turned back to the front and studied the fabrics, in deep shades of red and a dozen variations of white, used in the squares. They were mostly solids, with some small-scale calicos and chintzes, which were the types of fabrics you would expect to find on a quilt made around the turn of the century. Sadie felt certain this quilt was an authentic antique, just as the auction material had promised. She pulled out one of the reference books she kept on a shelf on the far wall. She couldn't possibly keep information about all the sorts of antiques she would encounter in this shop in her head, and these books often provided historical context, information about manufacturers, and recent sales prices. This book featured pictures and prices for quilts of all kinds, and she consulted the section on turn-of-the-century quilts.

Based on what the reference book said about the quilt and what she'd paid for it, Sadie figured a fair price and carefully wrote it on a tag and pinned it to the corner of the binding. She heard the bell over the door ring, but since she knew Julie was out front, she went back to her box of quilts.

Sadie had just folded the quilt neatly and pulled out the appliquéd quilt when she looked up to find her best friend, Roz, standing over her.

"You know, you're easy to sneak up on," Roz said, smiling. "You should watch that."

Goodness. "I suppose I don't expect people to be sneaking up on me in my own shop," Sadie said, laughing. "But it's good to see you anyway."

"Nice to see you too. And that is beautiful," Roz said, pointing to the quilt done in shades of rosy pinks and creams.

"It is nice, isn't it?" Sadie turned the quilt so she could see it better.

"I don't know how you work here. I would just end up taking everything home," Roz said.

"I'd very quickly run out of space and lose a lot of money if I did that," Sadie said. "Though I have to admit that sometimes I am tempted." She set the quilt down and straightened up. "So what brings you here today?"

"Maybe I just wanted to say hi," Roz said with a knowing smile.

"Maybe." Sadie laughed. She'd known Roz since the first day of kindergarten. "But I doubt it."

"Well, you're right." Roz let out a breath in mock indignation. "You know me too well. I'm actually here because the church is organizing a meal train for the Radcliff family and I wanted to see if you wanted to contribute. I know you were working with Virginia, so I thought you might."

"Of course. Sign me up." Sadie loved a lot of things about Campfire Chapel, but one of her favorite things was how its members cared for each other and for the people in Silver Peak who were in need.

Roz pulled a sign-up sheet from her purse and handed it to Sadie. Sadie spread it out on the top of the oak cabinet next to her and looked at the dates available. No one had signed up to make them dinner tonight. Well, Sadie didn't have any plans tonight. Besides, maybe this would be a good opportunity to talk to David, who still hadn't called her back.

"Do you have a pen?" she asked, setting down the quilt. Roz handed her a blue fountain pen, and she signed her name on the line for dinner tonight.

"So?" Roz crossed her arms and looked at Sadie expectantly.

"So what?" Sadie noted the address and the time frame she was supposed to drop the meal by. She'd have to leave a few minutes early, but she had all the ingredients for pesto tortellini at home, and that was a quick dish.

"So I keep hearing all over town that you know something about Virginia's accident Wednesday night, but I haven't heard it from my best friend." Roz looked at Sadie knowingly.

Sadie sighed. "I wouldn't say I know much of anything, but yes, it's true that I was on the line with her when it happened."

"And that you're running your own investigation into who did it?"

"Seriously, where does everyone in town keep hearing this stuff?"

Roz didn't answer, just waited expectantly.

"I'm not 'running an investigation.' I'm just looking into things." Sadie explained that Virginia had just told her who had started the old fire at the time of the accident, and the connection Sadie suspected between that and the crash. Sadie didn't mention the threatening note or the fact that someone seemed to want to keep the old news quiet pretty badly.

"Well, next time you should ask your best friend what she knows about it." Roz sniffed. She was smiling, but Sadie could see that underneath it she was a little bit hurt. Roz had helped Sadie solve a few puzzles in the past, and Sadie realized she probably should have at least let Roz know what she'd been up to.

"I'm sorry, Roz." Sadie shook her head. "I should have talked to you about it."

"It's okay," Roz said, and her face brightened a bit. "But Roscoe saw something on Wednesday night that I thought you might be interested to hear about."

"Oh?"

"Roscoe had a building committee meeting at church Wednesday night, and afterward, he went out to dinner with Don Sweeting and a couple of the other guys on the team."

"So you had the night off. Lucky you."

Roz beamed. "I made myself a frozen burrito and watched all the shows Roscoe hates. It was lovely. But the point is, they were at Los Pollitos and saw something strange."

Sadie's ears perked up at the mention of Los Pollitos. "What happened?"

"They had just been seated. The meeting had gone long, so it was almost eight o'clock by this point, and you know Roscoe. If he doesn't get his meals regularly he gets cranky."

Actually, Sadie had rarely known Roz's husband—a kind, generous man—to be cranky, but Sadie understood that wives often saw a different side of their husbands.

"So he was watching the Garza family, trying to get their attention so they could order, but just as they sat down he said Ramon got a phone call on his cell phone. He got visibly agitated, then hung up and immediately started to leave the restaurant. Gloria asked him what was wrong, but he wouldn't tell her, and he just grabbed his coat and left."

"This all happened in the middle of the restaurant?"

"Apparently. Roscoe said he could tell that Gloria tried to play it down so customers wouldn't notice, but again, he was hungry, so…"

Sadie nodded. She had been married for decades. She understood the single-minded focus men could have when they were hungry.

"Anyway, once he heard about Virginia's accident, the timing of it all seemed a bit strange. Neither of us wants to suggest Ramon was responsible, but… well, I heard on *The Chatterbox* the car that hit her was maroon, and I know Ramon does drive a maroon car."

Sadie nodded, and she wasn't surprised that the fact that the car was maroon had made its way to *The Chatterbox* blog. "The timing does seem odd." She didn't mention that she'd already witnessed tension between the Garza family last night at dinner, or that Ramon's maroon car had a scrape along the front panel.

"Thanks for letting me know."

"Of course. And I'll let you know if we hear of anything else that might be relevant."

"I'd appreciate that." Sadie sighed. "And thanks for heading up meals for the Radcliff family. That's going to be really helpful for them."

"We all want to help however we can," Roz said, and gave a little wave as she turned to go. Sadie stood there, her mind spinning, after she walked out the door. Ramon Garza again. Could he have—

Sadie didn't want to believe it. What possible motive could he have? He hadn't even been alive back when the old fire had been set. Sadie was pretty sure that his family had been in town, though—could he be protecting someone else? A family member from an earlier generation? Sadie would have to find out more.

Sadie looked out of the back room and around the shop. It was quiet now. But it was just about time for Julie to go out for lunch, so Sadie couldn't really run out and talk to Ramon right now. She should finish pricing these quilts, but suddenly she couldn't focus on antiques. She was itching to find out more about Ramon Garza and why he had left the restaurant so suddenly on Wednesday night, but she had a whole list of other names to find out more about as well. Now would be the perfect time to start on that. Sadie set the appliquéd quilt down and headed over to the desk. She sat down and shook the mouse to wake up the computer.

Sadie reached into the desk drawer and pulled her journal out of her purse. She flipped to the pages of notes she'd taken yesterday and studied the list of names cited in the articles and in the police report.

Vagrant/hippie? Ask Judith Marley.

Joe Curr reported the fire.

Melvin Loffredo, fire chief

Samuel Bradley, school superintendent

Robert Greene, sheriff

High school boys: Martin Goring, Justin Orr, Michael Leonard, and Tully Stewart

Burn pattern?

Orville Montgomery, maintenance worker, smoked Victory cigarettes, unaccounted for night of fire.

Jim Sharlett, officer who disagreed with conclusions
Tortoiseshell glasses

Thinking over what she had learned that morning, she decided it made the most sense to try to hunt down Robert Greene, the sheriff who had declared the fire an accident, apparently despite the evidence. Maybe he could shed some light on what led to his decision.

If he was still around, that was. This had all happened fifty years ago. Sadie wasn't sure how many, if any, of the key players were even still alive. Joe Curr, the neighbor who reported the fire, had been a friend of her father's and a faithful member of Campfire Chapel, and Sadie knew that he'd passed on almost a decade ago. Judith Marley was another former schoolteacher and Sadie ran into her occasionally in town. Sadie could talk with her. Samuel Bradley, the former superintendent, was very much alive and part of what passed for high-society life in Silver Peak. But the other names were anybody's guess.

Sadie wasn't sure where to start trying to track down information about Sheriff Robert Greene, or the other officer, Jim Sharlett, who had disagreed with the sheriff's conclusions, but Sadie decided a phone call to the police station would be a logical first step.

She dialed the number for the Silver Peak Police Department, and a moment later, Janet Parks picked up and spoke in her efficient, clipped tones.

"Silver Peak Sheriff's Office."

"Hi, Janet, this is Sadie Speers." Sadie always tried to sound warm and friendly with Janet, but especially when she was calling to ask something she just knew Janet would find frustrating.

"Hello, Sadie. Did you find what you were looking for yesterday? I didn't see you leave, so I wasn't sure." Janet's words were polite enough, but Sadie heard the silent accusation behind them: Sadie should have checked in with Janet on her way out. Sadie had left the file on her desk, but Janet hadn't been there. But it wouldn't do any good to try to explain to Janet that she had been away from her desk when Sadie went to leave; better to simply play nice.

"I did. Thank you so much for your help. I never would have been able to find what I needed without your help."

Janet made a noise, halfway between a grunt and a cough, that Sadie took to be acknowledgment.

"And now I'm calling with what I'm afraid is a bit of a strange question. I'm trying to track down some police officers whose names were listed in the files I saw yesterday. I was wondering if you might be able to give me any information about them."

Julie waved as she headed out the door for her lunch break, her purse slung over her shoulder. Sadie gave her a quick wave in return.

"I'm not really at liberty to divulge information about our staff," Janet said.

"Of course, of course," Sadie said. She'd been prepared for that answer. "I totally understand that and, of course, I'm not asking about current staff. I'm pretty sure these officers retired or moved on years ago. I was just hoping I could get a general idea of when they might have stopped working for the police force." Sadie wasn't sure if it mattered that the officers no longer worked there, but it didn't hurt to push that angle.

Janet grunted again, but then she sighed. "What are the names?"

"The first is Sheriff Robert Greene, and the other name I'm interested in is Officer Jim Sharlett."

"Well, I can tell you about Jim Sharlett. He was still working here when I started here fifteen years ago. He retired soon after that and moved to Colorado Springs."

"Wonderful. You wouldn't happen to have his contact information by any chance, would you?"

Janet sighed. "Even if I had it, I wouldn't be at liberty to share it with you." Sadie heard her typing on a keyboard. "But off the record I can tell you that I saw pictures of his new house in a retirement community high up in the mountains, and it was beautiful, perched on the edge of a hill overlooking a golf course. I don't know if that will help or not."

"Of course it does. Thank you so much." There couldn't be that many retirement communities on golf courses in Colorado Springs. It would take some legwork, but with luck she could track it down.

"But I'm afraid I don't know anything about a Sheriff Greene. That must have been well before my time."

"Is there anyone else there who might be able to tell me anything about him?"

Janet paused, and Sadie imagined her debating whether to go out of her way to help or not.

"I can ask around, but I'm not sure how likely it is anyone here will know of him," she said finally.

"It would be very helpful if you could ask. I really appreciate it," Sadie said. Janet grunted again, but Sadie heard a grudging respect in it. "Thanks so much for your help."

"I'll let you know if I find out anything about this sheriff," Janet said.

Sadie thanked her again and hung up. She hoped she would hear back about Sheriff Greene, but in the meantime, she opened a browser window on the computer in front of her and searched for retirement communities in Colorado Springs with golf courses. She was directed to a Web site that listed communities for residents fifty-five and up in Colorado, and was quickly able to sort the possibilities by limiting the options to those with a golf course. There were five listed, but only one was in the vicinity of Colorado Springs.

Sadie clicked on the link for Roaring Fork Ranch and was taken to a glossy Web site with beautiful photos of tasteful homes perched on craggy cliffs overlooking miles of green fairway. There were photos of a lodge-style community center building with floor-to-ceiling windows, as well as a workout facility and a crystal-clear turquoise lap pool. There were photos of laughing seniors meeting together over elegant meals and walking the trails in the nearby hills. Sadie had never really been tempted by planned communities like this one, preferring the more authentic feel of small-town life, but she had to admit this place looked nice.

She clicked to the site's main page and found a phone number to call for more information. Sadie reached for her phone and dialed the main number.

"Hello?" A chipper woman who didn't sound any older than a high schooler answered the phone.

"Hi, my name is Sadie Speers, and I'm hoping to get in touch with a resident of Roaring Fork Ranch."

"Certainly. Who is it you're trying to reach?"

"I'm looking for a Jim Sharlett."

"Oh, Jim." The woman's voice took on a sad tone. "I'm sorry to say Jim passed away about eighteen months ago. We all miss him terribly. He was such a character."

"Oh dear. I'm sorry to hear that." Sadie's heart sank. "Is there anyone there who would be able to talk to me about Jim? Maybe a widow?"

"I'm afraid not," the woman said. "His wife passed away a few years before Jim, and after Jim, the house was sold. I'm afraid I don't have any contact information for their estates. However, we do have some beautiful homes available, if you're interested. One just came available with a view of the ninth hole, and it's really a stunning home with great amenities. I think if you check it out, you'll see why people love living at Roaring Fork Ranch."

It did sound like a warm, inviting place. You had to like any place where the saleswoman knew the residents by name. But Sadie wasn't in the market for real estate, so she thanked the woman and left her contact information in case she thought of how to find out more about Jim.

Sadie hung up reluctantly. Even if she could get a hold of someone who had known Jim Sharlett, the chances were small that anyone would know what he'd been thinking when he made that note in the police file more than five decades ago. Sadie wasn't willing to think of it as a dead end, but she couldn't figure out how to move forward to find more information about Jim Sharlett at the moment. She'd come back to him and Sheriff Robert Greene later.

Sadie turned back to her list of names. It would be quite helpful to talk to Melvin Loffredo, the fire chief who had been quoted in the article and who had prepared the report on the fire. Sadie wasn't optimistic about her chances of talking to Chief Loffredo;

in the photo she'd seen in the paper, he'd had gray hair. He would no doubt be extremely elderly and frail if he were alive today. Still, she called the fire station and talked to Tyson, who had gone over the report with her yesterday, and Tyson confirmed that Chief Loffredo's name was on the plaque where all the past fire chiefs were listed, but that he had retired several decades before. No one in the firehouse now knew a thing about him. That didn't surprise Sadie either. For the most part, fighting fires seemed a young man's game, and most of the men she'd encountered at the station yesterday had been young enough to be her grandsons. She was doubtful most of them had even been born when Melvin Loffredo retired.

Still, if he was out there somewhere, Sadie wanted to find him, so she turned back to the computer on the desk and typed his name into a browser window. The first few links that came up were social media sites for people with similar names, but then Sadie came across a link from the *Denver Post*. Sadie clicked on it and quickly saw that it was an obituary for a Melvin Franklin Loffredo, who had passed away more than fifteen years ago. The obituary said that he was predeceased by his wife, Libby, but it listed three children as survivors. Sadie hovered the mouse over their names. She could try to track down the children. But would that do any good? Even if they were still around, what were the chances that they would have any idea about a fire their father had investigated when they were young? Sadie decided to wait and try more likely leads for now. She would come back to the Loffredo children if she didn't find more information elsewhere.

Sadie looked back at her list and decided to try to find Orville Montgomery next. Orville was the maintenance worker who was responsible for the historical schoolhouse site, and whose brand of cigarette butts had been found at the site after the fire, according to the police file. Sadie pulled out her phone and read back over the notes about Orville in the police file. He had been questioned by the police and had been vague about his whereabouts the night of the fire. That was suspicious, Sadie thought, but Orville had been saved from further questioning by the quick declaration that the fire had been electrical.

It sure sounded like someone was covering something up, and Orville seemed a likely place to look. Sadie started by searching for his name online, but even with such a unique name, Sadie couldn't find any results turn up for him. She tried to figure out where to look next. It was possible the school district had some contact information for its former employee, but after working for the district for several decades, Sadie knew how unlikely that was. The Silver Peak schools were continually financially strapped and running on a shoestring, and keeping up contact information for staff from fifty years ago would be low on anyone's priority list. Maybe she'd swing by the district office later and see just in case, but for now Sadie wanted to focus on more likely avenues.

She sat back and tried to think of how to locate Orville. The shop was quiet aside from the Merle Haggard song that floated gently through the store, but there was a low hum coming from Arbuckle's. Maybe coffee would help her think. Sadie pushed herself up and walked to the adjoining store, and by the time she'd returned to the desk with a steaming hot latte, she had a game plan. She set her drink down, walked to the back room and retrieved a phone book, and returned to the desk, flipping to the *Ms.* There were eight Montgomerys listed in Silver Peak and the surrounding area, but no Orville. Still, he'd lived in the area, and there was a chance at least one of the Montgomerys listed there was related to him.

Sadie decided to start at the top, and called the number listed for Alan Montgomery. There was no answer, so Sadie left a voice mail and her phone number and moved on to the next number. She'd called three numbers before she got a hold of anyone, but the woman who answered had never heard of an Orville Montgomery. On the seventh call, just as Sadie was starting to lose hope, there was some good news.

"Hello, my name is Sadie Speers, and I'm looking for a man named Orville Montgomery," Sadie said.

"Yes, Orville is my grandfather," the man said. Sadie could hear the sound of a baby crying in the background.

"Oh, that's wonderful!" Sadie said. "I'm hoping to get in touch with him. I live in Silver Peak, and I'm interested in speaking to him about his job in maintenance at the Silver Peak Schoolhouse. Do you know how I might get in touch with him?"

"Oh yeah, I remember him talking about that place," the man said. "I'm sure he'd be happy to talk to you, but I'm afraid he lives over in Leadville now, in a nursing home."

"Oh." Sadie tried to choose her words carefully. "Is he… Do you think he would welcome a visitor?"

"He loves visitors, especially those who want to talk about the old days," the man said. The baby had stopped crying now, and Sadie could hear the sounds of some children's program on a television in the background. "Here, let me get you the name of the home."

A few minutes later, Sadie hung up, the name and phone number of the nursing home in hand. She immediately called the number for Shady Grove Nursing Home, and was greeted by a cheery receptionist.

"Hi, my name is Sadie Speers," Sadie said, trying to choose her words carefully. She suspected the facility wouldn't let just anyone off the street waltz in and visit a patient, so she wanted to give the impression that Orville would be glad to talk with her. It was true, she suspected—most men loved taking about the jobs they did in their prime. "I'm hoping to find a good time to come see one of your residents, Orville Montgomery. Is there a time of day that's usually best?"

"Oh, Orville loves visitors," the receptionist said. "He's not having a good day today, I'm afraid, but he's usually at his best in the mornings. I'd try again in the morning and see if he's doing better then."

"Will do," Sadie said, and hung up after making a note in her notebook.

Sadie knew it was a long shot, but it still felt good to finally have a solid lead. She'd try getting in touch with him tomorrow.

Sadie turned back to her list and studied the names there. She still had to tackle the matter of the four high school boys who were seen going into the woods the night of the fire. She studied the list of names. Martin Goring, Justin Orr, Michael Leonard, and Tully Stewart. None of them meant anything to her. Did any of them still live in the area? If so, she didn't know them, but that didn't mean much.

The first step was to see what the Internet had to say about them. She did a search for the name Martin Goring and came up with a few possibilities, one of whom sold life insurance in Florida and another who was featured in a collection of photos by a camera-happy granddaughter.

Julie came back from lunch, and Sadie gave her a wave without really looking up from her screen. Sadie searched for the next name on the list and found a handful of Justin Orrs, dozens of potential Michael Leonards, and no results for a Tully Stewart.

Well. That clarified just about nothing. It would take forever to go through each of these results and see if they were the boy listed in the police report decades ago. She could see no way to narrow the results down, either, at least, not without knowing something more about these boys than their names. If only she knew something about what they were like when they were in high school, or saw photos of them, that might shed some light on her search, but…

And then she realized how she could find out more about what these boys were like in high school. It was so obvious she couldn't believe she hadn't seen it right away. She checked in with Julie, grabbed her coat, and a few minutes later she was out the door.

7

SADIE PULLED INTO THE STAFF PARKING LOT AT THE SILVER PEAK High School out of habit more than anything else. Technically, she should probably park in the visitor lot at the front of the school, but after two decades of teaching there, it was hard to think of herself as a visitor. She slid into a space right next to Hal Moyers's old beat-up Subaru; the gym teacher had been driving the same station wagon since well before Sadie retired. She parked the car, slung her purse over her shoulder, and headed toward the brick high school building. Sadie's ultimate destination was the library, where she knew there was a collection of yearbooks going back to the early days of the high school, but first she wanted to stop in and say hello to the principal, Anne Hastings, who had become a friend through the many years they'd worked together. Sadie also hoped to see if she could poke around Virginia's classroom while she was there. Virginia had been working in her classroom when she made the discovery about the fire on the night of the accident, and Sadie hoped she might have left some notes or records behind. Anne would be the one to grant her access to the classroom if she could get it. Besides, even though Sadie knew most of the adults at this school, she knew that school security was tight these days, and with good reason, so it wouldn't do to just start wandering around the campus without letting someone know that she was there.

Sadie walked up the steps and in through the double doors that led to the main hallway. She was greeted by the familiar scent that was impossible to define—some floor wax, a hint of teenage sweat, a bit of musty paper. It smelled like home to Sadie, and she took a deep breath as she made her way down the linoleum-covered hallway. There were posters for the prom hanging on the bulletin boards, as well as advertisements for upcoming cheer squad tryouts.

A wave of nostalgia washed over Sadie. It was all the same, in so many ways, and yet so different being here as an outsider. The kids who were now sitting in these classrooms had been in elementary school the last time Sadie had been in front of a classroom, and yet in so many ways it felt like it was just yesterday. Over the years, she'd grown weary of the paperwork and grading that came with teaching, and she'd never gotten used to the irate parents and the students who failed to live up to their potential, but she'd never grow tired of that spark in students' eyes the moment they grasped a tricky concept for the first time. Seeing a young mind turned on to the love of learning—that was what had made Sadie get out of bed for so many years, and that was what she missed most now as she made her way to the administrative office at the back of the ground floor.

"Sadie Speers!" Deedee Henderson was sitting at the front desk of the office, just like she always had, and she pushed herself up and gave Sadie a wide smile. "It is so good to see you."

Deedee was cheerful and outgoing, and if she missed a few scheduling details or dropped a few phone calls here and there, it was all forgiven because she was good at disarming everyone who came in through the front door. Even an irate parent bent on complaining about some new policy or a low test score was no match for Deedee's warm, heartfelt welcome. She could calm anyone and make everyone who walked through the office door end up feeling good about the school, and for that she would always have job security, Sadie knew.

"It's so good to see you, Deedee," Sadie said as the secretary came around the front counter for a hug. "And that's a lovely blouse you're wearing." Deedee was heavy, but she always wore cheerful print blouses and she always looked sharp.

"Why, thank you. I felt like I needed a bit of color this time of year, you know?" Deedee straightened the top, dotted with flecks of light pink and royal blue. "Now, what brings you here today?"

"I was hoping to say hello to Anne."

"She's in her office." Deedee gestured to the door at the far side of the office. "And I think she's free. I'm sure she'll be happy to see you."

"Thank you." Sadie knew that the receptionist should probably buzz the principal's office to see if now was a good time for visitors, but instead of pointing that out, she simply smiled and poked her head into Anne's office.

"Hello?" Sadie called. Anne was squinting at something on her computer screen, her eyebrows furrowed. She looked up when she heard Sadie's voice, and she sat back, her face breaking into a smile.

"Sadie. It's good to see you. Come in." Anne pushed back from her desk and gestured to the open visitor's chair. Her shoulder-length brown hair was streaked with gray, but it somehow looked elegant paired with her long, narrow face and her warm smile. Anne was dressed like a corporate lawyer, in a pantsuit and tailored blouse, but Sadie knew that on weekends she liked nothing more than to get outdoors and hike in the summer and ski in the winter. "What brings you here today?"

"I wanted to check out something in the library, but thought I'd pop in and say hello first," Sadie said, settling into the chair. She couldn't count the number of hours she'd sat in here talking through classroom management problems or going over questions about specific students over the years. Anne was a good fifteen years younger than Sadie, but she was wise beyond her years and had been something of a mentor to Sadie in the latter part of her time at Silver Peak High School.

"Sounds like a nice break. I've been working on plans for this fund-raiser next week, and my eyes are starting to glaze over." Anne gestured at a binder marked SCHOOL FUND-RAISER on the edge of her desk.

Sadie felt a wave of panic wash over her. She still hadn't started putting together the presentation, and it was now looking more and more likely she'd be giving it on her own next week. Or maybe she could get out of it? Surely Anne would understand, given the circumstances.

Just as she opened her mouth to ask, Anne started talking. "For some reason, we're having such a hard time pulling it together this year. You know what happened to Virginia, obviously?"

Sadie nodded mutely.

"Isn't it horrible?" Anne shook her head. "I was so shocked when I heard. I can't even imagine what that family must be going through." Anne had two teenage sons, and Sadie suspected she was thinking about what would happen to them if she were in an accident.

"It's terrible. It's so hard to imagine."

"And on top of that, ticket sales are down, and we've just had the caterer cancel, so we're scrambling to find someone who can fill in at the last minute. And it just has to come together. Our budget is getting slashed again next year, and if we don't find a way to bring in some more money, it's going to be difficult to keep going on as usual, forget about things like upgrades to the library."

Sadie felt her stomach clench. The idea of standing in front of a crowd wasn't what worried her—years of teaching had made her immune to that. But the presentation was supposed to be done with some fancy computer software and displayed on a big screen, with photos and videos and whatnot, and Sadie felt helpless at the idea of trying to pull that together on her own.

"You're still on for your presentation about the old school-house, right?" Anne asked, looking at Sadie pleadingly. "I know it'll be harder to do it without Virginia, but can you still give the presentation? We're counting on you."

Guilt burbled up. As much as she dreaded it, she couldn't let her friend down.

"Of course."

The relief on Anne's face was palpable.

Sadie felt chastened. She wasn't looking forward to figuring out how to put this presentation together, but maybe tonight she could carve out some time to start working on that.

"Actually, I wonder if you might be able to help me pull things together for the presentation," Sadie said, her mind spinning quickly. "You see, I know Virginia Radcliff was working in her classroom just before her accident, and I was hoping she might have left some of her notes behind. If I could get a hold of those, they would help me prepare for the part of the presentation she'd been working on." There. That was one hundred percent true, not to mention the fact that whatever notes she'd left might very well point the way to whatever answers Virginia had found about the old fire.

"The substitute who's handling Virginia's classes hasn't mentioned seeing anything like that, but I'm not sure that's the sort of thing she'd mention," Anne said, looking up at the clock by the door. "You know I'd be happy to let you look around for anything you might need, but fifth period just started. I'd hate to interrupt in the middle of class. Could it wait until after school?"

It would be a few hours before class ended for the day, and Sadie wasn't sure she'd still be around, but she nodded. If she couldn't get access to Virginia's classroom today, she'd come back some other time.

"Absolutely. Thanks so much for your help."

"Thanks for *your* help with the fund-raiser. I'm anxious to see what you put together."

Sadie nodded. She needed to figure out that software, and soon.

"Well, I'll let you get back to work," Sadie said, standing. Anne groaned, but she turned back to her computer and started typing before Sadie was even at the doorway. It made Sadie even more grateful for the relaxed pace of her own work schedule. Sure, she missed certain things about working at the school, but she wouldn't trade the freedom and flexibility—and the sheer number of antiques she got to handle—for anything.

Sadie waved to Deedee and stepped out of the administrative office into the hallway. Class was in session, and the hallways were quiet. She turned toward the library, and passed right by the display case that held the historic school bell. Sadie paused to take it in. It was huge—nearly two feet in diameter, and cast from solid silver. It had tarnished with age, but you could still tell, even behind glass, that it was finely crafted and beautifully made. And it had to be worth a fair penny, with all that silver. It was strange to see it like this, placed between old trophies and plaques like any other piece of memorabilia. She wondered how many people ever even noticed it was here or knew what it was. Well, she hoped her presentation would draw some attention to it.

Now that she was standing here in front of it, it occurred to Sadie that some modern pictures of the bell could work nicely in her slideshow, so she pulled out her phone and opened the camera app. She tried to get a good shot, even with the glass in front of it, and she managed to get a few that she thought might work. Sadie slipped her phone back in her pocket and turned back down the hallway, headed toward the library.

Sadie passed by a row of classrooms and stopped to peek in through the small glass pane on the door at what used to be her own room. Now it was being used as an English classroom, and the walls were lined with posters of literary figures. There was a high-tech projector shooting a video of some sort onto a screen at the front of the room, and half the students were taking notes on laptops and tablets. Huh. So much here was the same, but so much had changed.

Just as she was about to turn, Sadie saw her granddaughter, Sara, sitting at a desk in the second row doodling idly, her eyes glazed over. Sadie gave a little wave, and Sara's eyes widened and she slunk down in her chair when she saw Sadie's face. Sadie chuckled and turned back down the hallway. There was nothing wrong with scaring Sara a little bit. Maybe that would teach her to pay more attention in class.

At the end of the hallway, just past the main stairway that led to the second floor, Sadie found the door to the library and went inside. There was a class of kids milling about the nonfiction stacks, but Sadie steered clear of them and approached the check-out counter to let Laura Holbert, the school librarian whom Sadie had worked with for years, know she was there and what she was doing. Sadie chatted with Laura for a few minutes, catching up on Laura's grandbabies and the new house she and her husband were building, and then headed off to the far corner of the library, where she knew the yearbooks were kept. Sadie scanned the shelves. At the top were the recent books, and she recognized a couple of the colorful spines from seeing them in Theo's bedroom. She followed the spines all the way to the bottom shelf, where leather-bound editions of the school's first yearbooks, published in the late 1950s, were kept. Sadie loved all old things, but books were among her favorites, and she longed to grab the oldest book and soak in the smell of the paper, the feel of the spine, and the rich historical context the old photos would provide, but she forced herself to focus. The schoolhouse fire was in 1965, so she grabbed the books for that year, as well as the years before and after, and settled down at a table.

Sadie opened the yearbook for 1965 first, and she flipped through the pages. The front of the book was filled with photographs from around campus—scenes from the winter play, shots of the Homecoming Queen being crowned, pictures of teachers and administrators posing in front of their cars. She scanned the captions, looking for any mention of the four names: Martin Goring, Justin Orr, Michael Leonard, and Tully Stewart. She didn't find them in the front pages, and moved on to the pictures of the freshman class. She didn't see any of them listed there, though, and moved on to the sophomores. Sadie did love how all the boys wore suits and ties, hair slicked back carefully, and the girls all wore formal gowns and had their hair carefully styled. Back then, having a picture taken meant something. These days, kids took photos of themselves—*selfies,* Sara called them—and posted them online for the whole world to see, but back then, things were more civilized. The yearbook might be the only picture your classmates would ever see of you, so you dressed up.

Sadie was most of the way through the sophomores before she saw a name she recognized. There he was. Tully Stewart. Well, he was listed as Thomas Stewart, with Tully in parentheses. He had dark brown hair and dark eyes, and a thin nose and high cheekbones. That was about all Sadie could tell from this photo, but at least she now knew what he looked like. She'd see if he showed up in any of the other photos in the book that might prove more helpful. For now, she'd keep looking for the other boys.

Sadie was just starting to look through the juniors when a noise at the far end of the library caught her attention. One of the students had dropped an armload of books onto a table. Sadie hated to see books mistreated so, but she reminded herself it wasn't her place anymore to scold high schoolers, so she turned back to her books. But wait—was that...

Over there in the corner, it almost looked like Theo. Sadie blinked, and peeked again. It was Theo, and sitting next to him was Elena Garza. They were huddled over a book, and it looked like Theo was explaining something to her. Sadie gave a small wave, but Theo didn't see her at all. He was…well, oblivious was the best way to describe it. He was completely absorbed in whatever subject he was teaching her. No, that wasn't it, Sadie realized. He was completely absorbed in Elena. He might be tutoring her, but he was definitely enjoying the task. And Elena didn't seem to mind either.

Unless Sadie was reading the whole thing wrong, things were looking pretty cozy over there in the corner. And she'd seen them working on something just yesterday. Surely the girl didn't need help that badly. Elena must be sweet on Theo, just like he was on her.

She wondered if Alice knew anything about this. Had they been together for a while? Did everyone know except Sadie?

She watched them a few minutes longer, alternately bursting with pride and fearful that her family was keeping things from her, until the bell rang, signaling the end of fifth period, and Theo and Elena, along with the other students, all started throwing their books into their backpacks and clearing out.

Huh. She had a thousand questions for Theo. And, well, now that she thought about it, Theo was a whiz with technology. He would probably be a big help in trying to make sense of that infernal software program she needed to figure out for her presentation. Maybe she'd see if Theo could come by later tonight and help her get started on her presentation. She'd ply him with cookies, and maybe she could have a heart-to-heart with him about his new love interest. She just about burst with excitement at the thought.

For now, though, with the library cleared out, she turned back to the yearbook in front of her. Funny how the pictures, which just minutes before had filled her with such delight, now seemed so flat and lifeless compared to the love she felt when she thought about her handsome grandson. Still, she couldn't help feel a thrill of excitement when she found a picture of Martin Goring among the juniors.

Martin was small, bony under his suit jacket, with big ears. And a little further into the juniors, she found Michael Leonard, a beefy, round-faced boy with curly brown hair. His shoulders made him look big enough to play football, and Sadie made a note to check out the photos of the sports teams later in the book. For now, she kept flipping through the juniors until she came across the photo for Justin Orr.

She sucked in her breath.

It didn't mean anything for sure, she told herself. And yet, as she stared at the picture of Justin Orr, she couldn't help but feel like a piece of the puzzle had possibly just fallen into place.

8

Sᴀᴅᴇ ʟᴏᴏᴋᴇᴅ ᴅᴏᴡɴ ᴀᴛ ᴛʜᴇ ғᴀᴅᴇᴅ ᴘʜᴏᴛᴏ ᴏғ Jᴜᴛɪɴ Oʀʀ on the browning yearbook page. Justin was good-looking, with blond hair and light eyes, but that wasn't what caught Sadie's attention. Justin Orr wore tortoiseshell glasses. Sadie pulled out her notebook and flipped back to the notes she'd taken when she read the police file. Yes, she'd remembered correctly. A pair of tortoiseshell glasses had been discovered by the site of the fire.

There was no reason to assume the glasses were Justin's, Sadie reminded herself. Surely lots of people wore glasses like this, especially back in those days.

But so far, Justin was the only one she'd come across in this investigation. And he was one of the boys who had been seen heading into the woods the night of the fire, which meant he'd been placed in the vicinity of the fire. It was enough to make her look at him a little more closely, at any rate.

Sadie continued flipping through the yearbook and noticed that Michael Leonard did, indeed, make an appearance in the football team's group photo, while Tully Stewart was a male cheerleader and on the homecoming court. Justin Orr, Sadie saw, was in the chemistry club. Could he have been trying out some new experiment that night at the schoolhouse site?

When Sadie got to the end of the 1965 yearbook, she reached for the next year's, and quickly located Tully Stewart among the junior class. Both Michael and Martin were listed among the seniors, as she expected, but… She flipped all the way through the seniors once, and then again. Justin Orr did not appear in this yearbook at all. Had he stopped attending Silver Peak High? Why hadn't he come back to school his senior year?

Sadie knew there were many possible reasons, most of which did not involve illicit activity. But after seeing all of this, she knew she would be looking into Justin Orr just a little bit more.

Sadie flipped through the rest of the yearbook, but didn't see anything worth noting, so she slid the books back onto the shelf and headed back out to the car. It would still be another hour and a half before school let out, so Sadie decided to head back to her shop and see if she could gain access to Virginia's classroom another time. For now, she was headed back to her shop to try to track down every Justin Orr she could find.

9

LATER THAT AFTERNOON, SADIE HAD E-MAILED, CALLED, AND sent private messages to five different Justin Orrs she found online. One, a doctor in California with light hair, seemed the most promising, but there was really no way to tell. Now all she had to do was wait and pray someone got back to her.

Sadie checked the clock. School was out by now, if the parade of teenagers streaming into Arbuckle's was any indication. Now would be a good time to call Theo and see if he could help her tonight with her presentation.

Sadie looked around the shop while the phone rang and she waited for Theo to pick up. There were a couple of people browsing the vintage records, and Josh Ralston, a woodworker who often sold pieces in the shop, was arranging a set of new chairs in his stall, but they all looked content for now. The sweet strains of Dolly Parton's favorites played out softly over the shop.

"Hey, Grandma," Theo said. He was walking outside, Sadie could tell by the wind whipping past the phone.

"Hello, Theo," Sadie said, trying to suppress the rush of excitement that rose up remembering the vision of him and Elena together this afternoon. "I was wondering if I could ask a favor of you. I'm trying to put together a presentation for the big school fund-raiser next week, but the software I'm supposed to use to make the presentation is giving me fits. Do you have time to come over for a little while this evening and help me figure it out?"

"Oh, sure. Are you using PowerPoint?"

Sadie wasn't positive that was the name of the software, but it sounded close enough, so she said yes.

"That's supereasy. I can show you that—no problem. I have basketball practice but could come over after. Maybe around eight?"

Supereasy. Ha! Easy for him to say. He'd grown up using computers. Still, she was grateful he was willing to help her, and since she had agreed to bring a meal over to the Radcliff house early in the evening, the timing worked out just perfectly.

"Will that leave you enough time to get your homework done?" she asked. The last thing she needed was Alice upset at her for keeping Theo from his schoolwork.

"It'll be fine. I did most of it during school anyway."

Sadie wasn't sure working on homework during his classes was the best use of his educational time, but she wasn't going to argue with him about that now. She was grateful to have a grandson willing to give up his time to help her.

"Wonderful. I'll see you around eight then."

"See ya, Grandma." The line clicked off before she could say anything more. Sadie stared at the phone a moment, shaking her head. That kid. As much as she loved him, he could use a lesson or two about phone etiquette.

A few hours later, Sadie climbed the steps to her house and wiped her feet on the doormat. She pushed open the door and stepped inside gratefully and then took off her shoes and hung up her coat. She gave Hank a good rubdown while he tried to lick her hand. It was always nice to come home to a greeting like that. Then Sadie went into the kitchen, washed her hands, and set to work throwing together the ingredients for cheese tortellini with grilled chicken and pesto. She had enough of the ingredients on hand to make a double batch, so she would have enough to bring to the Radcliffs and still have dinner here at home for herself.

As she worked, she went over all the things she'd learned that day, and all the questions that still had no answers. She'd have to find a way to talk to Orville Montgomery, the janitor whose cigarette butts had been found at the site, and she hoped she'd hear back from a Justin Orr, who wore glasses like those discovered there. She needed to track down Sheriff Robert Greene and find out why he had declared the fire an accident in the face of the evidence. It seemed she still had a lot to track down, and those were just the clues she was tracking for the schoolhouse mystery. That was only the first step in finding out who had knocked Virginia off the road. To get there, she still hoped to get access to whatever files Virginia had been working on just before the crash, and she was still very interested in what had caused Ramon to leave the restaurant suddenly just before the time of the accident on Tuesday night, and who the man in the security footage who had called to report the accident was.

Sadie tossed the warm pasta and chicken strips in pesto, added some fresh chopped cherry tomatoes for color, and poured the dish into a plastic container. She put some baby spinach into a plastic bowl and added more tomatoes, as well as cucumbers, avocado, cheese, and some oily black olives, and took a package of frozen rolls from the freezer.

For now, she'd bring this meal to Virginia's family. She hoped it would nourish them, as well as give her an opportunity to find out what they could tell her about what Virginia had been working on.

A few minutes later, Sadie was pulling up in front of the Radcliffs' well-maintained ranch-style house on Jefferson Street. Through the open garage door, Sadie could see a blue sedan and a handful of bicycles of different sizes, as well as a wide assortment of sports gear. Sadie walked up the cement path to the front door and knocked gently. A moment later, a wide-eyed blond boy who looked to be about six pulled open the door. This must be Thomas. Or Matthew? Sadie couldn't remember which of Virginia's sons was older.

"Hello, I'm Mrs. Speers. I'm a friend of your mother's. I've brought dinner."

"Hi. Dad says to come on in." He smiled a little and ducked his head. He was wearing basketball shorts and a Superman T-shirt, despite the cool temperature, and it wasn't clear whether his hair had been combed that day.

Sadie stepped inside the tiled entryway, and he closed the door behind her. It was cool in the house, and from the next room she heard the sound of a television playing cartoons.

"He's on the phone. He'll be right here," the boy said, and led her into the kitchen. Sadie set the dishes she was carrying on the laminate counter and looked around. It wasn't huge, but it was cozy, with white cabinets and robin's-egg blue walls. The fridge was covered with photos of the two young boys and plastered with various art projects they'd produced. Dishes were piled in the sink, and it smelled like the garbage needed to be taken out. Fast food containers were scattered on the counter.

A moment later, David Radcliff stepped into the kitchen, a cordless handset in his hand. He was tall, with dark brown hair. Sadie had met him a few times, and thought he was an engineer of some sort, but she couldn't be sure.

"I'm so sorry about that," he said, setting the handset back on its base. "I feel like I've done nothing but fight with the insurance company since this whole thing started." He turned to the young boy. "Thank you, Thomas. Can you go tell your brother to get ready for dinner?"

The young boy scampered off into the room with the television.

"It's quite all right, and I'm sorry about the insurance. I know how maddening insurance companies can be sometimes." When her husband, T.R., had been sick, she'd felt like it had been a constant battle. "I do hope this will make things a bit easier." She gestured to the dishes she'd set on the counter. "It's pasta, salad, and rolls. You'll need to bake the rolls, but they only take about ten minutes." Sadie glanced at the kitchen table, which was piled high with backpacks and stacks of mail. This looked like a home in need of a mother's touch. "Would you like me to get them started for you?"

David sighed and thanked her. "That would be wonderful." Sadie turned on the oven and opened the cabinet next to the stove, where she easily located a cookie sheet.

"I'm sorry, we must look like a mess. I guess we don't realize how much Virginia does around here," David said, shaking his head. He gestured at the dishes in the sink. "The dishwasher is

broken, and I've been spending most of my time at the hospital…"
His voice trailed off.

"You've got more important things to worry about right now
than a few dishes," Sadie said, arranging the frozen rolls on the baking sheet. "And I'm thrilled for the opportunity to do something
to help." Sadie opened the oven door and slid the sheet into the
warming oven. She knew you were supposed to wait until the oven
got hot, but Sadie had never understood why the food couldn't just
get hot along with the oven itself.

"I really appreciate it. And thank you so much for your call the
other day," David said. "I have been meaning to call you back, but
I haven't quite managed to yet."

"Don't be silly. I totally understand." Sadie looked around the
kitchen. She didn't want to be presumptuous, but it was pretty
clear David was feeling overwhelmed. Caring for two small children while your wife was fighting for her life would be more than
most people could handle. Surely a little more help wouldn't be out
of line. Without another word, Sadie moved over to the sink and
began to run hot water over the dishes piled there. "I just wanted
to see if there was anything I could do. I'm not sure if you know,
but I was actually on the phone with Virginia when the accident
happened." Sadie found a bottle of dish soap under the sink and
squirted a hefty dab into the hot water rising around the dishes.

"You don't have to do that." David gestured weakly at the sink.
Sadie smiled. "I want to help."

He was quiet for a minute, and for a moment Sadie worried
she'd overstepped her bounds, but then his face relaxed. "Thank
you," he said. "And I did hear that you were talking to Virginia.
That's part of why I've been meaning to call you back. The police

told me they talked to you, but I wondered... Well, obviously we're anxious for any little clue that might lead to who did this."

"Of course." Sadie grabbed a sponge from the counter and plunged it into the warm soapy water. She recounted her side of the phone call, telling him how Virginia had said she'd been working in her classroom and she had just discovered who had set the old fire, as well as all the details she could remember of the moments just before the crash. "I was actually wondering if she might have left some of the papers she'd been working on about the fire here," Sadie said, adding a freshly cleaned plate to the handful she'd already set in the dish rack.

"I haven't come across anything," David said. "But then, I haven't really been looking for anything like that. I can take a look around and see if I can find anything."

"Thank you. I'd appreciate that." Sadie scrubbed at a coffee mug. "Have the police found any leads yet?"

"Nothing solid, though they're looking into a few possibilities. They think the other car was maroon, so they're trying to track down all the maroon cars in the area. And they have some security camera footage of a mysterious man calling nine-one-one to report the accident. I guess they're hoping he saw something, and if they can track him down, he'll be able to tell us more about what happened."

Sadie rinsed off a juice glass and set it on the dish rack. "Yes, I saw that too. Have they found out who the man in the tape might be?"

"Not that I know of." He shrugged. "Personally, I think the best option they're looking into so far is one of Virginia's students."

Sadie stopped scrubbing the mug and turned a little. "A student?"

"Yes, for a few months Virginia had been having trouble with one of her seniors. At first it was mostly typical second semester senior stuff—cutting classes, blowing off assignments, that sort of thing. But in the past few weeks, he'd gotten more difficult, acting out in class, missing tests and large projects. Virginia had tried to warn him that his behavior and missed assignments were jeopardizing his chance at a passing grade, and therefore graduation, and he just became more difficult. Then, just last week, she held him back after class to let him know that he was failing the class and likely would not graduate, and he threatened her."

"Goodness. Threatened her?"

He nodded. "He cursed at her, said she would be sorry, and that his parents would fix it and they would find a way to make sure she never worked in this town again, apparently. I get the impression he's a bit of a spoiled child of wealthy parents, and isn't used to being told no."

"Wow." Sadie had had her share of unpleasant interactions with students over the years, but she'd never been threatened like that. Either things had changed a lot in the past ten years or this boy was seriously out of control. "I can see why they're looking into him, but is there any reason to believe he may have been involved?"

"Well, he drives a dark red Thunderbird," David said, sighing. "Apparently he got it for his sixteenth birthday. The police were going to investigate him more today, but I haven't heard yet what they've found."

Sadie scrubbed a bit of dried-on cereal from a bowl, then rinsed it and set it in the dish rack. "Do you know what this boy's name is?"

"It's Curtis Younts," David said, brushing a hand across the stubble on his chin. His voice was flat, and his eyes looked defeated.

Sadie felt bad. This man was clearly struggling. The last thing he needed was someone bringing all this up. "I'm sorry to pester you. I know this must be hard to talk about."

"No, it's okay. It's almost good to get it out. Since the accident, everyone has sort of been tiptoeing around us, and I haven't really had the chance to say all this out loud and see how it feels."

"And how does it feel?" Sadie knew she was pushing again, but David seemed to welcome the chance to talk about it.

"I don't really know. On the one hand, I certainly hope this boy had nothing to do with it. I would hate for a teenager to be involved. It's so hard to contemplate how devastating that would be for him, and for everyone, you know?" He looked down at the floor. "And yet, at the same time, I just want answers."

Sadie nodded and she wiped off the last plate. It really would be horrible to think that a child could be behind such a sinister act. And yet, at least then they would know the truth and could begin healing.

"I'm sure the police are looking into it thoroughly." She gave him what she hoped was an encouraging smile. "And I'll be praying that they find answers soon."

Just then the two young boys came into the room and climbed into chairs at the dinner table. David nodded, then turned to clear away stacks of paper to make room for plates. Sadie set the last dish into the rack, looked around, and, satisfied that she'd gotten them all, drained the sink and rinsed her hands. Then she located a pot holder in one of the drawers, pulled the golden rolls out of the oven, and set the baking sheet down on top of the stove. She took one of the freshly cleaned serving bowls, wiped it dry with a paper towel, and dumped the rolls in, then set the bowl, along with the other food containers she'd brought, onto the table.

"I don't know how to thank you," David said, looking down at the fresh food. Even the boys were looking at the food with wide eyes. Sadie wondered how long it had been since they'd had food that hadn't come from a fast-food drive-in.

"You just take care of your family and be strong. That's all the thanks I need. And I'll keep trying to figure out what happened. Please let me know if you get any answers from the police."

"I absolutely will," David said. "And thank you again."

"I'll talk to you soon." Sadie showed herself out, and as she drove back through the hilly streets of town, Sadie thought about what David had told her. Was it possible that a teenager with a grudge had been the one to drive Virginia off the road? As hard as it was to imagine a student nearly killing his teacher over a few test scores, she had seen teenagers behave in some irrational ways, and she could see how it could happen. Teenagers often thought they were invincible and acted without thinking through the consequences. Was that what had happened here? Sadie knew the police were looking into him, but it still wouldn't hurt to see if she could find out more about this Curtis Younts.

The visit had taken a bit longer than she'd anticipated, and by the time Sadie got home, she had just enough time to reheat the remainder of the pasta dish and start dinner before her front door opened and Theo came inside. Looking through the file of Virginia's notes would have to wait until later.

"Hey, Grandma," he called, and Sadie heard his shoes thunk against the floor of the entryway. Sadie finished buttering her roll.

She knew it wouldn't take her grandson long to follow the smell of food into the kitchen. A moment later, he appeared in the doorway, a grin on his face. "Hey there. Whatcha eating?"

"Pasta. Would you like some?" Sadie stood up to get a plate even as she spoke. She'd spent enough time around teenage boys to know the answer to that question. "Did you have dinner?"

"Yeah, but I'm still kind of hungry," he said, eyeing her plate. It did look good, Sadie had to admit. She set a plate and silverware at the table, and Theo sat down across from her and started telling her about something funny he'd seen on television earlier. Sadie ate, contented. This was what she loved about having her daughter and grandkids nearby—they were in each others' lives so much, it was easy and comfortable. They didn't have to worry about making a big deal of things; they could simply enjoy being together.

Theo wolfed down his second dinner in minutes flat, and Sadie was done shortly after. Then they set their plates in the dishwasher, and Sadie retrieved her laptop and her notes for the presentation and set them up on the table.

"This is the program I'm supposed to use to make my presentation," Sadie said, clicking on an icon at the bottom of the screen. A moment later, a window opened. It had a blank part taking up most of the screen, but there was a column at the left side and a row at the bottom, and Sadie wasn't sure what to do with any of them.

"Okay, what's your presentation about?" Theo asked, scooting his chair closer to Sadie's so he could see the screen.

"It's supposed to be about the historic Silver Peak Schoolhouse and how education has always been a priority in Silver Peak." She flipped open the folder that contained the notes she'd made before

Virginia's accident. It seemed so long ago now. Theo nodded and typed the words *Silver Peak Schoolhouse* in the middle of the open part of the screen. Sadie was surprised to see a box appear around the words. "I was supposed to be working on this with Virginia Radcliff, and she was going to handle this part of things."

"Oh yeah, that stinks about Mrs. Radcliff. We had a big assembly about it at school the day after it happened." Theo added Sadie's name and Virginia's in a smaller font below the title. "I sure hope they catch whoever did that to her."

"I sure hope so, too. If I have anything to say about it, we will," Sadie said.

"*We?*" Theo smiled at his grandma. "How did I guess you would be trying to figure it out? Have you found the answer yet? You're ahead of the police, aren't you?"

Theo's eyes sparkled with excitement. It seemed he found this subject more interesting than making a PowerPoint presentation. Theo had helped Sadie solve puzzles in the past, and was even considering a career as a detective, and she knew he loved nothing more than hearing about the details of whatever she was working on.

"No, I'm not ahead of the police. Let's just say we're approaching the mystery from different angles."

"Which means?" Theo tapped his fingers on the keyboard and added the date of the presentation. "There. That's your first slide. You can add more to it or change it later." Then he clicked on a button at the top of the page and a new blank sheet, just like the first one, appeared. "So what are you doing that the police aren't?"

"I think Virginia was run off the road because in doing research for this project she discovered who set that old schoolhouse fire, and someone didn't want the secret to get out."

"Whoa." Theo's eyes widened, and he looked to the file folder Sadie had set on the table. "I thought the old fire was an accident. That's what they told us in school. Something about electrical wiring."

"It appears that was what they wanted people to think, but when you dig a little deeper, it seems that might not have been the case. Virginia became fascinated with it and had been looking into the old evidence. She had just figured out who she thought set the fire. She was on her way over here to tell me who it was when she had the accident."

"And someone knew what she'd discovered and wanted to keep her quiet, so they ran her off the road." Theo nodded, his fingers hovering over the keyboard. "That's nuts." He shook his head, and a lock of his hair flopped in his face. He brushed it back.

"It's pretty hard to imagine, I know." Sadie turned back to the presentation and flipped open her folder. "I have an etching of the first one-room schoolhouse that was on that site, and I was thinking that should go early in the presentation. How do I insert that picture into one of these screens?"

"Do you have the file digitally?"

Sadie shook her head and pulled out a printout of the old one-room schoolhouse she'd found at the Historical Society.

"You don't have a scanner, do you?" Theo asked, and when Sadie shook her head, he gestured for her to hand him her cell phone. Sadie did, and Theo took a photo of the old photo and then started typing something on her phone's screen.

"So what are the police working with?" Theo asked without looking up from the phone.

"Well, they know the second car is maroon, so they're looking into that. And just before the crash, Virginia read me a string of numbers that might have been the license plate number of the car, so they're tracing that. And they're looking into some security footage of a man calling nine-one-one to see what he knows about the crash."

Theo set her phone down and nodded. "They're working with the technical stuff. So obviously you're trying to retrace her steps and see if you can figure out who she thought set the old fire, because that will lead you to whoever ran her off the road to protect their secret, right?"

Sadie felt a surge of pride. Theo really would make a good detective someday, if he chose that path. He'd figured that all out without much help from Sadie. She nodded.

"So. What have you found out so far?"

"What did you do with my photo?" Sadie looked down at her screen.

"It's right here." Theo clicked over to an icon of an open box on her desktop and pulled the photo he'd just taken from it, then scrolled back to the presentation and dropped it onto the page. "How's this?"

Sadie pointed to the left side of the screen, indicating where she wanted the photo to go.

"So far I haven't found much," she said. "Just more questions. But enough to make me think Virginia was on the right track."

Theo created a text box next to the photo of the old schoolhouse and typed THIS IS WHERE YOU WRITE ABOUT WHEN THE SCHOOL WAS BUILT in it. Then he turned back to Sadie. "So what's our next step?"

Sadie laughed. "Our next step is you showing me how to make this silly program work on my own so I can put together my presentation and not look like a fool at the fund-raiser."

"That's easy." Theo waved his hand. "I mean, what's our next step toward finding out who tried to hurt Mrs. Radcliff?"

Sadie knew what had happened, but still, the words sent chills down her spine. Someone truly had wanted to get her out of his way. Sadie thought uneasily back to the note that had been slipped under her door, warning her to stay away from the mystery. Someone had tried to injure Virginia, and they knew Sadie was on the trail as well.

It wasn't enough to scare off Sadie—she would find out who hurt her friend, no matter what—but the idea of bringing Theo into the fray was unthinkable. There was no way she would put her grandson in any danger, and this project was already proving to have plenty of that.

"I'm afraid this is one project I won't need your help with," Sadie said, shaking her head. "If someone really did try to hurt Virginia, they want to keep their secret pretty badly, and I don't want you anywhere near them."

Theo rolled his eyes. "Oh. Come on, Grandma. What are they going to do, try to hurt a kid because he traced some old records?"

"I don't even want to think about it. The answer is no. I don't need your help this time around."

"You can't be serious." Theo's eyes were wide, like he couldn't believe what he was hearing.

"I'm totally serious," Sadie said. "Now, what if I want to add something in between these two screens you made?"

"Grandma, I promise I'll be careful. You can't leave me out of this."

"I very much mean to leave you out of it. Now, can we focus on this presentation please?"

Theo looked hurt, and Sadie felt a pang of guilt. He just wanted to help, she knew, but he needed to understand that she was serious. He still seemed shocked that she'd dared to say no, which was probably a sign that she didn't say no to her grandkids enough. Well, grandmas did tend to let their grandkids get away with a lot, but she meant it this time.

A few minutes passed, and Theo showed Sadie how to change the order of slides and how to format the text. Sadie was following, but she was also thinking back to her conversation with David Radcliff a little while ago. Theo went to school with that boy David had mentioned, Curtis Younts. How could she ask what Theo knew about him without raising his suspicions?

"Theo, do you know a student named Curtis Younts?"

Theo rolled his eyes. "Yeah, why? Did he do it?"

"No. Of course not." Sadie didn't need to let on that Curtis was on the list of suspects. "What do you think about him?"

"I think he's a spoiled rich kid who thinks he can have whatever he wants." Theo typed something on the laptop keyboard.

"I take it that means you're not friends?"

"No, I wouldn't say we're friends," Theo said, his eyes on the screen. Theo's was voice was tight, and the muscles in his shoulders stiffened. She'd hit a nerve somehow.

"Did something happen between you two?" Sadie asked gently.

"No," Theo said a little too quickly. He typed some more, and Sadie thought he was done with the subject, but then he added, "He's a player. He thinks he can get any girl to go out with him, so he asks out like every girl he meets. It's not cool."

Ah. Sadie was starting to see where this was going. She should have known.

"Did he ask out a girl you want to go out with?" Sadie ventured.

"No," Theo said, just a hair too quickly. His eyes were trained firmly on the screen. "What do you want on this next slide?"

Sadie tapped a black-and-white photograph of the wooden schoolhouse being constructed, and Theo digitized it and dropped it into the slide.

Sadie thought about Theo's reaction and what she'd seen in the library today, and tried to figure out how to broach the subject of Elena Garza. If she could get Theo to open up, maybe she could help.

"You know, I was at the high school today and saw a bunch of posters for the prom," Sadie said, trying to sound nonchalant. "Are you going to go?"

"Probably not," Theo said, his eyes still trained directly ahead.

"Oh, come on, a handsome boy like you? I bet there are dozens of girls who are hoping you'll ask them. You wouldn't deny them the opportunity, would you now?" She elbowed him playfully.

"I don't think so," he said, typing.

"Well, you don't need dozens anyway," Sadie said, trying a different tactic. "I can't believe there's no one you'd like to go with."

Theo kept typing, like he hadn't heard. Sadie was afraid she'd pushed too far, but a moment later Theo sighed and said, "There's someone I was thinking of asking, but I don't know if she'll say yes."

Of course she'll say yes, Sadie wanted to shout. Sadie knew she was partial, but a girl would have to blind not to see how special Theo was. Still, it couldn't hurt to give him a few pointers.

"I'm sure she would say yes anyway, but I bet I know how to make sure she does."

Theo's eyes went away from the screen, just for a moment, when he looked at her and then quickly looked away.

"You just need to treat her like a lady. Show her that she's special to you. Girls want to be romanced."

Romance was how Sadie's husband, T.R., had won her over. When he'd first asked her out, Sadie had not been interested in him. She had thought he was too rough, too wild. But he had made his intentions clear, and brought her flowers and sent her sweet notes, and it was all so different from what she had expected from the rough-and-tumble cowboy that she hadn't been able to help falling for him. It had been the same with Edwin—she hadn't been looking for a relationship, but he'd pursued her, letting her know with thoughtful words and gestures that he had feelings for her, and she had slowly felt the spark they'd had in high school rekindle.

Theo now turned and looked at her, square-on. "What do you mean?"

"Well, when you go to ask her to the prom, tell her she's beautiful and you can't stop thinking about her. And bring her flowers. That will show her you're serious about your feelings."

Theo looked skeptical, but he was listening.

"You could write her little notes, letting her know you're thinking about her. When you're with her, hold doors open for her, always let her walk into a room first. When she comes into a room, stand up until she sits down."

"Stand up when she comes into a room?" Theo scrunched up his nose.

"It's old-fashioned chivalry, and it shows a girl you respect her and think she's worth treating well."

"I've never seen anyone do that stuff," Theo said, narrowing his eyes.

"All the better. You'll stand out as the one boy who knows how to treat her well. She won't be able to resist."

Theo watched her, uncertain.

"It's one of the things I like about Edwin," Sadie said. "He always goes out of his way to be a gentleman. It's important. Girls want to be cherished and feel safe, and if you can show her that you think the world of her, she won't be able to resist falling for you."

Theo looked back at the screen and typed something on the keyboard. He was acting like he hadn't heard, but Sadie knew he was processing what she'd said. These days, too many young people had no idea what proper romance looked like; they were too caught up in their hormones to be intentional and gentle-manly about it, but in Sadie's mind, old-fashioned courtship rituals had worked well for hundreds of years and they had stuck around for a reason. Times might change, but what girls wanted did not.

"What else?" he finally said.

"Well, you'll pay for everything on your dates, obviously."

Theo balked. Sadie ignored that and went on. "Show respect to her family. When you pick her up for the prom, go inside the house and talk to her parents. Let them know you're responsible and plan to treat their daughter well. It wouldn't hurt to bring some flowers for her mom."

Theo was still staring at the screen, but he was nodding softly.

Sadie thought for a minute, and thought of one more thing. "And every girl likes the grand gesture."

"The what?"

"Think about movies you've seen. Isn't there always some big, public romantic gesture the guy makes that wins her over?"

"I don't really watch movies like that."

"Well, trust me, girls love them, and they imagine themselves in them. When a guy confesses his feelings for you, it's wonderful. When a guy confesses his feelings in front of your friends, so everyone sees how much he cares about you—well, there's not a girl alive who could resist that."

"I don't know. Kids don't really do stuff like that these days, Grandma."

"Again, all the better. She'll see what a catch you are." Sadie saw his cheeks turn pink, but she continued. "Although I'm sure she already knows that anyway."

Theo didn't say anything for a while, and Sadie began to think that he was done with the conversation, but then he shook his head and simply said, "Thanks, Grandma."

10

ON SATURDAY MORNING, SADIE STOPPED IN TO VISIT VIRGINIA, who still showed no change. Sadie sat by her friend and prayed, and then, her heart heavy, she headed to her shop.

The Antique Mine was busy from the time Sadie opened the doors. The day had dawned clear and beautiful, and the temperature was up into the sixties. It seemed like everyone in town was taking advantage of the weather to get out and walk around. Julie had the day off to be home with her boys, and Sadie was glad her daughter, Alice, was there to help out. Alice worked in the store on weekends whenever she could, and she had promised that Theo and Sara would be in later as well, as soon as they had tackled their homework for the weekend.

Sadie sold a set of beautifully painted jelly glasses and one of the new quilts—the cream and pink appliqué—and was perusing an online auction for a lot of vintage records when the bell over the door dinged. She looked up to see Theo walk into the shop. Alice was in the back cleaning up a set of Herman Miller scoop chairs that had come in yesterday from an estate sale. Alice loved midcentury design, and she had welcomed the opportunity to polish and restore the classic pieces.

Sadie smiled and waved, and Theo nodded and came around behind the desk to drop his backpack. Sadie figured he'd go check in with Alice, so she was surprised when she looked up to find him standing next to her, holding out a list of names with numbers and letters.

"Check it out, Grandma," he said, shoving what she now saw was a printout from an online site in front of her.

"What's this?" She squinted at the numbers.

"It's a list of people in the state of Colorado whose license plates start with 510-O," Theo said.

Sadie sucked in a breath. 510-O were the first four digits of the string Virginia had been reading off to Sadie just before the crash. "How did you get this?"

"It was easy to find online. It's all public record, and there are Web sites that track this kind of stuff," Theo said, shrugging.

Sadie thought that through. It might well be possible to get ahold of public information like license plate numbers, but how in the world had Theo known to do so?

"But where did you get 510-O?"

Theo plopped down in the chair next to Sadie. "Well, you told me Mrs. Radcliff had given you a string of numbers. When I found these numbers written on a paper by your phone last night, it didn't take a genius to figure out what it was."

Had Sadie left the paper with the numbers out? She supposed she had, in the kitchen. She certainly hadn't expected Theo to find them, let alone guess what they were. "When did you find that?"

"When you were in the bathroom." He leaned forward and ran his finger down the list of numbers. "And look what else I found." His finger stopped on a name. Sadie leaned in and saw that he was pointing at the name Curtis Younts. He moved his finger along to the full license plate number and to the address where the car was registered, in Silver Peak.

"Oh my." Despite the clear delight on Theo's face, Sadie felt dread in her belly. No matter how obnoxious a teenager was, he was still young, and it didn't make her happy to see a high schooler emerge as a lead suspect in the case.

"I thought I said I didn't want to get you involved in this mystery," Sadie admonished, shaking her head. The last thing she wanted was for Theo to be put in any danger, and so a part of her was frustrated that he had deliberately disobeyed her and gone ahead and found this list. But a small part of her couldn't help but be proud about how smart and resourceful her grandson was.

"No one will find out," Theo said. Sadie shook her head. She didn't see how anyone *could* find out, and she certainly wasn't going to tell, but it still made her nervous.

"Just please don't do any more," Sadie said, but she took the paper and folded it in half and then stuck it in her purse.

"Sure, sure," Theo said. Sadie pretended not to notice he hadn't exactly agreed to stay out of things. "So what's on the agenda for today?"

"For you?" Sadie eyed him like she was mad, but they both knew she couldn't stay upset at him long. That was no doubt what he'd been banking on. "A lot of ringing up sales, I hope. Is your sister coming in today?"

Theo shrugged. Sadie knew he liked working the register. The old-fashioned machine was kind of fun to operate, and in between sales, he could read a book or work on homework.

"Yeah, I think so. She went over to a friend's house to work on some group project, though I suspect that project had a lot more to do with goofing off online than actual schoolwork."

"You're such a pessimist."

"I know my sister."

Sadie had to admit that Sara wasn't as studious as Theo, and she did spend more time with friends. Relationships were very important to her, as they were to most teenage girls, though it often looked to everyone else like a lot of giggling nonsense.

"And what about you? What are you going to do today?"

"Well, I was hoping to head over to a nursing home in Leadville to talk to someone."

"Sounds like a blast."

"Even better that you stay here, then." She reached for the store's phone and picked up the handset. She pulled up the number of the nursing home, and the woman who answered told her that Orville was having a good day and would no doubt welcome a visit.

Just then, Jane Remington came up to the register holding a porcelain pitcher and basin delicately painted with pink and white flowers, and Sadie greeted her.

"Hi, Jane. This is a lovely piece. Is this for the inn?" Jane and her husband, Jerry, ran the Silver Peak Bed-and-Breakfast out of a beautiful old Victorian on Jefferson.

"Yes, we need something for on top of the bureau in one of the guest rooms, and I think this should do nicely," Jane said, admiring the piece as she set it on the counter.

"I'm sure it will be lovely," Sadie said, and then turned to Theo. "Think you can ring Mrs. Remington up and hold down the fort at the register for a while?"

"I got this. Go have fun at your nursing home."

Jane gave Sadie a strange look, and Sadie laughed and grabbed her purse. She'd explain that she wasn't actually looking into a nursing home for herself later. She popped her head in the back to tell Alice she was heading out. Alice was knee-deep in fiberglass cleaner, but she waved, and Sadie got ready to head out. The store had a constant stream of customers, but most were just browsing, and she knew that Theo and Alice could handle whatever might come up. She started to head toward the door, but thought a cup of coffee couldn't hurt—it rarely could—and she decided to pop in to Arbuckle's and grab one to go.

Arbuckle's was hopping on this sunny Saturday morning, she noted as she waited in line to order. There were a few people sitting quietly reading the paper or working on laptops. There was a group who looked like they'd just come in from a run gathered at a table by the door, and at a table at the back a group of women and their small children were gathered for some sort of moms' group. And over there—Sadie saw a group of older men gathered around a small table by the far wall, and noted that it was full of some the town's wealthiest residents. There was Simon Riley, whose great-grandfather had owned one of the more profitable silver mines. Next to him was Howard McNaught, a lawyer who had represented some big developers who had bought up plots of land on the outskirts of town. And there was Samuel Bradley, the former school superintendent who, since his retirement decades ago, had become known as the town's biggest supporter of the arts. His thin white hair was brushed over carefully to hide the balding spot on top of his head, and his clothes all looked too big on his thin frame. Sadie did some quick math. If he had been the superintendent back in the 1960s—well, Samuel Bradley looked frail, but he seemed to be doing all right for his age. Sadie could only hope she would be in such good shape in her mid-nineties. The men around the table all lived in some of the town's nicest old Victorians, and they were the first people Edwin would typically go to for support when he wanted to make improvements in Silver Peak.

Sadie watched the little group as the line moved slowly toward the register. Samuel Bradley was on her list of names, since he'd been interviewed in the old newspaper accounts of the fire. Could she find a way to talk to him now? Sadie watched his little group and noticed that they seemed to be just chatting, not in the middle of some serious discussion. She was almost at the front of the line now, and several people had joined the line behind her. She'd get her coffee, and then see if she could find an excuse to pop in and say hello to Bradley. She didn't know him well—they hardly moved in the same social circles—but she had met him several times when she'd been with Edwin.

Finally, it was Sadie's turn to order, and she asked Luz Vidal for a latte. She glanced back at the group around the table and saw that they were starting to gather their things. She hoped they'd stick around long enough for Sadie to snag Bradley. Sadie paid for her drink, then moved down to the far end of the bar by the espresso machine to wait for Hector to finish making it.

"Hey there, Hector," Sadie said. Hector looked up from the jug of steamed milk and smiled.

"Hi, Sadie. Your latte is coming right up." He fitted the espresso holder into the machine and turned the handle, then pushed a button on the top of the machine. Sadie tried not to panic when she noticed that Samuel's group was starting to push back from the table. Could she walk away now and stop them? And say what? Better to wait until her drink was done, so she could make it look casual. And Hector was almost done with her latte. She silently willed him to hurry.

Hector scooped a bit of foam onto the top of the milk, then added a lid and handed the cup to Sadie. "Here you go."

"Thanks so much," Sadie said, and reached for the cup. Sadie took the cup and turned around, but in the time she'd been waiting, the little group of Silver Peak's elite had broken up. McNaught was still throwing his cup into the trash can, but the others seemed to have already left. Sadie felt a surge of disappointment. Well, no matter. She tried to be positive. She'd find an opportunity to catch up to Samuel Bradley soon enough. Maybe Edwin could help her arrange a meeting. That might be better than approaching him cold, anyway, she mused as she headed for the door.

Sadie stepped out into the bright spring sunshine, and the sun's warmth felt delicious on her skin. And the coffee was wonderful—just the right amount of milk. Sadie dug out her car keys and unlocked the doors, and she arrived at the Shady Grove Nursing Home a short while later. The drive to Leadville had been spectacular, with astonishing views of snowcapped peaks against a brilliant blue sky, and Sadie pulled into the parking lot, grateful, as always, to live in a place where God had showered so much beauty.

Sadie stepped out of the car and smiled as a group of distance runners sped by on the street, their sinewy legs pumping quickly beneath their loose running shorts as they went by. Because of Leadville's high elevation—almost identical to Silver Peak's own—it was well-known for its endurance running races, and it was often used as a training ground for runners of all sorts. It had been a long time since Sadie had run like that, and though she envied how fit the runners were, she was glad she was not among them. She smiled and headed into the low brick building.

Just inside the front door, there was a desk, and when Sadie stopped in front of it, a young woman in nurses' scrubs looked up from a folder.

"Hi there," Sadie said. "I called earlier about visiting Orville Montgomery."

"Oh yes, Sadie, right?" The woman smiled. "He loves visitors. I just need you to sign in here, if you don't mind." She pushed a visitors' log across the counter, and Sadie dutifully filled in her name, address, and phone number, and the reason for her visit. "Do you know where his room is?"

Sadie shook her head.

"Just go down this hallway and turn right at the bend. He's halfway down on the left." The woman gave Sadie a cheerful smile, and Sadie thanked her and started off toward his room. The hallway was painted a soft green and hung with pictures of sunsets and waterfalls, but the blue industrial carpet was stained and worn. Sadie found Orville's room without much trouble, as the label outside the door identified him and displayed a black-and-white picture of him from what must be decades ago. It was sweet, Sadie thought, to show photos of the residents as they had been in their prime. That was how she'd want to be remembered as well.

Sadie poked her head into the room and saw a man in an overstuffed recliner staring down at what looked like a large-print Bible.

"Hello? Orville?"

At first the man didn't move, so Sadie tried again, louder, and this time he looked up. At first he looked confused, but then he smiled.

"Hello," he said. "Have you come to visit with me?" He was thin, reedy, with longish gray hair that had receded on top.

"I have. I'm Sadie Speers," Sadie said, stepping into the room. "From Silver Peak."

"Ah. Welcome, Sadie from Silver Peak. Please, have a seat." He gestured toward a hard plastic chair next to the bed. "I'm afraid I can't get up and offer you the comfortable chair like a gentleman."

"This is lovely." Sadie sat, set her purse at her feet, and looked around. There was a big window that overlooked a small lake, and ducks were gliding across the surface as if they'd been staged. The walls of the room were a soft blue, and there was a blue quilt on the bed and posters with Bible verses printed on them on the walls. There was a row of books by authors Sadie knew wrote about Christianity and the church on a low bookshelf, as well as photographs of what Sadie assumed to be his family. It was cozy and neat, and somehow warm.

"So what brings you here to see me?" he said, closing his Bible. "Don't get me wrong. I'm happy to see a new face. I get tired of looking at the same old mugs here every day. Don't tell anyone I said this, but the other people who live here?" He shook his head. "Most of them are old!"

Sadie laughed. Orville obviously had a good sense of humor, and he seemed friendly and genuine. "I'm actually working on a project about the fire at the old Silver Peak Schoolhouse," Sadie said. She watched as he processed this news. His smile faded a bit, and his hands clenched up. "I was reading some of the old records, and saw that you worked in maintenance for the district, and I wondered if you might be able to tell me about it."

"Oh yes, the old schoolhouse fire," Orville said, shaking his head. Some of the excitement had gone out of his voice, but his eyes still reflected a friendly attitude. "If you've been looking into the records, I assume you must realize that I was considered a prime suspect for having set that fire." Orville gave her a wry look. From the next room, Sadie could hear the sound of a television playing some game show.

"I did see that," Sadie said gently. "I also saw that you were cleared." Sadie wasn't sure that meant that he was innocent; he'd been let off the hook when the fire had mysteriously been declared an electrical fire despite all evidence, but there was no sense in making him feel that she thought he was guilty.

"Yes, I suppose I was. It was lucky how quickly they closed that case, wasn't it?" Orville shook his head. Sadie wasn't sure what to make of that.

"I suppose it was, although I assume they were acting on some evidence. The thing is, I haven't been able to figure out what that was, and I was wondering if you would mind telling me what you know about it."

Orville was quiet for a moment, his fingers pressed against the cover of his Bible. Sadie listened as a cheer went up on the television in the next room, followed by the dinging of bells. Someone must have just won a prize. Finally, Orville spoke.

"I don't much like to think back on those days," he said, shaking his head. "I did a lot of things then that I am not proud of. But a lot has changed since then. Most notably, I found the Lord, and

He has changed my heart. I know I've been forgiven, so all that stuff I did doesn't weigh on me anymore."

"I'm a Christian too," Sadie said. "I go to Campfire Chapel."

"That's a good church," Orville said, nodding. "Good people."

"The people are wonderful," Sadie agreed.

Orville was quiet again, and Sadie heard that a new contestant was on the game show now.

"I didn't have anything to do with that fire," Orville said. "I know a lot of people thought I did, because I was responsible for cleaning it and my cigarette butts were found there. People saw cigarettes and thought they must have started the fire. The thing is, the cigarette butts were there because every time I went to clean the site, I had a smoke. I smoked a lot in those days. Like I said, I did a lot of things back then I'm not proud of." He shook his head. "But I wasn't anywhere near there the night of the fire. But I wouldn't tell anyone where I had been, so naturally they all assumed..."

Sadie nodded as his voice trailed off.

"Well, like I said, I'm a new creation now, and if it helps at all, I can tell you what was really going on. I was drinking a lot and gambling away my paycheck, that's what."

Sadie felt her eyes widen, but she just nodded to keep him talking.

"It was wrong and I know it. I knew it then. But Clara and I, we were having problems. Had been for a long time. We married too young, and with the baby coming so soon after, things had been rocky pretty much from the beginning. That doesn't excuse it, but at the time I felt like it did. But she was threatening to leave. I know this doesn't make much sense, but as hard as things were with her, I didn't want her to leave, so I promised I'd stop."

For a moment, he was quiet—a faraway look in his eyes. "I know it's silly, but I felt like I worked so hard, I had earned the right to a little fun, and sometimes me and the boys... well, we fell into the old patterns a bit too easily. It wasn't fair to Clara. I shudder now to think that there were some months I drank away our money and left her with nothing to feed the baby." He shook his head.

"I was doing better, though, after I made my promise to Clara. But, well, the night of the fire, me and the boys got together. I had just gotten paid, and I told Clara I was putting in overtime, but we went over to the gambling tables in Central City and wasted our money. And then, when the police came calling the next morning, asking where I had been and whether I'd set the fire, what could I say?" He shrugged. "If I admitted the truth, I knew Clara was going to leave. If I said I'd been working overtime, it would have taken the police about two minutes to check with the district and figure out that was a lie. So I didn't say anything, and I know how suspicious that looked, but what was I to do? And then I was saved when the police determined it was an accident and I was off the hook."

"So you weren't anywhere near the site that night?"

"No, ma'am. I was in Central City, drunk as a skunk and gambling away my baby's milk money." Sadie could hear the shame in his words. "I've changed a lot since those days," Orville said, seeing her face. "The Lord is good. By His grace, I've been on the straight and narrow for decades. But back then, I was wild."

Sadie took a minute to absorb all of this. If Orville was telling the truth—and she had no reason to doubt him; his hands were literally on a Bible as he spoke—he was cleared from suspicion.

Sadie was glad about that. She liked Orville, and he seemed genuine about his life and his faith. But though it did cross a suspect off her list, it didn't, ultimately, get her any closer to figuring out what *had* happened the night of the fire.

"I believe that you had nothing to do with the fire," Sadie said, and that acknowledgment seemed to set him at ease a bit. His hands relaxed, and he sat back a little in his chair. "But something did happen there that night, and it has never fully been explained. From what I've seen, there's not much chance the fire was actually started by faulty wiring." Sadie glanced at him. He was looking away, not quite meeting her eye. "I believe you didn't have anything to do with it, but I am curious about what you think might have happened."

He was quiet for a minute. The television in the next room had gone to a commercial.

"There was talk of a drifter who'd been seen around town," he finally volunteered.

"I've heard that. Did you see this drifter?"

He shook his head.

"Is that who you really believe is responsible?" Sadie asked. He still didn't look at her, and she hoped she hadn't pushed too far.

"I don't want to spread rumors," he said.

"If you do know something, it would be an enormous help to me," Sadie said. "You see, my friend has had an accident, and we think it might be related to what happened that night." She filled him in quickly on Virginia, and he listened without saying anything. Then, finally, he spoke.

"Like I said, I don't want to spread rumors. Lord knows I've had plenty of rumors spread about me in my day, and I know how much they can hurt. And the Bible says, "'When words are many, sin is not absent, but he who holds his tongue is wise.'"

Sadie nodded. She agreed with that, but still hoped he would share what was on his mind. "That's true. But if you knew something to be true, would it be wrong to share it, if it could help us find who hurt Virginia?"

He shook his head, like he was trying to work it out. "I don't know." He sighed. "All I know for sure is this. I thought it was strange how fast the sheriff declared the fire an accident, but it got me off the hook so I didn't question too much. But my wife, Clara, she worked down at the hardware store, and the day before the fire she sold Robert Greene a big bottle of kerosene. I always thought the timing was strange."

Sadie thought back to what Tyson Wynan, the fireman, had told her, about how it looked like an accelerant like gas or kerosene had been used at the schoolhouse.

"That is very strange timing indeed," Sadie said. "Thank you for telling me, and I promise not to spread that around. I really appreciate your honesty."

"It's not too often folks want to talk with me about the old days," Orville said, smiling a little. "It's hard to think about some of what went on, but it's kind of nice too."

Sadie smiled. Some of her favorite memories were of when she and her family were young as well. She understood.

Orville yawned, and Sadie realized she was tiring him. She pushed herself up and thanked him for his time.

"Thank you for coming. Come back and see me again, why don't you?" He gave her a lopsided grin. "I always love to see visitors."

"I hope to," Sadie said, nodding. "It was great to meet you."

"You too."

Sadie slung her purse over her shoulder, waved, and turned to go. She thanked the nurse at the front counter and headed back to her car. On the drive back to Silver Peak, Sadie thought about what he had told her. Sheriff Greene had purchased kerosene the day before the fire. That could be fairly significant, or it could mean nothing, Sadie realized. There were plenty of reasons people used kerosene, especially fifty years ago. Though certainly most homes in Silver Peak had been wired for electricity by 1965, Sadie knew that kerosene- and gas-powered appliances were still common enough back then. Her grandparents had used a kerosene-powered refrigerator until it finally gave up the ghost well into the seventies, simply because they already owned it and it still worked. Living through the Depression had taught them never to waste anything. Sadie knew that those old refrigerators were now considered retro and could fetch a nice price at auction if you could get your hands on one. But, as Orville had pointed out, the timing was odd, given the certainty that something like kerosene had been used to start the fire, and given how quick the sheriff had been to ignore the evidence and declare it an accident.

Sadie wasn't sure what to make of it, but one thing was certain. She would be looking more into Sheriff Robert Greene, immediately.

11

SADIE STOPPED IN AT HOME TO GRAB A QUICK LUNCH OF LEFTOVERS, then hurried back to the Antique Mine. When she got there, Alice was helping a customer sort through some beautifully illustrated prints of birds and other wildlife Sadie had cut from a damaged Audubon book, and Theo was carrying some boxes to the back room. The new shipment of glassware she had been expecting must have come in. There was no sign of Sara yet, but Sadie supposed she must still be working on her project—or, more likely, enjoying her day off from school. No matter. Sadie wanted to see her, of course, but things looked to be under control here.

Sadie sat down at the desk. She would help Theo unload those boxes in a minute, but first Sadie thought she might see if the Internet could tell her anything she didn't already know about Robert Greene. She shook the mouse to wake up the computer, and smiled when she saw what was up on the screen. It was the Web site for Silver Peak Florist, and the webpage showcased a variety of different bouquets and corsages available for purchase, as well as their prices. Theo must have been using this computer last. It was nice to see that he was taking her advice to heart. She scanned the options and saw that there were several beautiful choices at good prices. She hoped Elena would be pleased and flattered.

Sadie left his page open and opened a new browser window. She'd see what she could find about Robert Greene here, and then maybe head to the town hall and see what she could dig up in the public records. But first she scanned her e-mail, and was pleased to see a response from a Dr. Justin Orr.

She clicked on the e-mail quickly, and was delighted to read that this Justin was indeed the Justin Orr who had grown up in Silver Peak. He said that he remembered the night of the fire, and would be happy to talk to her about it. He asked if she had some time Tuesday afternoon to chat. Sadie quickly replied that Tuesday would be fine, and suggested a time. She clicked on a link at the bottom of his e-mail and was taken to a Web site for his pediatric practice. Dr. Orr, according to this Web page was married and had three kids, and had an office that focused on reaching out to low-income patients who wouldn't otherwise be able to afford care as well as more traditional patients. Well, that certainly seemed noble and upstanding, but that didn't mean he hadn't had anything to do with the fire. And Tuesday she could ask him all about it.

Her heart was beating faster just thinking about it. Justin was one of the four boys who had been seen in the woods the night of the fire. Finally, she would be able to talk to someone who had actually been spotted near the scene of the crime that night—and someone who had, possibly, left evidence there as well, in the form of his glasses. Sadie couldn't wait for Tuesday afternoon.

In the meantime, Sadie poked around online, seeing what she could find about Robert Greene that she might have missed before. The short answer was nothing. It was a common enough name, and he had lived so long ago, that there was almost nothing on the Internet about him. Sadie sat back in her chair and tried to figure out what to do next. At the town hall offices you could often find things like marriage certificates and property records, but she couldn't see how that would be too relevant here. If only she knew someone who had been in the police force back then…

And then she realized she did. Well, not someone who had actually been on the police force, but the next best thing. She picked up the phone, and a few minutes later, Sadie was on her way to visit her good friend Roz.

A short while later, Sadie reached the outskirts of town and pulled up in front of the small cottage where Roz and her husband, Roscoe, lived. Crocuses and peonies lined the walkway, and the house looked neat and cheerful. Sadie rang the doorbell, on the off chance Roscoe was home. Roz just came straight into her place these days, and Sadie loved that, but she'd hate to surprise Roscoe and give him a fright. A moment later, Roz appeared at the door and ushered Sadie inside and out though the back door onto the back deck. The backyard sloped down away from the house into a stand of pine trees. From the deck, a breathtaking view of the treetops and, beyond that, the highest peaks of the Rocky Mountains were visible.

"Do you mind if I keep at this while we chat?" Roz said, gesturing to an array of clay pots and a bag of potting soil. Dozens of colorful blooms sat on the deck in small plastic tubs from the garden center.

"Not at all," Sadie said, and took a seat in one of the wrought-iron chairs that surrounded the Putnams' outdoor table. "I see you're digging up dirt today too." Sadie grinned, and Roz laughed out loud.

"Is that what you're doing here? Digging up dirt?" Roz brushed her hands together. "And here I thought you'd just missed your best friend."

"Well, of course I did. But I'd be lying if I said I didn't have an ulterior motive." Sadie looked around the gorgeous yard and sighed. "It's so lovely out here. And it's wonderful to see signs of spring." She studied the annuals Roz had gathered around her. "Those dahlias are going to be especially lovely."

"Roscoe thinks I'm being too optimistic about the weather and I'm going to lose these guys, but I choose to believe our last frost is past us," Roz said, kneeling in front of one of the pots and pulling on garden gloves. "And I'm so ready for the warmer weather, I just couldn't bear to let the first nice weekend pass us by."

"I sure hope you're right," Sadie said, turning her face toward the sun. It felt lovely to sit outside and enjoy the warmth, and though there would likely still be plenty of cool days and nights before the long, hot days of summer came along, it did give her hope that the worst of winter's storms had passed.

"So you want to know about the police," Roz said, gently tugging on a dahlia stem to free it from its pot. The flowers were bright pink with yellow centers, and they really brightened up the back deck. "I'm not really sure how much I can help you there."

"I'm not really asking what it's like to be a policeman." Sadie laughed. "I just want to know what you remember about growing up with a dad in the force."

"I don't know. He was pretty much like any other dad, I guess," Roz shrugged. "You knew him. It wasn't like Silver Peak was some

major urban crime center. It was mostly finding lost cats and helping old ladies cross streets."

It hadn't been that idyllic, Sadie knew, even through the rose-
tinted glasses of childhood. But Roz was right that Silver Peak had
always been a safe place to live, especially back in the sixties.

"Do you know if he helped investigate the old schoolhouse
fire?" Sadie pressed.

"I'm sorry, Sadie, but I don't know." Roz scooped potting soil
from the bag into the bottom of a clay pot and then gently rested
the roots on top. "We were what, twelve? And he tried not to bring
his work home with him. I remember my mom being pretty insis-
tent about his not talking about it around us kids." She used a
trowel to scoop more soil around the plant and patted it down
gently with her fingers.

Sadie nodded. It had been a long shot, she knew. Maybe it was
silly to think that Roz might be able to tell her anything about
Robert Greene just because he'd been her father's boss. But she
still had to ask.

"I'm mainly interested in finding out more about the sheriff at
the time. By any chance do you remember your dad saying anything about Sheriff Robert Greene?"

Roz sat back on her heels. "You know, I don't know much, but
I do remember that name. And I do remember feeling like he was
something of a bully."

"How so?"

"Well, again, I don't know how much of this to trust, since I
was just a kid, but I remember overhearing my parents talking
about how to handle Dad's boss, how he was unfair and didn't
listen and just bossed everyone around, that sort of thing."

"I suppose that's what a boss does." Sadie laughed. "Boss people around."

"That's true," Roz said, reaching for the next pot. "You know, I do remember my dad's frustration with his boss, but some of my feeling about all this might be coming from the fact that Selma Greene was so horrible to me in school."

"Selma Greene?" Sadie scrolled through her memories, trying to place the name.

"You remember her," Roz said. "Tall, dark hair, athletic. She always seemed like she could eat you for breakfast."

Selma's face was coming back to Sadie slowly. Selma had been kind of standoffish, and she did seem to exude a sort of athletic aggressiveness. But though they'd gone to school together for years, Sadie hadn't really interacted with Selma all that much and hadn't thought about her in decades.

"I vaguely remember her," Sadie said. "She was horrible to you?" Roz was her best friend. How had Sadie not known about this?

"Just sort of snotty. She couldn't help reminding me whenever she could that her dad was my dad's boss. Tried to boss me around as well. That kind of thing." She reached for the next dahlia plant in its plastic tub.

"I had no idea."

Roz shrugged. "I don't know why you would have. It wasn't some big thing that dominated my childhood. It was just annoying, like she actually thought I would be cowed by the fact that her dad ranked above mine."

Scraps of memories were coming back to Sadie now. She could see Selma playing basketball with the boys in their class in elementary school, and remembered seeing her say something cutting to one of the weaker girls in their English class in sixth grade. Sadie couldn't remember what she'd said, but she vividly recalled the shame she felt that she hadn't stood up to Selma and defended the girl.

"Anyway, if you're looking for information about the old sheriff, you could maybe look Selma up. Last I heard, she lived over in Breckenridge."

That was an interesting possibility. "Do you know anything else about her?"

"She married that cretin Marshall Matthews from school. Remember him?"

There was another name Sadie hadn't heard in a while. Marshall had been the captain of the basketball team when they were in high school.

"But I think they got divorced a while back. I'm not sure what name she would be using now."

Sadie pulled out her phone and pulled up an Internet browser. She typed in "Selma Greene Breckenridge," and a list of results came up. Sadie clicked on the first link, which was the Web site for a café and pastry shop that catered to tourists in Breckenridge. The bottom of the page said Selma Matthews, Proprietor.

"Here she is," Sadie said. "She owns a café."

"Good for her."

Sadie was pleased to see that Roz was genuinely happy Selma had done well for herself, even after the way Selma had treated her in childhood.

"Here's an e-mail address," Sadie said, clicking on the address on the contact page. "I'm going to e-mail her." Sadie typed out a message on her screen, asking if Selma remembered her and asking if they could meet up, then sent it off to Selma.

"Let me know if you hear anything back," Roz said, brushing her hands together to shake the dirt off her gloves.

"I will. And thanks for your help," Sadie said, pushing herself up. She should get back to the shop. She'd hardly been there at all today.

"Anytime. I'll let you know if I think of anything else," Roz said. Sadie waved good-bye and said Roz didn't need to get up, then showed herself out.

As she drove back to the shop, Sadie thought about Selma Greene and Marshall Matthews. If Sadie remembered correctly, they had been prom king and queen Sadie's senior year. She'd forgotten that. It was funny how things like that mattered so much when you were in high school, but now they seemed like such trivial matters. Still, after decades in the schools, Sadie knew how seriously kids took that sort of thing, and she was grateful she'd had the chance to talk with Theo about his upcoming prom. She said a quick prayer that all would go well for him as he worked up the nerve to ask Elena.

When Sadie got back to the shop, her granddaughter, Sara, was sitting at the desk, staring down at her cell phone.

"Hi there," Sadie said, and tucked her purse behind the desk. "When did you get here?"

"A while ago." Sara looked up from her phone briefly, then looked back down. Her strawberry-blonde hair was pulled back into a low ponytail, and Sadie could see the rubber bands on her braces were a new aqua color. She must have gone to the orthodontist recently.

"Did you get your project done?"

"Done enough for now." Sara shrugged, her phone buzzed, and a moment later her fingers were flying over the buttons again.

Sadie tried not to be frustrated. As annoying as it could be to be ignored for whoever was on the other end of the text conversation, Sadie did remember what it was like to be fourteen, how your friends were your lifeline and being in touch with them seemed like the most important thing in the world. Sadie sighed and looked around the shop. Two of the tulip chairs Alice had cleaned up earlier were set out next to a sixties-era television set. Alice was helping Mary Sue Abbot sort through a collection of old maps, and there was a group of women about Sadie's age browsing the vintage sewing patterns.

"Is Theo here?"

"He's hiding in the back."

"Hiding? From what?"

"Humiliation."

"What?" Sadie started toward the back.

"I'd stay out of there if I were you," Sara said. "He's not in a good mood. He asked Elena Garza to the prom. Can you imagine?"

So he'd done it then. And by the sound of it, it hadn't gone well. Oh dear. Sadie ignored Sara's warning and started off toward the back room.

"It's your funeral," she heard Sara mutter. Sadie ignored her and threaded through the store and found Theo on the floor, using fiberglass polish on one of the Herman Miller chairs Alice had been working on earlier.

"Hi there," Sadie said, but her voice sounded overly cheerful, even to her. "How's everything going?"

"Fine," Theo said, but he didn't look up, just moved the rag in his hand in a circular motion over the scooped back of the chair. There was an edge to his voice Sadie wasn't used to hearing.

"I hear you asked Elena to the prom," Sadie said, lowering herself into one of the chairs that still needed to be cleaned up.

"Has everybody heard already?"

"I don't know about everybody. But Sara told *me*. I don't assume she's alerted the media."

She waited for Theo to laugh, but he didn't.

"So how did it go?" Sadie asked.

"Fine," Theo said. He continued polishing the chair.

"I don't know how to interpret that," Sadie said. Though, really, the tone in his voice told her probably as much as she needed to know.

"It means I don't know. She said she had to think about it."

"She had to think about it?" What kind of answer was that? What was there to think about? She either wanted to go to the prom with Theo or she didn't. "When will she decide?"

Theo sighed and set down the rag, then turned and faced her.

"I don't know. She said she doesn't know if she can go because she's grounded. And then Makayla Henderson said she'd be off restriction by then, but Elena wasn't sure."

"Wait." Sadie tried to envision what Theo was telling her. She knew Makayla was another high schooler. "Makayla was there when you asked her?"

"Yeah. A lot of people were. I did what you told me to." His voice sounded hurt, like he was smarting and blamed Sadie.

"How so?" Sadie had a sinking feeling in her stomach.

"You said girls like the grand gesture, that they want people to see how much you like them. So when she came into Arbuckle's a while ago with a group of her friends, I went out and got her flowers, like you told me to, and then I went over and said I was sorry to interrupt, but I had a question I had to ask her. In public, just like you said."

Sadie had said that. But she hadn't exactly meant that he should interrupt her while she was with her friends to ask her. There was a definite note of anger in his words. Sadie tried not to notice that and focused on how to reassure him.

"And then what happened?" Sadie said weakly.

"I said the other stuff you told me. That I would pay for everything and treat her like a lady, and all that."

"Oh boy." Sadie could see that this had not played out like she had hoped. She hadn't actually meant for Theo to actually say those things to her, only to expect to *do* them. Theo was naïve when it came to girls, and while Sadie stood by her advice, maybe she should have been more careful about how she had phrased it. "How did she react to that?"

"She seemed confused, mostly."

Theo didn't say so, but Sadie had been around enough teenage girls in her life to imagine there must have been a fair amount of giggling from her friends. Her heart ached for her grandson.

"But she didn't say no, right?"

"No." Theo shook his head. "But she didn't say yes, either. And, I don't know, it kind of seemed like maybe she didn't want to go but didn't know how to say no."

"Well, you'll just have to wait and see."

"I guess so." Theo picked up the rag and started polishing the fiberglass again.

"Did she say when she'd have an answer?"

"I don't really want to talk about this anymore, Grandma."

Well, that stung, but she got the message. Sadie wanted to say more, to comfort him and give him hope. She suddenly wished he were small again, so she could gather him up in her arms like she had when he'd hurt himself as a small boy. But it sure seemed like Theo just wanted to be left alone.

"Okay. If you want to talk, I'm here."

Theo didn't say anything, just nodded, and reluctantly, Sadie went back out to the front of the store and left Theo to lick his wounds.

12

AT CHURCH ON SUNDAY MORNING, THE CONGREGATION PRAYED for Virginia Radcliff, and Pastor Don Sweeting reported that there had been no change in her condition. The church had been providing meals for David and the boys, though, and Pastor Don encouraged them to keep it up, and to pray without ceasing for Virginia's full recovery. In her head, Sadie added a silent prayer that the Lord would help them find whoever had caused the crash in the first place.

She left church feeling refreshed, and she and Edwin went for brunch at Flapjack's. Predictably, there was a wait, as there usually was on Sunday just after church, but Sadie and Edwin browsed in the shops nearby and were seated in a cozy booth in the corner before too long. They talked about the church services as they ate pancakes smothered in strawberries and real maple syrup. Edwin had heard, as Sadie had been sure he would, about the threatening note that had been slipped under her door, and he asked her again to please be careful. Sadie promised she would, and then as they got ready to go, Edwin invited Sadie to go on a hike in the canyons surrounding Silver Peak with him. Sadie was tempted—she loved nothing more than hitting the trails, especially on such a nice spring day—but she was supposed to have dinner with Alice and her grandkids, and in the meantime there were still several people on her list that Sadie had yet to contact, and she decided she should probably spend the afternoon trying to track them down.

She thanked Edwin, and promised to call him later that evening, then she drove home to change out of her church clothes and figure out her next step. First, she checked her e-mail on her laptop, and was thrilled to see a response from Selma Matthews, née Greene, in her in-box. Sadie clicked on it and saw that Selma had remembered Sadie and was glad to hear from her. She said she would be happy to talk to Sadie, and she invited her to come by her house Sunday afternoon around four—her day off—or to drop by the café any time. Sadie looked at her watch. She had plenty of time to make it to Breckenridge by four, even if she made some other stops first, so she e-mailed Selma back and said she'd love to stop by that afternoon.

She still had a few hours before she needed to get on the road, so in the meantime, Sadie settled in an Adirondack chair on her porch, Hank at her feet, and studied the notebook she'd used to take notes on this case:

Vagrant/hippie? Ask Judith Marley.

Joe Curr reported the fire.

Melvin Loffredo, fire chief

Samuel Bradley, school superintendent

Robert Greene, sheriff

High school boys: Martin Goring, Justin Orr, Michael Leonard, and Tully Stewart

Burn pattern?

Orville Montgomery, maintenance worker, smoked Victory cigarettes, unaccounted for night of fire.
Jim Sharlett, officer who disagreed with conclusions
Tortoiseshell glasses

Sadie took a pen out of her purse and started a list of those whom she was looking into for the crash Wednesday night. She put the name Curtis Younts at the top. He was the high schooler who'd threatened Virginia, and Sadie hadn't yet found out much about him. And, if Theo was right, his license plate number matched the number Virginia had started to read out to her. There was also Ramon Garza. He'd been seen leaving the restaurant agitated at exactly the right time, and his red car had a dent in it.

Sadie had already tracked down or reached a dead end with most of the people on the fire suspect list, she realized. She would see Selma Greene later today, and maybe find out more about the sheriff, she would talk with Justin Orr tomorrow, and possibly get some insight into what role the teenage boys had played in the fire then. She hadn't yet approached Judith Marley, who still lived here in town, or Samuel Bradley, the former superintendent. He was only on the list because he'd been interviewed in the newspaper article, but she'd decided to talk to everyone on her list, so she needed to figure out a way to connect with him.

Sadie pulled out her cell phone and called Edwin. Edwin, she reasoned, was her best bet for connecting with Samuel Bradley, and she hoped he'd help her arrange a quick meeting. The call went to voice mail, though—he must be out of cell phone range on his hike—and Sadie left a message asking him to call her back.

She studied the name of Curtis Younts. She knew the police were looking into him, but she still wanted to talk to him as well.

She tapped her pen against the paper. How could she find a way to get him to talk to her? She didn't know where he lived or really anything about the boy, including how to get a hold of him. Theo had made it clear he was not friends with Curtis, and Sadie didn't think there was much chance a senior boy was hanging out with her freshman granddaughter. Sadie would have to wait on him until she could find out more.

That left Judith Marley. She thought for a moment, and realized she could tackle her today. Sadie and Judith were friendly, even though for many years there had been a rivalry between their two families. Sadie looked down at her phone. She was pretty sure she had Judith's number in there. It was a beautiful sunny day, and perhaps Judith, who lived alone, would welcome a visit. Sadie stood up, ushered Hank inside, and arranged some leftover snicker doodles she'd made for coffee hour at church on a plate. Then she grabbed her light coat and headed out to visit Judith.

Judith Marley lived in a small redbrick house on Adams Street, and when Sadie pulled up in front she was pleased to see that tulips were starting to push up through the soil in Judith's carefully manicured yard. Sadie carried the cookies to the porch and rang the doorbell, and a moment later, Judith answered the door. She was wearing pressed wool pants and a pink twinset with pearl earrings, and her hair was perfectly styled. Sadie wanted to laugh—that was hardly the kind of outfit Sadie hung around the house in—but that was Judith. Proper and put-together, no matter what. Sadie admired her for it, though she knew it would never be how anyone described her. She now felt dowdy in her jeans and fleece vest.

"Hello Sadie," Judith said, and gestured for her to step inside. "This is a nice surprise."

"I was hoping you wouldn't mind a visitor," Sadie said, holding out the plate. "I brought cookies."

"How perfect. I would have been glad to see you anyway, but the cookies seal the deal," Judith said. She closed the door behind Sadie and led her down the hallway to her living room. "I was just working on a quilt I'm piecing together, and my eyes were starting to get buggy." Sadie knew quilting was a hobby Judith had taken up in retirement. "Would you like some tea?"

"Some tea would be nice," Sadie said. Judith nodded and gestured for Sadie to sit on one of her high-backed crewel-work love seats—reproductions, Sadie could tell, but high-quality—and then she left the room and returned a few minutes later with a china teapot and a set of dainty porcelain cups. Sadie recognized the set. Judith had bought it from Sadie a while back. It was a lovely set by Royal Worcester, in the willow pattern, and though a few of the cups had some small nicks, it had been in very good condition, and Sadie was thrilled to see Judith using it. She set the tea service down on the carved cherry coffee table and began pouring out the tea. Sadie's plate of cookies looked woefully underdressed next to such finery.

"So what brings you here today?" Judith asked. Judith was known for her bluntness, and though Sadie supposed some might find the question rude, she appreciated it. It wasn't as if Sadie and Judith often visited each other, and Sadie was glad the older woman felt free to get straight to the point.

"I was doing some research on the old schoolhouse fire," Sadie said, dropping a sugar cube into her tea with a pair of tiny silver tongs. "And I read in a newspaper article that you remembered seeing a vagrant around town about that time who might have had something to do with the fire. I was wondering if you might remember anything about this vagrant."

"Goodness." Judith dropped two sugar cubes neatly into her cup. "That was a long time ago. I was still fairly new to teaching back then." She shook her head. "That was so scary. There were all these reports of this unkempt fellow appearing in people's backyards, stealing things…it was just—" She shook her head. "It made you afraid to go outside, you know? And I had just moved out into my own place, so there was no one to call for help if something happened." She added cream from a small pitcher and stirred her tea.

Sadie nodded. "I can imagine." Part of her was simply placating Judith, trying to keep her talking, but truthfully Sadie did understand that very real, if irrational, fear as a woman who lived alone.

"Did you ever see the man?"

Judith set down her teaspoon with a neat *click*. "Not directly. But some things did go missing from my house some nights, and it had to be him who took them."

"What sorts of things?" Sadie took a sip of her tea. It was Earl Grey, one of her favorites, and hot and sweet, just like she liked it.

"Oh, wood from the woodpile. That happened a couple of times. And one time it was my milk—this was back when you could still have it delivered. He took it straight from my doorstep."

Sadie took another sip and processed this. It sure seemed like someone had been taking things from Judith, but so far she hadn't heard anything that convinced her it had been the vagrant everyone kept mentioning.

"So you never saw this vagrant yourself?" Sadie tried again, just to clarify.

"I never saw him myself, but plenty of people did." Judith looked at Sadie over the top of her teacup.

Sadie smiled, trying to encourage Judith, but the more Judith talked, the less sure Sadie was about what to believe. She needed to find someone who had actually seen this vagrant everyone kept mentioning.

Sadie and Judith chatted for a while longer, and Judith showed Sadie the quilt she was working on, a baby quilt for a niece who was about to have her third child. Then Sadie thanked Judith for her time and headed off.

As she climbed into her car, she pulled out her notebook and updated her list. She had now talked to Judith, and was no closer to finding answers about this mysterious vagrant, or anything else.

Sadie sighed, tucked her notebook back in her purse, set her GPS to the address Selma had given her, and pulled out of the driveway. Then she steered her car toward the edge of town, where she would pick up the highway that led out of Silver Peak toward Breckenridge. The road was steep and curvy, traversing the mountain pass that separated the two towns, but Sadie had been driving on mountain roads her whole life, and she pulled into the resort town in just over twenty minutes.

Breckenridge was a charming mountain town with a lovely historic district downtown, much like Silver Peak, as well as tons of rental apartments that, in winter, were filled with skiers and snowboarders drawn by the famous ski resort. Sadie navigated past the downtown and onto a side street that led her to a neighborhood of modest homes. This must be the part of town where the people who worked at the resort lived, Sadie realized, as she made her way to the address Selma had given her. She pulled up in front of a neat wooden bungalow, simple but well cared for, and stepped out of the car. Sadie took a minute to prepare herself for meeting up again with Selma. High school had been many decades ago, but somehow you never quite got over the social pecking order, and it took Sadie a minute to work up the courage to face one of the more popular kids in her class. She reminded herself that Selma might be the only one who could tell her about what her father, the sheriff, had been up to on the night of the fire, and slowly, she headed up to the door.

Sadie rang the bell, and the door opened, and Selma Greene stood there, smiling at Sadie. Her dark hair, which had always been long and lush in school, was cropped short now and shot through with gray, and though she was still long and lean, just as she'd always been, she was wearing a velour track suit that made her seem a bit dowdy. Instead of the stunning cheerleader Sadie had been cowed by in school, Sadie now saw a middle-aged woman very much like herself.

"My goodness. Sadie Wright." Selma shook her head and gestured for Sadie to step inside. "I couldn't have been more surprised to see your e-mail pop up in my in-box, but I was so glad to hear from you." Selma seemed warm and genuine, and Sadie reflected again on how the years had changed things. "Come in, come in. Sorry for the way I look." She gestured down at her outfit. "On my day off, it's hard for me to get motivated to try too hard."

"You look just fine," Sadie said, gesturing down at her own casual outfit. "And I'm hardly dressed to the nines."

"You look just the same," Selma said, and started to lead her down a short hallway. Sadie spotted an antique mirror in an elaborately carved mahogany frame hung on the entryway wall, and she itched to stop and examine it, but she followed reluctantly behind Selma. "You always were too practical to worry about keeping up with trends." Sadie wasn't sure how to take that, which sounded a lot like a backhanded compliment, but she smiled anyway. "I sure could have saved myself a lot of stress if I'd figured out how to do that sooner."

She led Sadie into a living room filled with exquisite Queen Anne furniture. Sadie sucked in a breath. "This is beautiful," she said, looking from the armchairs upholstered in rich brocade to the coffee table with perfectly turned legs to the highboy dresser against the far wall. A large flat-screen television and some hi-fi equipment ruined the look of a Victorian parlor, but the furniture itself was stunning, and not at all what she expected to find in this suburban tract home.

"Thank you." Selma shrugged. "It all belonged to my parents. They were big antique lovers. Didn't I see that you now own an antique store?"

So Selma had looked up Sadie, just as Sadie had done for her. She supposed that made sense; she probably would have done the same if an old classmate had contacted her out of the blue after forty years.

"I do. The Antique Mine, right in Silver Peak. So I can say with authority that you have some lovely pieces." Sadie eyed a mantle clock and a set of burnished silver candlesticks over the fireplace. There were a number of photographs in lovely cut-glass frames there as well. Sadie looked at one, a picture of four boys, ranging from about five to fifteen, and realized they all bore a striking resemblance to Marshall, the basketball star Selma had married out of high school. They must be Selma's grandchildren.

"Thanks." Selma sat down on the couch and indicated that Sadie should sit in one of the armchairs. "My parents spent a lot of time trolling antique stores and estate sales, looking for the right pieces. Of course, it all looked a lot better in the house I grew up in, one of those old Victorians on Jefferson Avenue, but I love it, even if it doesn't exactly fit in here."

Sadie ran her hand over a beautiful cherry side table with delicately turned legs. It was built solidly and polished to a high sheen. "It makes a charming room," Sadie said, and then noticed an interesting lamp on the table. Sadie turned to study it. It had a white glass dome-shaped shade, and beneath that was an ornate brass base with a wide belly that narrowed down to a delicately detailed footprint. Sadie had seen a lamp like this before. She ducked down and peeked up under the shade. There was a light bulb in there now, so it had been modernized and wired for electricity, but when this lamp was new, there would have been a cotton wick that fed from the belly to the burner under the shade.

"Did this start life as a kerosene lamp?" Sadie asked, touching the lamp gently.

"Sure did." Selma picked at an invisible piece of lint on her pants. "Mom and Dad loved that thing. I had it wired for electricity when I moved it here, but they used to light that ridiculous wick long after every house in town had electricity. They liked the glow better than the artificial light from light bulbs." Selma smiled, but it was a bit pinched, like she was trying to figure out what Sadie was really doing there.

"That's fascinating," Sadie said, though fascinating wasn't really the word she was looking for. She realized another clue was being crossed off her list. "Where did they get the kerosene? You can't just buy that anywhere these days."

"Oh, it's been almost twenty years. I'm not really sure where you'd get it now, but it was easier to find when we were younger. Dad always got it at the hardware store when we were kids, if I remember right."

Sadie nodded. So that explained that, then. That was where Orville Montgomery's wife had seen him buying it the day before the fire. It seemed Robert Greene had a perfectly valid reason to be buying kerosene that day. That didn't guarantee he'd only used it for the lamp, and it didn't do anything to explain why he'd been so quick to declare the fire an accident, but it did help explain one key piece of evidence against him.

"It's great to see you after all this time, Sadie…" Selma said, and let her voice trail off. Sadie understood what Selma was politely asking. Why was Sadie there?

"It's great to see you too, and thank you so much for having me." Looking at Selma now, it was hard to see the mean girl who had held herself so above most of the kids in high school. Selma was a grandmother trying to run a small business in difficult times, and Sadie felt more open and free to talk to her than she could have imagined. "I came across your name because I have been looking into the old fire at the Silver Peak Schoolhouse, and I read that your father had been involved in the investigation."

Selma's face didn't change; if she knew something she wasn't supposed to tell about the fire, she had done a good job covering it up.

"No doubt he was. He was the sheriff, you know, so he was involved in just about everything that went on in Silver Peak back then."

"I read that," Sadie said. "It must have been interesting, having your father be so involved in what was going on around town."

Selma shrugged. "I guess. I was really just a kid. It's not like he talked about his work around me much."

"I suppose that makes sense," Sadie said. "But do you remember him talking about the schoolhouse fire at all? It would be so helpful to hear anything you might remember from that time."

Selma sat back against the couch and thought for a moment, then shook her head. "I'm sorry, Sadie, I'm afraid I'm not going to be much help. We were, what, twelve at the time?" Sadie nodded, and Selma shook her head. "I vaguely remember something about some high school boys being involved, but only because I thought Tully Stewart was cute."

Sadie laughed. That sounded more like the Selma Greene Sadie remembered. She tried a few more questions, but it quickly became clear that Selma really didn't know anything about the fire or her father's involvement, so Sadie asked what she'd been up to for the past forty years, and they spent the next little while catching up. It turned out Selma had been married to Marshall for twenty years. They'd lived in Colorado Springs and had three kids, and when they split up shortly after Selma's parents passed away in quick succession, she moved to Breckenridge to help her sister run the café. Selma now owned it herself, and while it was extremely busy during peak ski season, things had quieted down a bit now that spring was on the way. They conferred about the challenges of owning a small business and laughed about some memories from high school.

The clock over the mantle bonged, and Selma looked at the time. "Goodness, I'm sorry to run, but I didn't realize it was getting so late," Selma said, pushing herself up. "I am supposed to help my aunt go return a rental car in a few minutes."

Sadie pushed herself up as well. It was nice that Selma had so much family nearby, and it was nice of her to help out.

"Thank you so much for taking the time to talk with me," Sadie said. "It was great to catch up." Sadie had enjoyed the visit, but she still tried to keep the disappointment out of her voice. Instead of learning how Robert Greene might have been involved in a cover-up, all she'd gotten was an explanation for what had seemed such a damning piece of evidence before.

"Thank you for coming by," Selma said, and Sadie started to follow her around the furniture back toward the hallway. But as she walked past the mantle, Sadie's eye caught on one of the photographs. Sadie stopped and took a closer look. It was a picture of an older couple perched on a cliff, with what looked like Grecian ruins behind them, the sun just setting over azure waters. Sadie squinted at the picture. It had to have been taken a few years back, but that was definitely Samuel Bradley there, and his wife, Meredith.

"This is a beautiful photograph," Sadie said. "Look at how blue that water is."

"Yeah, that's my Uncle Brad and Aunt Meredith. They went to Turkey for their fiftieth anniversary and gave us all copies of that photo afterward."

Sadie tried to feign causal interest. "I recognize him. He lives in Silver Peak, doesn't he?"

"Sure does. He and Aunt Meredith live in my grandparents' house. Aunt Meredith is Dad's older sister."

Sadie's mind was spinning. So Samuel Bradley and Robert Greene were brothers-in-law. That didn't necessarily mean anything, of course, but it was a connection she hadn't realized before this. Interesting. Sadie realized Selma was waiting for her to say something, and so Sadie straightened up and said, "I've never been to Turkey, but if that's what it looks like, I'd sure like to go there someday."

Selma smiled, and then she led Sadie to the door. "Thanks again for taking the time to talk with me," Sadie said, and Selma leaned in and gave her a hug.

"It was great to see you again," Selma said. "Take care of yourself, and let me know if there's anything I can do to help."

Sadie thanked her and headed back to her car. Clouds were rolling in, and the late afternoon sky had gone from brilliant sunshine to a gloomy gray. As she drove back to Silver Peak, Patsy Cline crooning on the radio, she tried to process what the connection between Samuel Bradley and Sheriff Robert Greene could mean, and while she came up with a lot more questions, she didn't get any closer to finding the truth. She needed to talk to Samuel Bradley. She hoped Edwin would be able to arrange that soon.

Sadie turned off the radio and spent a good chunk of the drive praying for Virginia's recovery, for clarity of thought, for preparations for the upcoming presentation, and that God would help her to find the answers she was looking for. Then, as she got close to Silver Peak, Sadie plugged in her hands-free headset and called David Radcliff to see if there was any update on Virginia and ask if there was anything the family needed. David said the doctors had seen some promising brain activity in some scans earlier in the day, but there was no outward change to her condition. He also said that they were being well-cared for by churches and friends of Virginia's, so he couldn't think of anything they needed at the moment. He thanked Sadie for calling, and Sadie promised to keep chasing answers.

Sadie stopped at home long enough to bake a batch of peanut butter cookies, which she knew were Sara's favorite, and then she headed over to Alice's house for Sunday dinner. Storm clouds were starting to build up over the mountains to the east. It looked like their stretch of nice weather was about to change; then again, it wouldn't be spring in Colorado if the weather didn't do its best to confuse you.

Alice's 1940s-style cottage house smelled like roasting garlic when Sadie stepped inside, and she took a deep breath. It smelled wonderful.

"Hi, Mom," Alice called from the kitchen. Sadie ventured in to say hello, and they chatted for a minute about their afternoons. Alice was just draining a pot of linguine, and Sadie could see a pan of shrimp cooking in garlic and olive oil. Her mouth started watering. Alice always had been a good cook, and this meal looked delicious.

"Where are my grandchildren?" Sadie asked, looking around. The house was small, and the kitchen could use a bit of updating, but the house was full of beautiful antiques, many of which came from the Antique Mine, and it felt comfortable and warm.

"I know Sara's in the living room watching TV," Alice said, as steam from the hot pasta rose up around her. "And Theo—"

Just then, a door slammed upstairs. Alice laughed. "It sounds like Theo's in his bedroom. Maybe that's for the best. He's not exactly in the best mood today."

"Oh?" Sadie certainly hoped he wasn't still upset about what had happened with Elena yesterday. "Maybe I'll go say hi."

"Can you let him know dinner will be on the table in a minute and to wash his hands?" Alice asked. Sadie nodded and headed down up the stairs to knock on Theo's door.

"What is it?" Theo called. His words were short, but it was the tone of his voice that worried Sadie. He was definitely upset.

"Can I come in?" Sadie asked.

There was a pause. "I'm kind of busy right now."

Oh dear. Their relationship wasn't always perfect, by any means, but Sadie couldn't remember a time when Theo had refused to talk with her. He was upset, and he was upset with her.

"Okay," Sadie said, trying to keep her emotions under control. "Your mom says it's time to wash your hands for dinner."

Theo mumbled something in response, and Sadie turned and headed back to the kitchen. Sara was just setting out plates around the table, and Sadie chatted with her about the television show she'd just been watching, a reality show about a family who made duck calls, then Theo and Alice came in and they all sat down. After they prayed, Sara kept chattering away, and Sadie was grateful, as there was a decided lack of participation from Theo's end of the table. He hardly said a word, and as soon as he was done eating, he asked to be excused and retreated to his room.

Sara rolled her eyes, and Alice gave her a look, which caused Sara to laugh. Somehow the tension was defused, but when they were all done, Sadie pushed her chair in and craned her neck down the hallway, looking toward Theo's room.

"I'd just give him some space, Mom," Alice said, shaking her head. "I think he just needs some time."

Sadie turned away reluctantly. She hated to know he was upset, and she wanted to talk it through with him, but she trusted Alice's insight about her children. She would wait. Instead, she helped carry the dishes to the sink. Alice went to her bedroom to make a phone call, and while Sara started filling the sink with warm soapy water, Sadie started boxing up the leftovers into Tupperware containers.

"He's been pouting all day," Sara said, plunging her hands into the soapy water.

"Do you know what he's upset about?" Sadie wasn't sure she wanted to hear the answer.

"Yeah. Some kids at school were posting things online about how he asked Elena to the prom." Sara rinsed a glass and set it on the top rack of the dishwasher. Sadie had never understood Alice's insistence on washing the dishes before putting them in the dishwasher—wasn't that what the dishwasher was for?—but Sara was so used to it it didn't seem to phase her anymore.

"What kinds of things?"

"Oh, you know, how weird it was that he did it in front of everyone, how he brought her flowers, the strange things he said." She shook her head and scrubbed off a plate.

"How could they complain about him bringing her flowers?" Sadie felt anger rising up. "That shows he's a gentleman."

Sara gave her a look, eyebrow raised.

"What? Maybe I'm being old-fashioned, but I honestly can't see how that would be seen as anything but polite."

"Um…" Sara rinsed off the plate and set it in the lower rack. "That's not really how kids do things these days."

"Do you mean to tell me that if some boy arranged a whole big to-do to show how much he wanted to go to prom with you, you'd turn him down?" Sadie dumped the leftover pasta into a container, but not before snagging one last shrimp and popping it in her mouth.

"Oh, I'd be totally psyched that I got to go to prom, for sure," Sara said, "But I'm only a freshman. Elena is older and can go with anyone she wants." She rinsed off a glass, held it up to the light, and scrubbed at it again. "And honestly, yes, I would be weirded out if a guy went on about how he was going to pay for everything and open doors and whatnot, and in front of my friends too. I mean, who says stuff like that? It's like he got advice about girls from someone's grandpa."

Sadie didn't say anything for a moment, and Sara's eyes widened. "Oh, Grandma, you didn't..."

"I told Theo to treat her like a lady. That's how a girl with any self-respect should expect to be treated. That's how I expect any guy you go out with to treat you too. If he can't be bothered to treat you like you're worth holding doors for, then I don't want him anywhere near you."

Sara shook her head, her cheeks flaming. "But Grandma, that's just not how things are done these days. If you want all that, I'll never get to go out with anyone."

Sadie didn't necessarily think that would be such a bad thing, honestly, at least not for a decade or so, but she didn't need to get sidetracked by that now.

"So how exactly are things done these days?" Sadie tried not to let her anger come out at Sara. It wasn't Sara's fault these other high schoolers were ingrates. "How *should* he have asked Elena on a date?" She resisted the urge to add air quotes to the word "should." She didn't need to stoop to their level.

"Well, for one thing, people don't really go on dates much anymore. I mean, not like you're thinking. Usually people just hang out."

"Hang out?"

"Yeah. You know, with a group, or not, but, like, actually setting up a date? That's a little old-fashioned. And no one expects the guy to pay for stuff. That's just weird."

Sadie processed this, trying to make herself believe what she was hearing.

"But for something like prom, where it's a little more expected that you'll do the whole date thing, he should have just texted her, like everyone else does." Sara set the clean glass on the top rack of the dishwasher.

Sadie couldn't believe her ears. The "whole date thing"? Asking a girl out by text? What was wrong with kids these days? Sadie felt a rush of affection for Edwin, who knew how to treat her like a lady should be treated. But she also felt sad. If this was how kids these days behaved, they didn't know the first thing about healthy relationships.

"And the girls stand for this? For being asked out, or whatever it is you all do, by text?"

"Sure." Sara shrugged. "Or the guys. Why does it always have to be the guys initiating things? That's, like, from another century."

Sadie couldn't help it. She let out a sigh. Sara laughed, and it actually helped lighten the mood, which had somehow become quite tense. Sadie finished boxing up the meal and rearranged the contents of the refrigerator to find room for it all. This gave her a minute to think. She wanted to argue with Sara, to point out all the things wrong with what she was saying, but Sadie knew that wasn't the point right now. She couldn't change the whole culture by arguing with a fourteen-year-old, as much as she'd like to. And that wouldn't help Theo. In light of Sara's words, Sadie could see how the advice she'd given him probably seemed out of touch. That didn't make it okay for the other kids to make fun of him—

what was wrong with kids these days? Sadie wondered again—but Sadie was starting to see now that in trying to help, she might have made things far worse for Theo.

"So do you think there's any chance Elena will say yes?" Sadie asked.

"I don't know." Sara set the last of the dishes in the dishwasher and pulled the drain out of the sink. "I mean, they're kind of in different social worlds, you know? And I think she has been seeing someone, but I don't know. He's a poser."

A poser. What in the world did that mean? Sadie decided not to get off on that particular bunny trail. Instead, she marveled that though Sara was several years younger than Elena and probably had rarely talked to her, she seemed to know all about what was going on in her personal life. It always seemed to be that way with the more popular kids.

"But I do think his chances would have been better if he'd asked her like a normal person instead of someone from the 1800s." Sara sprayed out the sink. "Don't worry, Grandma, I know you were only trying to help. And he knows it too, even if he's not acting like it right now."

Sadie processed all this for a few moments while Sara washed her hands and turned off the water. She should go try to talk to Theo again. Apologize. She didn't get or approve of teen social customs, but she had led Theo astray, and she needed to atone for that. She turned and started up the stairs again.

"Good luck," Sara called. The tone in her voice said that Sadie would definitely need it.

Sadie knocked on Theo's door. She heard music playing inside. "What?" Theo called.

"I want to talk to you," Sadie said, gently. "To apologize."
There was a pause.

"Not right now, Grandma," Theo finally said.

"Please? Just open the door for a minute," Sadie said.

"Some other time."

Sadie stood on the other side of the door, waiting. Should she
barge in anyway? Insist he talk to her?

But that wouldn't do any good, Sadie knew. It might make her
feel better to get an apology out there, but if Theo wasn't ready to
talk, it would only make him more angry.

Reluctantly, Sadie turned and headed back to the kitchen. Her
heart ached, knowing she'd caused her grandson pain, knowing
he was hurting and there was nothing she could do about it. She
would pray about the situation. For now, that was just about all
she could do.

Later that night, Sadie lay awake in bed, turning over the
things Sara had said in her mind. After a quick evening phone call
with Edwin, in which he told her he'd left a message for Samuel
Bradley, Sadie had turned in and headed to bed, but sleep wouldn't
come. She'd been trying to get to sleep for over an hour, but she
couldn't stop thinking about Theo, and about Sara, about what
she should have done differently.

And then, she heard it. A noise, like someone was yanking
open the back screen door. And then a *thud*. Sadie held her breath.
The *thud* again, and this time, it was clear what it was. Sadie
screamed and turned on the light. Someone was trying to wrench
open the back door!

13

SADIE SAT UP IN BED, HER HEART POUNDING. SHE DIDN'T HEAR the noise again. Had her scream and the light turning on scared away the intruder? She hoped so, but she wasn't sure she was brave enough to go downstairs and check it out. She reached for her cell phone, which was on her bedside table. Should she call 911? Sadie sat still for a minute, listening. She heard light rain falling against the roof, but nothing like the noises she'd heard a few minutes before. Sadie considered for a moment, then dialed a number.

A moment later, Edwin answered, his voice groggy. Sadie explained what she'd heard, and Edwin said he'd be over as quickly as he could. He made Sadie promise to turn on as many lights as she could and to stay on the second floor, just in case someone was actually in the house. The sound of his calm, reassuring voice soothed Sadie, and as the minutes ticked by with no noises coming from downstairs, Sadie's courage came back. She had pulled on her robe and turned on every light on the second floor, and she was starting to feel silly hiding out when Edwin called to say he was at the front door. He hadn't wanted to knock, for fear of scaring her again. She hurried down the stairs, threw open the door, and ushered him inside. He was dripping wet from the rain, but as she helped him take off his coat she noticed that even now, just minutes after she'd called, her always-proper boyfriend had shown up in pressed chinos and a cashmere sweater.

"Show me where you heard the noise," Edwin said, and went ahead of Sadie toward the back of the house, turning on lights as he went. They walked to the back door, and didn't see or hear anything out of the ordinary. Slowly, Edwin pushed open the back door. Sadie stood a few feet back, trying to see over his shoulder. He looked around, and stepped out onto the back deck. Sadie could see rain streaming down from the black night sky, bouncing and dancing in puddles on the wooden slats. Big gusts of wind were blowing the rain at a strong angle. A moment later, Edwin stepped back inside, carrying a large stick.

"I think I might have found your problem," he said, indicating the stick, then tossing it back out onto the deck and closing the door. "There's quite a storm going on out here, and I suspect it must have been the wind that yanked open the screen door, and then that tree branch must have blown off and knocked into the back door."

"That branch?" Sadie said skeptically. "But how could it…" Sadie tried to picture it, and played back the sounds she'd heard in her mind. She supposed it could have been…

"I'm afraid you've got a bunch of branches down," Edwin said, running his hands through his wet hair. "There's going to be some work to do clearing it all up in the morning."

Sadie gestured for him to step farther in, then led him to the kitchen. She pulled out a clean kitchen towel and handed it to him to dry off. "Do you really think it was just the storm? It sounded so much like someone was trying to get in."

Edwin ran the towel over his hair and used it to dry off his glasses.

"Thankfully, there's no sign that anyone was out there, though, of course, it's hard to say for sure. But that's my guess, and frankly, I'm glad about it."

Sadie felt relief sweep through her, but then, almost simultaneously, embarrassment flooded her. She'd dragged Edwin out of bed in the middle of the night in a storm, and all for a tree branch. She couldn't believe she'd been so jumpy. And she couldn't believe how lucky she was to have a boyfriend who would gladly be wakened from a deep sleep to drive through a storm in the middle of the night just to make sure Sadie was safe.

"Thank you so much for coming," she said, and stepped forward to wrap her arms around Edwin. He pulled her in close and returned the hug. "I'm so sorry to drag you out of bed for this."

"Of course I came," Edwin said, laughing softly. "My heart just about stopped when I thought someone was trying to break in to your house. Nothing could have prevented me from getting here as soon as I could to make sure you were safe."

Neither of them mentioned the threatening note Sadie had received. Neither of them had to. Sadie knew he was thinking about it, just as she was.

They stood that way, arms around each other, for a few minutes, while Sadie's heartbeat returned to normal. She was so thankful for Edwin. She had never been more glad to have a man in her life who would rush to her side, no matter the circumstances, to protect her. Kids at the high school might not understand yet how important it was for a man to be willing to do this for his partner, but Sadie had never been more grateful that Edwin knew how a true gentleman acted.

Edwin yawned, and reluctantly, Sadie let go and remembered that it was the middle of the night. Now that the excitement was over, he needed to get home and get to bed. She thanked him again for coming, and she stood on the front porch, watching his headlights disappear down her long driveway, until he turned off onto the road. Then she went back inside and crawled into bed, and slept like a baby, reassured at how cherished she truly was and how lucky she was to have Edwin in her life.

By the next morning, the storm had cleared, and after Sadie tidied up the yard a bit, she drove to work, sipping a travel mug of coffee, praying for strength to make it through the day after the night she'd had. As she followed the road around the wide mountain curves, she saw Mickelson's Garage up ahead, just off to the right. Virginia's car was still sitting in the parking lot, waiting to be repaired. Sadie had already examined the car at the crash site, but maybe there was something more she'd be able to tell by looking at it again. And she *could* use some gas…

Sadie flipped on her blinker and pulled over into the parking lot of the garage. The gas station area was in front, with a repair shop behind. This place had been here forever, Sadie realized. Or at least, long enough that it felt like forever. She remembered coming there with her dad, back when he'd needed to fill up his old Ford, and it maintained a sort of old-fashioned charm, with vintage signs and a small, uncovered gas pumping area with historic pumps. She pulled up to one of the pumps and waited for Charlie to come out. That was the thing about this place—there was no self-serve option; the old pumps weren't easy to use and they certainly didn't have a credit card reader. Often Sadie chose to fill up at one of the more modern chain stations in town for this reason, but she wasn't in a rush this morning, and there was something charming about having a face-to-face interaction with the person pumping your gas. And when it came to repairs, Charlie's work was second to none.

The door of the little convenience store next to the repair shop opened, and Charlie came out, his round belly leading the way. Charlie's father had started the business decades ago, but Charlie had been running it since his father retired. He waddled toward her now, wearing stained jeans, a dark blue T-shirt, and a sweat-stained ball cap embroidered with *MICKELSON'S*.

"Hi there, Sadie," Charlie said. His voice was deep and gravelly, but his hands were unexpectedly small and graceful, and Sadie had always thought it was a funny contrast. "Fill 'er up?"

"Yes, please." Sadie climbed out of her Tahoe and closed the door. "Charlie, do you mind if I take a closer look at Virginia Radcliff's car while I'm waiting?"

Charlie gave a small shrug, like it didn't matter to him either way. She took that as permission and started off across the lot to the wreckage, which was parked alongside the garage. The body of the car looked just like she'd remembered it—white, crumpled in the front, dent and maroon streak on the back right panel. She peeked into the driver's side window and saw that the interior was clean; nothing looked out of place. She studied the car for a few moments, trying to see if there was anything that looked suspicious, but nothing stood out to her. The police no doubt would have taken anything that did seem suspicious in any case. She turned back and headed toward her car.

"I'm waiting on the police to give me the go-ahead to start fixing it," Charlie said, nodding at the car. "Right now it's still evidence."

Sadie nodded. That made sense. In case there was some clue there, you couldn't just go fixing it while the investigation was open.

"Have they found much of anything?" Sadie tried to keep her voice neutral, like she had only a casual interest in the answer.

"Danged if I know. But they do come out and stand around and look at it for a while just about every day."

Sadie had to laugh. Charlie had always had a unique way of expressing himself, but he was the nicest man you'd ever meet. He finished pumping the gas and returned the nozzle to the pump. A few drops of gasoline splashed out onto the ground, but Charlie didn't seem to notice.

It gave Sadie an idea, though.

"Charlie, gasoline is pretty flammable, isn't it?"

He laughed and nodded, and squinted at the numbers on the pump. "Sure is," he said. He pulled a pen and small clipboard out of his pockets and started recording the numbers on a small slip of carbon paper. "Burns better than just about anything."

"How much gasoline would you need to start a fire?"

Without looking up, he said, "Depends on how big a fire you're looking to start."

"What if you wanted to set a building on fire? Not a huge building, just an average-sized one, smaller than a house."

"In that case, probably a half gallon would do you, though you might get a gallon, just to be safe. Half-gallon would be easier to carry, though." He looked up from his clipboard. "Do I need to be worried about you lighting a fire, Mrs. Speers?" He gave her a sly smile and told her her total.

Sadie laughed. "The only thing I'm burning these days is the cash in my wallet." She reached into her car for her purse and handed him a credit card. He smiled good-naturedly. "I've actually been looking into the old schoolhouse fire. Do you remember that?" Sadie watched him carefully to see if this news elicited any sort of response. If he knew something about the old fire, she hoped he would betray it now. He gave the slightest nod, but his hand froze. "I've found some evidence that gasoline or something like it might have been used to start the fire," Sadie went on. "So I was curious."

Charlie didn't say anything more for a moment, but he quickly finished filling out the slip and handed it to her to sign, along with her credit card.

"I don't know anything about that," he said, and though his voice was even, she saw that his hand was now shaking.

"I suppose this would have been one of the few places in town to buy gasoline back then," Sadie said, and Charlie nodded, but stepped back quickly.

"There were others," he said, a little too quickly. "They're just closed down now. But this wasn't the only place."

His reaction was strange. Sadie hadn't actually thought he could possibly know anything about the fire; she was simply asking about gasoline. But here he was, acting jumpy because of her questions.

"Charlie, were you working here yet when the fire happened?" Sadie did some quick math in her head. He was about half a decade older than she was, she guessed. Even though his father would have still been running the place back then, he would have been in high school or so. *Could* he have known something about the fire?

"I'm sure I don't know," Charlie said, and tipped the brim of his hat. "If you'll excuse me, I have to get back inside." And with that, he walked away, toward the small shop. Sadie climbed back into her car and sat there for a moment, processing what had just happened. Was it possible he knew more than he was saying? Sadie shook her head. It was hard to say. But he had clammed up when she had mentioned the fire, she was sure she wasn't imagining that. It seemed that he knew something about the fire and didn't want to say it. Sadie turned on the engine and pulled away from the pump, resolving to find out more.

The shop had a steady stream of customers that morning, and Sadie was kept busy helping them. In her downtime she rearranged the display of vintage linens to best showcase the remaining quilts she'd unpacked and priced last week. She was so busy she didn't notice Samuel Bradley come in until he was standing right next to her.

"Oh!" Sadie looked up from the embroidered silk tablecloth she'd been folding to see him standing there. "Hello, Samuel."

Though she'd met him before, Sadie was once again surprised by how slight Samuel Bradley was. He was such a big presence in town, funding so many of the arts and cultural events that happened there, that she always expected him to be larger than life. But he only came up to Sadie's shoulder, and he was rail-thin, his belt cinched tight around his waist, and he looked rather frail. Up close, the thin white hair and the liver spots on his hands verified his ninety-plus years of age.

"Hello, Sadie." He grinned, laughing at her surprise. "Edwin told me you wanted to talk to me, and I was nearby, so I thought I'd come see how I could help."

"Thank you so much," she said, setting the tablecloth down. "I really appreciate it." Sadie knew such an important man must have dozens of things that needed to be done, and she was honored that he had taken the time to come by. "I don't know how much Edwin told you, but I'm looking into the old schoolhouse fire, and I'm trying to find out everything I can about what happened that night. I saw that you were quoted in one of the articles because you were the school superintendent back then, and I wondered if you could tell me what you remember about the fire."

He nodded. "I'm happy to help if I can, but the truth is, I don't know much more than what was in the articles that came out around that time. It was terrible, for sure. To lose a piece of our history like that—" He shook his head. "Well, it makes me sad just thinking about it now."

"It really was a tragic loss for Silver Peak," Sadie said.

"Thankfully, no one was hurt, but there were so many rumors flying. People blamed our maintenance guy, people blamed some of our high schoolers, some people thought it was a bum who'd been spotted in town." He tapped his fingernail on a bureau next to him. "It was such a relief to find out it had been an accident all along. It still didn't make the loss any easier, but at least no one was to blame."

"I'm sure it must have been a relief." Sadie paused, trying to decide how much to say. "From what I've learned, though, it seems like maybe it wasn't a complete accident. The records indicate there might have been foul play involved."

"Oh?" He started and tilted his head, and seemed genuinely surprised to hear it.

"There's some evidence that gasoline or something similar might have been used to get the fire started," Sadie said.

Samuel's eyes widened, and he shook his head. "If that's true, this is the first I'm hearing of it."

Sadie studied him. Was he telling the truth? Surely he would have been told about the rumors at the time. Someone in town knew the truth; the note that had been slipped under her door was proof of that. Could it have been Samuel Bradley, eager to protect some long-buried secret?

Looking at him now, a stooped, too-thin man known for his generosity, it sure seemed hard to imagine. He seemed genuine. And what motive could he possibly have for setting fire to the property he was responsible for protecting?

Sadie thought about what she'd just told him. She had a hard time imagining he'd never been made aware of the possibility of foul play. But then again, the evidence had been buried so quickly and so completely that hardly anyone in town seemed to have heard about the fire department's report.

"Who do they think set it, if it was set on purpose?" Bradley asked.

Sadie shook her head. "The records don't say. I guess that's what I'm trying to find out."

Samuel tilted his head and looked toward the front window. He seemed to be lost in thought for a moment.

"You know, as I mentioned, there were all these rumors that there was a vagrant seen around town right at that time. I wonder if there's any chance..."

He let his voice trail off.

"Yes, I've heard about him. Did you ever see him?" Sadie asked.

Samuel shook his head. "No, but enough people reported seeing him that I'm sure he was around. If there was any evidence of foul play, that's where I'd look."

Samuel checked his watch. "I'm sorry, Sadie, I've got a meeting of the Opera Board of Directors in a few minutes, so I've got to go. But if you have any other questions, please don't hesitate to let me know."

Sadie thanked him for stopping by, then watched as he shuffled off. There was another vote for the mysterious vagrant. But so far, all she'd heard was a bunch of rumors. No one had actually seen him. She was starting to believe that the man had never existed.

Sadie was growing more frustrated the more she learned. It seemed like every conversation led her toward a dead end. She shook her head, and turned back to her antique linens. The rest of the morning passed quickly and she reconciled some invoices as she ate lunch. Before she knew it, the after-school crowd was filling up Arbuckle's and the sidewalks were crowded with people. She looked up from the display she'd been arranging, and was surprised to see Elena Garza walk past the shop through the big front window. A rush of emotions flooded through her—anger, frustration, shame. Sadie knew she'd caused Theo to embarrass himself, and more than anything, Sadie wanted to make it right, to make Elena realize it was Sadie's fault, not Theo's, and to make the girl see that she should go to the prom with him. Sadie hesitated. In the back of her mind, she could hear Alice telling her that she was meddling, to stay out of it, but Sadie pushed that thought aside. Every parent knew that when your child was hurting, you'd do anything to take the pain away, and that feeling only intensified with your grandchildren. If there was anything Sadie could do to make this right, she had to do it now.

Before she really thought about what she was doing, Sadie was out the door. Elena was just up ahead, crossing the street, headed toward Los Pollitos. Sadie walked quickly and caught up to her just outside the bank.

"Elena," she called. Elena pulled earbuds out of her ears and turned to see who was calling to her, and her brow knit and eyes narrowed when she saw it was Sadie. "Sorry to bother you, Elena, I just wanted to say one thing," Sadie said, scrambling to come up with words that made sense.

Elena stopped and waited, and Sadie walked up and stopped next to her. She seemed confused. Elena knew who Sadie was, as they'd interacted a number of times, and Elena said hi whenever Sadie came into the restaurant, but they weren't exactly used to chatting.

"I know Theo asked you to the prom, and I know he did a strange job of it, but that's because I gave him some bad advice," Sadie said in a rush. In all honesty, she wasn't at all sure the advice had been bad—more timeless; the current culture for dating in high school was what was bad—but thinking about that wasn't going to help her here. "I wanted to apologize to you for that, and say that it was my fault, but Theo would really love to go to the prom with you, and I hope you'll be able to go with him."

Elena's cheeks were pink, and she looked from Sadie to the ground and back to Sadie. "Okay…" she said. She seemed to struggle to come up with the words to say. "I—I'm not sure if I can go or not. I'm kind of grounded."

Sadie remembered Sara had said that now. But honestly, this was the prom. Sadie was sure Elena's parents would let her out for such a big event, especially if she was going with an upstanding boy like Theo. Sadie watched her. Was Elena telling the truth? Was that the real reason she didn't say yes to Theo?

"Well, anyway, I just wanted to make sure you knew that," Sadie finished. It felt lame, halfhearted, but she didn't know what else to say.

"Thank you, Mrs. Speers." Elena fiddled with the strap on her backpack. Sadie nodded, but she wasn't sure what else to say and she could see that she was making the girl uncomfortable, so she turned away to go. "I—I really am grounded," Elena said. Sadie stopped and turned back to Elena. "I know it sounds like an excuse, but I went to a party on Wednesday night, and Papa had to come get me, and he was really mad, and I don't know when I'm going to get off restriction."

The words seemed to tumble out before Elena could stop them, and Sadie took that as a good sign, that she really wanted Sadie to understand. But also, something in what she said caught her attention, and she played the words back in her head. Wednesday night. That was the night of Virginia's accident.

"You say you were at a party Wednesday night?" Sadie said. "Where was the party?"

Elena looked around, like she was trying to decide whether to answer or run away, but she took a deep breath and answered.

"Travis Stewart was having a party at his house after the basketball game," Elena said. "He's one of the basketball players?" Sadie didn't know the name, but she nodded, encouraging Elena to continue. "Curtis Younts asked me to go with him." She shrugged, as if that explained it all.

Sadie started. Curtis Younts was the kid who had been threatening Virginia. So Elena knew where he had been Wednesday night! That realization was followed by a sinking feeling in Sadie's stomach. The way she said Curtis's name, and the shrug that indicated that obviously she had to go when Curtis had asked her, made Sadie think Elena had feelings for Curtis. What had Sara called Curtis? A poser? Sadie had seen enough lovestruck teenage girls to recognize the signs.

"So you were at the party with Curtis the whole evening?" Sadie asked, fighting the bitterness that threatened to creep into her voice. Why did girls always seem to fall for the bad boys? If what David Radcliff had said was true, this Curtis was not exactly a nice guy, and if Theo was to be believed, he used girls and discarded them like tissues. But for some reason, girls always seemed to fall for boys like him, instead of the good, upstanding young men who would treat them well. Sadie tried to push down her frustration and focus on what she could learn about Curtis's whereabouts on the night in question.

"Well, for a while." Elena looked down, and then up again. She pulled on the strap of her backpack. Sadie could only imagine she was hesitating because she had no real reason to tell Sadie anything. But then, she appeared to make a decision. "A lot of the kids were drinking. Curtis had had a few. Not enough to be really drunk or anything, but enough that I knew I didn't want to get in the car with him when he said it was time to go."

Sadie's heart almost stopped. Teen drinking was bad enough, but the idea of a teenager who'd been drinking getting behind the wheel of a car was enough to make her blood run cold.

"So did he—" If he'd been drinking and driving, that would make it very easy to understand how he'd—

"I called my dad," Elena said, shaking her head. "Curtis is cute, but I'm not an idiot. I know better than to get in the car with someone who's been drinking. Papa came right away."

A hundred thoughts floated through Sadie's mind—anger at the stupidity of high school boys; gratefulness that Elena had been smart enough to not get in his car; the fear Ramon must have felt to get the call saying his little girl was at a party and needed help.

"Do you know what time on Wednesday night this was?"

Elena shrugged. "Probably around eight or so."

So it lined up perfectly with what time Roscoe had reported Ramon receiving a phone call at Los Pollitos and leaving in a hurry. If Elena was telling the truth, Ramon had just been cleared from her suspect list. But Curtis Younts—who had been drinking and intending to drive anyway—had just risen right to the top.

"Do you know if Curtis drove home after that?" Sadie tried to think of possible scenarios to explain what might have happened next. She hated to think what might have happened if he'd gotten behind the wheel—

"I don't know." Elena looked down at the ground. "Papa was pretty mad, and he made me go wait in the car. He didn't come out for a few minutes. I don't know what happened in that time, but then Papa climbed into the car and wouldn't say a word to me the whole way home."

That also explained the tension she'd witnessed between the members of the Garza family the night after the accident. If Ramon was still upset—and what father wouldn't be?—there was every possibility that the tension between them would still be palpable. But it didn't answer her bigger question.

"So you don't know whether he drove home from the party or not?"

Elena shook her head. "I'm sorry. I don't. I haven't exactly…" She pulled on her backpack strap again. "I haven't really talked to him since then."

Based on what Sadie knew about the boy, he didn't seem like the kind of kid who would respond well to being snubbed by a girl. Unfortunately, Sadie was pretty sure by looking at Elena that she was still hoping Curtis would come around. Sadie wanted to shake the girl, make her see that there was a great guy who adored her and would never treat her this way, but Sadie knew better. She could never make Elena see things rationally, she knew that. Fewer things were less rational than a teenage girl's emotions.

"Papa was pretty angry that I was at a party where people were drinking, so that's why I'm grounded." Elena tugged at her strap again.

Sadie could understand that. If Alice had pulled a similar stunt—well, thankfully Alice had always had the good sense to avoid parties like that, or T.R. would have grounded her until she turned twenty-five. She was glad, again, that Elena had had the good sense to call and ask for a ride home instead of getting in the car with Curtis, and she was sure Ramon would feel the same way, but that didn't erase the anger that Sadie would have felt at her for being there at all.

Sadie shook her head. What was it that made teenagers do such dangerous, thoughtless things? She looked at Elena, and remembered the way she'd talked about Curtis, then realized she'd just answered her own question. Good-looking basketball-playing bad boys who showed girls some attention had a lot to do with it, she was sure. Her heart sank again. Curtis was no good, that was very clear to Sadie. But if life experience was any guide, Sadie was sure that she now understood at least part of why Elena was hesitating about going to the prom with Theo. She was hoping that Curtis would ask her.

Sadie thanked Elena for talking, and then when Elena hurried off into the restaurant, Sadie turned away. It seemed Ramon Garza was probably off the hook, but now she had even more suspicions about this Curtis Younts. She needed to talk to this kid, and soon.

But that wasn't what weighed heaviest on her heart as she walked away. Instead, Sadie couldn't help thinking about Theo. Sadie was pretty sure the girl her grandson wanted to go out with had feelings for someone else. What, exactly, was she supposed to do about that?

14

MONDAY EVENING, AFTER SADIE CLOSED THE SHOP, SHE WENT TO say hello to Scout, her chestnut gelding who was quartered at Milo Henderson's farm. After brushing him down and feeding him a special treat of apples, Sadie came home and had dinner and then settled down to work on getting her presentation ready. The big night was tomorrow, and Sadie had been so busy chasing the mystery she hadn't had time to work on pulling all the information together. She sat down in front of her laptop and checked her e-mail. She returned .a message from Roz, who asked if she wanted a ride to the fund-raiser the next night. Roz had been a teacher at the elementary school for decades, and she, like Sadie, was very enthusiastic about education in Silver Peak. But Edwin had already offered to give Sadie a ride to the event, so she responded that she'd meet Roz there, then turned to making her presentation.

She was surprised to see how easy it was to use the computer program now that Theo had shown her the basics. She had assembled several slides using the material Virginia had pulled together, and was starting to feel like maybe she really could do this presentation after all when the phone rang.

Sadie reached for the phone and was surprised to see Virginia's home number show up on her caller ID.

"Hello?" Sadie said, hoping against hope it was someone calling with good news.

"Hi, Sadie, it's David," he said. "I was looking through Virginia's work bag, and I found some stuff Virginia had been working on for the presentation. I flipped through it and don't really see anything that might be helpful, but you're welcome to look through it yourself."

Sadie felt her heartbeat quicken. Finally, she would get her hands on Virginia's notes. There had to be some useful clue or hint in there.

"I'd love to take a look." Sadie looked at the clock. It was getting late, probably too late to drive over to get it right then. "Could I come pick it up in the morning?"

"Sure thing. I'm planning to head to the hospital after I drop the boys off at school. Could you meet me there?"

"Of course." It would be nice to visit Virginia again anyway. "I'll see you there around nine?"

"That sounds perfect," David said.

She hung up, and though she was excited about the chance to finally see what Virginia had been working on, she tried to focus on the presentation. She worked until she couldn't keep her eyes open anymore. The presentation was in pretty good shape, and she could put the finishing touches on it tomorrow. She decided to head to bed. She prayed for wisdom, both for the Virginia mystery and for what to do about Theo, and then fell deeply asleep.

Tuesday morning, Sadie loaded up on coffee during her devotions. It was going to be a long day, what with her presentation tonight, and she needed to be ready, mentally—hence the caffeine—and spiritually, so she read one of her favorite passages, Hebrews 11, sometimes known as the faith Hall of Fame, and meditated on it. It listed great heroes from Scripture who were honored because they had had faith in the face of great odds. Sadie needed that kind of faith today, and she prayed that God would allow her to trust in Him as she tried to find the answers to this puzzle. Then she dressed, fed Hank, grabbed a quick breakfast, and headed to the hospital.

When Sadie stepped into Virginia's hospital room, David was there by her bed, holding on to her hand. Virginia looked the same—eyes closed, hands by her sides. She looked pale in the fluorescent hospital lights.

"Hi, Sadie." David pulled his hand back and reached down into the bag at his feet. His skin looked sallow, and there were dark circles under his eyes. "Thanks for coming."

"Thanks for sharing what you've found." Sadie nodded toward Virginia. "How's she doing?"

"The doctors say there are signs of some brain activity, but outwardly there's no change," David said. Sadie nodded.

"Is there anything I can do to help?" Sadie asked.

David thought for a moment, then shook his head. "Just keep praying." And then, a moment later, "And keep trying to find out who did this to her."

"I'll keep doing both," Sadie said.

"Here's what I found," David said, and pulled a manila folder out of his bag. "Like I said, I don't really see much here that would be useful, but I hope you see something I'm missing."

"Thank you," Sadie said, tucking the folder into her purse. "I'll let you know if I come across any clues."

David nodded, but his eyes were back on Virginia. Sadie stayed a few minutes longer, asking about the boys and how they were holding up, but Sadie could see that David was focused on Virginia and wasn't really in the mood to chat, so she said good-bye and headed back out to her car.

As soon as Sadie sat in the driver's seat, she opened the file and looked it over. Her heart sank as she flipped through the pages. Like David said, there really wasn't much of anything here. This appeared to be the folder where she'd kept all of her research on the history of the schoolhouse itself—all the information she'd been gathering to use in the actual presentation. It contained photocopies of many of the same documents Sadie had found at the Historical Society, and some scans from old books about Silver Peak history. As far as Sadie could see, there wasn't anything about her research into the cause behind the fire at all in there.

Sadie sat back against the seat, deflated. She didn't know what she'd been hoping for, but it didn't seem to be there. She tried to be positive. Now she was even more certain that she needed to get into Virginia's classroom and see if she'd left anything there the night she'd been working late. If there was anything to be found that pointed to who Virginia thought had set the fire, Sadie felt certain it had to be there. Sadie sighed and started to close the folder, but her eye caught on something. Scribbled on the inside of the back of the folder was a note. "School district records."

Sadie studied the scrawled note. Was this Virginia's handwriting? It was hard to say for certain. Sadie wasn't that familiar with her friend's writing, and whoever had written this appeared to have done so in a hurry. But who else would have written it? And what did it mean?

She closed her eyes and tried to make sense of the note. What could Virginia have been looking for in the school district records? What could she have found?

Sadie sat there a few minutes longer, then shook her head. There was only one way to find out, she decided. She made a quick call, and Julie agreed to open up the shop this morning, so Sadie turned on her car and started to drive to the school district office. She had no idea what she was looking for, but she hoped she might find some answers there.

The district office was next to the high school and shared the faculty parking lot, and she arrived just as the teachers and students were streaming onto campus before first period. To Sadie, it almost felt like coming home. Nostalgia tugged on her heart as she watched teachers she had worked alongside for years trudge toward the redbrick school building, but Sadie turned and headed toward the smaller, squat district office. The Silver Peak School District contained only four schools— two elementary schools, plus the middle school and the high school—but there was still a surprising amount of management that went into maintaining and running the schools, and Sadie had spent her fair share of time in this building during her teaching years. She stepped through the glass front doors and approached the front counter, where Barbara Mack was typing something into her computer.

"Sadie Speers!" Barbara looked up from her screen and smiled. She had tightly coiled dark hair and a broad face with a warm smile. Barbara was reed-thin and moved with the grace of a ballet dancer, though she'd spent her entire career working in education. "Good to see you. What brings you here today?"

"Well, I've got something of a strange request," Sadie said, and Barbara laughed.

"That's generally the kind we get around these parts." Something beeped on Barbara's computer, and she typed something quickly and then turned back to Sadie. "Could you be a bit more specific?"

"I was wondering if the district kept old records around here anywhere." There was nothing about Virginia's note that specified she'd been interested in historical records, but when Sadie had thought about it, that seemed the most likely.

Barbara tilted her head. "You know, that's funny. You're the second person to ask that question in just over a week. Who knew the old records were such hot items?"

"Did Virginia Radcliff come in to see them?" Sadie's heart beat faster. She was on the right track. She had to be.

"I guess it's not such a coincidence after all if you know that already," Barbara laughed. "She did indeed. I'll show you what I showed her." She pushed back from her desk and led Sadie down a short hallway through a doorway to a flight of stairs. They headed up the steps to a room at the end of the hallway on the second floor. Barbara flipped on the light, and Sadie saw that it was a storage room, filled with broken and unused tables and desks piled on top of one another. Chair legs stood upright, looking almost ghostly. Rows of old metal filing cabinets were pushed up against one end.

"A lot of the records have disappeared over the years, mostly when we moved into this building, I would guess." Sadie knew that move had taken place in the early nineties. "But Virginia was interested in the really old stuff, and we dug through and found that way over here." She led Sadie to a cabinet in the far corner and pulled out a drawer. The old warped metal squeaked and squealed as it opened. "She seemed most interested in this stuff, though I honestly can't say what she was looking for. I left her alone in here to search to her heart's content after school last Monday, and she was still in here when I left Monday evening."

Sadie thanked Barbara and promised she'd let her know if she had any questions. Then she grabbed a handful of files from the drawer, scooted a dusty rolling chair to one of the unused tables, and settled in.

Sadie was surprised to see that the folder had what looked like old budget reports. Sadie was familiar with reading financial documents—it was part of what she had taught in her Introduction to Business class—but she had always found it somewhat dull. Still, she looked dutifully at the lines of small print and did her best to make sense of it. The folder seemed to contain packets of financial statements, presented to the school board quarterly. The front page was a summary page, and behind it were records that broke out the budget into more detail. Since Sadie didn't know what she was looking for, she tried to study each page carefully, and it was tedious work. She made her way through the first few folders, which took her through the quarterly financial reports from 1957 through 1963. It quickly became clear that the district was in sorry financial shape in the early sixties, with the margin between expenses and the budget growing every quarter. She could see that they had let a number of teachers go, but the budget gap was still increasing. Sadie tried to figure out why, but the numbers were difficult to make sense of. Silver Peak's population was growing, and not enough tax money was coming in to support the exploding number of students, but, also, Sadie could see that the taxes and expenses the district was paying each quarter seemed strangely high. The number on the line marked "Facilities" seemed disproportionately high compared to the bulk of the budget.

Sadie dug through the next few folders, and noticed something odd. The district still struggled, but things seemed to balance out around 1965 and 1966. The number on the facilities line shrank, and without it, the schools seemed to regain solid financial footing. They even began hiring teachers again, instead of laying them off.

Well, that was interesting, but it didn't tell her what had changed, only that something had. She needed to find out more about that facilities budget.

She dug through the drawer and saw that toward the back, there were folders stuffed with pages from what looked like old ledger books. She pulled those out and started flipping through, looking for...well, she wasn't really sure what she was looking for, but she focused on the entries for 1964 and 1965. These logs didn't seem to list fixed expenses, like teacher salaries and taxes; they just tracked incidental expenses and income the district received. She saw lines for things like new textbooks, repairs to a classroom after a burst pipe, and petty cash expenses for the teachers' Christmas party. And then, in March 1965, she noticed something different.

There was a deposit for $5,100.40 from a Wilcox Company. The numbers were what caught Sadie's eye first. Those were the same numbers that Virginia had read out to her just before the accident. The numbers Sadie had assumed had been from a license plate. But then Sadie remembered what else

Virginia had tried to tell her the night of the crash. She'd said something about a "Wilc" before she'd been cut off. Could she have been trying to say "Wilcox Company"?

It could be a coincidence, but… Sadie's heart beat faster. She had to be on the right track. She looked for other information, a notation of what the entry was for or where it had come from, but all she had to go on was the amount and the name of the Wilcox Company. The entry was made just two months before the fire. She took out her notebook and copied down the information. That amount of money didn't sound like much these days, but back in 1965 it would have been a sizable sum.

Sadie pored through the records for another hour, but she didn't see anything else that stood out to her. All she knew for sure was that things started to turn around for the district after that unexplained credit and the fire. But what in the world was the Wilcox Company, and why had they paid the school district over five thousand dollars?

Sadie decided not to wait to look for answers to that question. If there was more she was supposed to find there, she wasn't seeing it. For now, she would pop over to the computer lab at the high school and see what she could find out about the Wilcox Company. She still wanted to see if she could get into Virginia's classroom anyway to take a look around, and now would be a good time to see if she could do that.

Sadie thanked Barbara on her way out of the building, then she headed across the parking lot to the high school. It must be a passing period, Sadie realized as she walked in the front doors. Kids were chatting in the hallway, opening and shutting lockers, and scurrying down the corridors. In addition to posters for the prom, Sadie saw advertisements for the big fund-raiser tonight, and a wave of nervousness passed through her.

She looked around, wondering if any of these kids was Curtis Younts. She wanted to talk to him and see what he had to say about his whereabouts Wednesday night. But short of stopping a random kid in the hallway to ask, she couldn't see how to figure out who Curtis was, so Sadie ducked in to the office and stopped in to see Anne Hastings, the school principal. They chatted for a few minutes, and while they were talking, the bell rang, signaling the start of a new period. Sadie asked about getting in to see Virginia's classroom, but Anne apologized and said it would have to wait until fourth period was over. Sadie agreed to come back after the next bell, and in the meantime, she let herself into the computer lab.

The school must have recently made upgrades to the lab, because the room was filled with sleek high-end equipment, most of which looked like something from that old cartoon *The Jetsons*. Sadie chose a computer that looked the most similar to what she had at the shop and shook the mouse to wake it up. She pulled up a browser and did a search for the Wilcox Company.

Pages and pages of results came up, and Sadie started dutifully clicking through them, but she hadn't found anything useful by the time a class of freshmen came in to type up some project twenty minutes later. Sadie ceded her computer and headed back to the school office. She would wait there until the bell rang. But on her way, she noticed that the lunchroom was packed with students. She remembered that a few years back the school had had to divide the students between two lunch periods, one quite early and one a bit later, due to space constraints in the cafeteria.

Sadie poked her head in, looking for Theo. She still wanted to apologize to him, and she knew he was there in the school somewhere. She scanned the room and didn't see him, but she did spot Sara, sliding down low in her chair, surrounded by girls, trying to avoid Sadie's eye.

Sadie smiled. If she didn't know better, she'd think Sara was trying to hide from her. Well, Sadie wouldn't do anything to embarrass her granddaughter, but she could use the opportunity to ask Sara to point out Curtis Younts.

Sadie threaded her way through the auditorium and came up to the table Sara was sharing with a gaggle of other freshmen.

"Hi, Sara," Sadie said, trying her best not to be conspicuous. She recognized a few of the other girls at the table, including Mia Garza, Elena's younger sister and Sara's best friend, and another girl she thought was named Lauren, and she waved a quick hello.

"Oh my goodness, Grandma, what are you doing here?" Sara said, sliding down even lower in her chair. Her cheeks were pink.

"I just have a quick question," Sadie said. "I was wondering if you could point out a young man named Curtis Younts."

The name brought forth a burst of giggles from the girls at the table.

"I think he might be a senior," Sadie said, "so you may not know who he is, but—"

"Everyone knows who Curtis Younts is," Lauren said, laughing. "He's only, like, the most popular kid in the school." This statement set off another round of teenage laughter.

"He's over there." A slight girl with stick-straight sandy hair and braces pointed to a table in the far corner of the room. Sadie turned and saw a group of students lounging around a big round table, laughing, chatting, and largely ignoring everyone else in the room. Compared to these freshmen, they looked like full-grown adults. "In the striped polo shirt," the girl added.

"Ah." Sadie spotted him immediately. He was talking animatedly with a boy across the table, his arm around a thin girl in a short pink skirt. "Okay, thanks," she said brightly. She turned and started toward the table of seniors.

"Oh my goodness, Grandma, you're not going over there right now, are you?" Sara turned to Mia, her eyes wide. "What if he saw you talking to us?"

"Don't worry, I won't tell him I'm related to you," Sadie said, and though the other girls laughed, Sara put her head down into her hands.

Part of her felt bad; she could see Sara was worried. But Sadie could tell that no one at what was clearly the popular kids' table was paying attention to the group of freshman girls or the old woman who had been talking to them. As she walked across the crowded lunchroom, she spotted Elena Garza at a table nearby, surrounded by friends. No one at Curtis's table seemed to notice when Sadie approached the table.

"Excuse me, Curtis?" she said, stepping close to him. He looked up, but didn't say anything. "Could I speak to you for a moment, please?"

The boy didn't look as much confused as bored.

"And you are...?"

Ooh, the insolence... Sadie had never put up with it in her classroom, but this wasn't a classroom and she wasn't in charge here. She needed to talk to him, and he had no reason to cooperate, so Sadie knew she had to play by different rules.

"My name is Sadie Speers. I've heard that you're someone who knows what's going on around school"—she tried to play to his vanity—"and I'd just like to ask you a few questions if you have time."

He looked around the table to see how the others were reacting to this. The girl next to him patted his leg. "She's right. No one knows more than you do."

Curtis nodded, affirming the truth of this statement. "Let's make this quick," he said, pushing himself up in a way that made sure everyone at the table noticed he had been singled out. Sadie nodded and led him out the side cafeteria door.

"I hear you were at a party last Wednesday night," Sadie said. He nodded, his eyes searching from right to left. "I'm trying to find out about something that happened after the party."

"Is this about Mrs. Radcliff's car crash?" he said, rolling his eyes. "I already told the police I had nothing to do with that."

Sadie didn't find it the slightest bit endearing that he rolled his eyes at Virginia's accident, but she pressed on. "I'm not working with the police, so I wondered if you might be able to tell me about it as well."

He muttered under his breath, and though Sadie couldn't make out his words, she thought she heard something about a "nosy old lady." He shook his head, then seemed to make some sort of decision.

"Look, like I told the cops, I couldn't have had anything to do with it, because that jerk took my car keys, all right?"

"That jerk?"

"Elena's dad." He shook his head a little. "Stormed right into the party, took her away, and demanded my car keys. He threatened to call the cops if I didn't turn them over."

Curtis was obviously still upset about it, but Sadie felt like thrusting her arm in the air to cheer for Ramon. That was exactly the right thing for him to do to keep the drunk teenager off the road, and Sadie was grateful on behalf of everyone in town.

"So how did you get home that night?"

"I didn't. I slept at Tyler's."

"And there are others who can verify that?" Sadie asked.

"Yeah. Tyler, for one," he said, as if Sadie was an idiot. "And his mom was there the whole time. The police already talked to her and she vouched for me."

"Did you get your car keys back?" Sadie asked.

"I stopped by that hole in the wall they call a restaurant and got them the next day." He looked back toward the door of the cafeteria. "Does that answer all your questions?"

Sadie had all kinds of questions she wanted to ask him, mostly about how he was raised and where he got off treating people the way he did, but she had to admit that if he was telling the truth—a big if—he did indeed seem to have an alibi for Wednesday night.

"I guess not. Thank you for your time," Sadie said, and without a word, the boy turned and stormed back into the cafeteria.

Well, he wasn't the most pleasant young man, and for the life of her she couldn't see how anyone would choose him over Theo, but he had answered her questions—and, as much as she hated to admit it, it did seem like he might be innocent if she could verify he was telling her the truth about his car keys. She shook her head, and started back toward the school office just as the bell rang. Students started streaming out from classrooms. Sadie dodged a few low-flying students headed for the cafeteria and made it to the principal's office again with no mishaps.

"Ready to go poke around?" Anne said, pulling a set of keys from her desk. "Virginia's lunch period is now and the substitute is probably in the teacher's lounge, so there's no class in her room at the moment."

Sadie had to stop herself from making one of her favorite jokes, about how there was no class in that room even when the students were there. Somehow it didn't seem appropriate right now. Instead, Sadie followed her friend down the familiar hallways. They chatted about Anne's son Mark, who was waiting to hear back from colleges, and for a moment, it almost felt like it could have been ten years ago, just chatting with her friend and boss as they both went about their days. But when they stopped in front of the classroom door, Sadie remembered why they were really there, and she felt a sense of sadness wash over her. She was there to find answers to who had tried to hurt her friend. She had to focus on that.

Anne pulled out a key and unlocked the door, and they stepped inside. This hadn't been Sadie's classroom, but it had the same beige walls, the same whiteboard at the front of the room, the same industrial blue carpet, and the same wooden desks that had graced Sadie's own room. Virginia had hung up posters of Benjamin Franklin and Thomas Jefferson to warm up the space a bit, and on the large teacher's desk at the front of the room, there were photographs of her sons, which lent a bit of a personal feel.

Sadie did miss teaching sometimes, but she definitely preferred the atmosphere of the Antique Mine to these sterile classrooms.

"Remind me what you're looking for exactly?" Anne said, walking to the center of the room.

"I'm not sure." Sadie headed straight for Virginia's desk. There were papers and some textbooks in neat piles on the surface, no doubt being used by the substitute teacher. She didn't see anything on the top of the desk that could be relevant to the fire, but she felt strange about poking through the drawers. "Virginia said she was working here in her classroom just before the accident, so I was hoping she'd left behind some trace of what she'd found."

Sadie pulled open the shallow top drawer tentatively. It contained a plastic desk organizer filled with pens and paper clips, and a few stray rubber bands, but no papers, or anything that looked relevant. She was hoping for a file folder, or a thumb drive, or—she didn't know. *Something* that could feasibly contain the name of who Virginia thought had started the fire.

Sadie opened the top drawer on the right side, and found nothing more than office supplies. Underneath that was a drawer that contained neatly organized answer keys and teacher-edition textbooks. The bottom drawer, large enough for hanging file folders, was the only one left. Sadie set her hand on the handle and pulled.

It didn't budge. She tried again, but still, the drawer remained firmly in place.

"Anne, do you have a key for this drawer?" Sadie crouched down and peered into the keyhole at the top of the drawer.

"No." Anne came over and crouched to see what Sadie was looking at. "It's locked?" She tried the handle too, but the drawer stayed firmly shut. "That's strange."

"Do you know who would have a key?"

Anne shook her head. "No, I don't. I would guess only Virginia does, and maybe the master set for the school. But even I don't have access to that." She jiggled the drawer, trying to get it to budge, but it didn't. "Huh." She raised an eyebrow at Sadie. "I wonder if whatever you're looking for might be in this drawer."

"I was thinking the same thing, if it's here at all," Sadie said. She studied the drawer. Short of breaking the lock, she wasn't sure how to get inside, which only made her more certain she needed to do so.

"I wish I knew what to tell you," Anne said, shaking her head.

"I guess I'll call David and see if he found a key among her things," Sadie said, and Anne nodded, acknowledging that was probably the best plan. She looked around the room a few more minutes, but she didn't seem much else worth investigating, so together, the two friends walked back toward the office.

"I'm sorry you didn't find more," Anne said. Sadie nodded. She hadn't found what she'd been hoping for, but overall, it was far from a wasted visit. She had eliminated a suspect, and she would see what she could find out about the Wilcox Company and why it made a deposit that matched the number Virginia had given her. And if David had a key to that desk drawer…

Sadie stopped in front of the display case just outside the office. The historic school bell sat there, just like it always did. If only that bell could talk, give up its secrets, tell her what had gone on that night so long ago when it was the only thing that survived the fire.

And then, Sadie saw something she'd never noticed before. How strange… She squatted down to get a better look at the rim of the bell.

"What is it, Sadie?" Anne said.

Sadie didn't know how to answer. She wasn't sure what she was seeing. It couldn't be…

She squinted, trying to make sense of things. She had to have her facts wrong. She'd need to do some research on this. Because if she was right—

Sadie shook her head. If she was right, everything she'd ever known about the schoolhouse fire had just been called into question.

15

"IS THERE SOMETHING WRONG WITH THE SCHOOL BELL?" ANNE asked, standing a bit behind Sadie.

"I'm not sure," Sadie said, straightening up. "Would it be possible to get a closer look?"

"Sure thing." Anne searched through the key ring until she found a small metal key, and with a flick of her wrist she opened the thick glass case. After a nod of permission from Anne, Sadie reached into the case and touched the bell. The metal was cold and hard under her fingers. She scratched at the surface with her nail. A tiny flake of something—dirt? paint?—scraped off. She examined it.

"What is it, Sadie?"

Sadie turned over the flake in her hand. It was brownish gray. It did look like paint, but it was hard to say for sure.

"I had never noticed this before," Sadie said in answer to Anne's question. She pointed to a small mark in the metal on the very rim of the bell. It was an elaborate G, but so small it was very easy to miss. "This is the maker's mark. It's the mark for Garrett and Sons smelters."

"Okay…" Anne looked puzzled, but there was a hint of admiration on her face. "How did you know that? Did you memorize the maker's marks for all the silver smelters or something?"

Sadie shook her head and ran her finger over the mark. It was pressed into the metal, just as it should be, but the surface of the bell was rougher than she'd expected.

"Unfortunately, no. And that's part of the problem."

Now Anne's face twisted up, and Sadie realized she wasn't making any sense.

"I recognize the mark because I've seen it on some antique horseshoes," Sadie explained. "Garret and Sons made a lot of iron horseshoes in the first half of the last century. And, apparently, they made other things, including school bells."

"Well, that's interesting," Anne said. Sadie shook her head. She wasn't getting it yet.

"The thing is, Garret and Sons specialized in cast-iron pieces. As far as I know, they didn't cast silver."

"Oh, but that can't be right. The bell is silver, brought over from England—"

"That's the other strange bit," Sadie said. "Garrett and Sons is an American company. And this"—she scratched at the surface with her nail again—"is not silver. It's cast iron."

"But, Sadie, that can't be true."

"I need to do some research, but I think it is, I'm afraid. See how the surface here is a bit rough? That's from the sand they used inside the cast-iron molds. And the color—"

Sadie couldn't believe she hadn't noticed the color before. This bell was a dull brownish gray color, but it didn't have the rich, varying undertones of tarnished silver. It was flat and uniform, almost as if it had been painted to look that way. Apparently she'd never taken the time to really look at the bell, and it seemed no one else had either.

"It's just tarnished. It probably hasn't been polished in decades."

Sadie let out a long breath. "It's possible," she said, though she knew in her heart that wasn't the answer. "Like I said, I have to do some more research."

"But if what you're suggesting is true, then it means..." Anne said, and let her voice trail off.

"Yes, if it's true, it means this isn't the original silver bell that survived the schoolhouse fire."

"But if that isn't the bell," Anne said, still trying to wrap her mind around this, "then what happened to it?"

"That's exactly what I hope to figure out," Sadie said. She had a strong suspicion that if she could find an answer to that question, a lot of other pieces of the puzzle would start to fall into place. "The good news is, I have an idea of where to look."

Sadie thanked Anne and promised to fill her in as soon as she did some more research, then she started off toward the front door of the school. Just as she stepped out into the sunshine, her cell phone rang, and she dug it out of her purse quickly. A number from an area code she recognized as northern California flashed on the screen. With a start, she realized it was time for her conversation with Justin Orr. Sadie rushed down the front steps and held the phone to her ear.

"Hello?" she said.

"Hi, this is Justin Orr calling for Sadie Speers." His voice was warm and rich.

"Yes, thank you so much for calling," Sadie said, and walked toward a metal bench off to the left, by the grove of aspens a long-ago senior class had planted as a gift to the school. "I really appreciate your taking the time."

"It's not a problem. So you said you had questions about the old Silver Peak Schoolhouse fire?"

"That's right. I'm trying to find some information about what happened that night, and I was looking through the old police file and your name was mentioned. I know it was a long time ago, but I was hoping you might be able to tell me what you remember about that night."

Justin laughed. "Goodness, it was a long time ago. It almost feels like another lifetime. My family moved away from Silver Peak that summer for my dad's new job in San Jose, and before I got your e-mail, I probably hadn't thought about the fire in thirty years. But I'm happy to help if I can. Now, I'm guessing that if my name was in the file, it made reference to me and three other guys being spotted in the woods right by there that night?"

"That's right." Sadie pulled her notebook out of her purse and flipped to the pages of notes about the high schoolers.

"Goodness. Wait, it was Michael Leonard, and Tully Stewart, right? And who else?"

He certainly wasn't acting like someone who had anything to hide about that night. Still, you never could tell. "Martin Goring," Sadie said.

Justin laughed. "That's right. I miss that guy. I kept in touch with them a bit after we moved, but you know how it is with high school boys. I wonder what he's up to these days?"

"I'm not sure," Sadie said, but Justin hadn't really seemed to expect an answer.

"Well, I was in the woods with those guys that night, but we had nothing to do with the fire. I swore that up and down with the police, but the fact that I lost my glasses that night sure made it hard for the police to believe that."

"So they *were* yours. I saw that a pair of glasses had been found at the site in the records, and I noticed they matched the kind you wore…"

"Oh yeah. They were mine. And believe me, the police did not overlook that fact either. I think I got very lucky that they determined it was an accident and let us all off the hook, because for a while there I know it was not looking good. But honestly, we had nothing to do with it."

"Can you tell me how your glasses did end up at the burn site?" Sadie asked.

"Of course. We were there, early in the evening. I don't know how familiar you are with the area—"

"I know it well," Sadie said.

"Great. Then you know how the schoolhouse was right up against the woods?"

"Yes, I can picture that," Sadie said.

"Well, there was an entrance to a path just beyond the schoolhouse. The path led to a campsite maybe a quarter mile in? A lot of us teenagers used to go there sometimes, and, well, drink and smoke mostly. I'm not proud of what we did, but it's the truth. That's what we were up to the night of the fire. We headed down to the woods, and were goofing off as we crossed the schoolhouse site. We'd, well, we'd already had a bit to drink before we got there, so we probably weren't being as quiet and discreet as we thought we were. That's no doubt why that neighbor guy noticed us going into the woods. And Tully smacked me, just goofing around, you know, and my glasses came off. He was always doing that kind of thing. At the time we all thought it was hilarious, but it was so dark I couldn't find them again right away. Plus, well, obviously without my glasses it was difficult. The others kept going, so I just went along with them and figured I'd search for them on the way back out."

Sadie had spent enough time around high school boys to be able to picture the scenario. It sounded plausible.

"But you didn't stop to find them on the way out?"

"No, because while we were in the woods that night, the fire broke out. We heard the sirens and saw the sky light up this fiery orange, and we knew we had to get out of there. I mean, we were underage and all, plus we were worried about the fire spreading and getting caught in the woods, so we went out the back way."

"The back way?"

"There was another trail that went out toward Silver Creek Road. It was a longer way around, but it got you out of the woods, so we took that and made it out and headed home. We thought we were safe, but then it came out of course that that neighbor guy had seen us, so the police were at our doors the next morning asking questions."

"What sorts of things did they ask?" A light breeze blew, and Sadie wrapped her cardigan around her a bit more.

"Oh, you know, what were we doing, did we see anything, where did we get the cigarettes, did we happen to drop any, that sort of thing. They never came out and told me they'd found my glasses, but they were asking questions that made it clear they'd found those."

"Is there any chance you did drop a cigarette?" Sadie asked.

"No, we didn't start smoking until we were at the campsite. They didn't love that answer, but it was the truth."

"And can I ask where you did get the cigarettes and beer? You were underage, right?"

"Sure were. But I worked part-time at Mickelson's Garage. You know that old place? It used to be out on Country Rock Road?"

"It still is," Sadie said. "I live not too far from there."

"Oh wow. Old Man Mickelson can't still be running it, right?"

Sadie hadn't heard Charlie's father called that, but she knew that was who Justin was referring to.

"Oh man," Justin continued. "Now that I think about it, I'm probably at least as old as Old Man Mickelson was when we called him that. That's a scary thought."

Sadie laughed. "I'm afraid not. But his son Charlie has been running it for years now."

"Charlie? That's great. He was a few years older than me, and we'd joke around sometimes. Didn't have a lot to say, but nice guy."

"So did you work in the little store at the gas station?"

"Nah, mostly I pumped gas, but when I wanted something from the store that I wasn't technically old enough to buy, they just sort of looked the other way." Justin laughed. "Of course, that summer was when they installed the second gas pump, so I did spent some time in the store while they were working on that."

"Second gas pump?" Sadie didn't remember a time when there was only one.

"Oh yeah. It was big news back in the day. Gas pumps were expensive, and somehow suddenly Charlie was putting in a second one. No one had two back then. We all joked that he must have robbed a bank to be able to afford it, but it sure paid off. Business about doubled. I expect that's why the station is still around today, in fact."

Well, that was interesting. Sadie didn't remember any of that.

"How do you think he did get the money to install the second pump?" Sadie asked.

"Oh, I don't know." Justin laughed. "It was probably something benign like a small business loan, though at the time that wasn't exciting enough for us to contemplate. But we moved away later that summer, so I don't really know."

It was interesting to think about, but Sadie didn't see how it was relevant, so she shifted her questions back to the night of the fire. "Did the police question all four of you who were in the woods that night?"

"I'm sure they did, though when my parents found out what I'd been up to, I was grounded so fast I wasn't really able to ask the other guys much of anything. And then, they decided it was an accident, and the questions stopped, and we all just kind of went on with our lives."

"That was lucky timing," Sadie said.

"I guess so, though at the time, it just seemed like they'd figured out what had really happened, and since we were innocent we were thrilled to be cleared."

Sadie could see that. She tried to picture the events of the night in her head to see what else she could ask him.

"You said sometimes other people gathered at the campsite in the woods too. Were there others there that night?"

"No, we didn't see anyone else that night. It was a Wednesday night, so that wasn't really all that surprising. Usually it was just weekends people went out there, but it was Michael's birthday, so that's why we were there."

"Can you think of anything else about that night? Anything that might shed light on what happened at the schoolhouse?" Two squirrels were chasing each other around a tree near Sadie.

"I'm guessing by these questions that you don't actually believe it was an accident," Justin said.

"No, I don't," Sadie said. "I think someone set that fire, probably deliberately, and I'm trying to figure out who it was."

Justin let out a breath. "Goodness. It was so long ago. I can't..." His voice trailed off, and he didn't say anything for a minute, but then he spoke. "You know, there was one thing. It didn't occur to me until later, but as we went out the woods the back way, we did see a car parked right at the entrance to the trail where it let off at Silver Creek Road."

"Oh really?" Sadie asked. "Do you remember anything about the car?"

"Oh yeah. Don't forget, we were teenage boys. We were into cars." He laughed. "It was a Buick Riviera. Chrome finishes. Really nice. It was night, so it was hard to tell for sure what color it was, but it was dark, probably black."

"That's interesting. What do you think it was doing there?"

"Hard to say," Justin said. "But if someone did want access to the schoolhouse site, it was only maybe a half mile walk through the woods to get there, and no one would connect a car parked there with whatever went on at the school. If I was going to set the place on fire, that would have been a good, inconspicuous place to park," Justin said. "Not that I did set the place on fire, let's be clear about that."

Sadie laughed. She admitted it did look suspicious, those boys in the woods just by the schoolhouse right when the fire was set, but something about Justin's tone and open manner made her believe that he didn't have anything to do with the fire in the end.

"I believe you," Sadie said. Something was niggling at the back of her mind. A Buick Riviera. Where had she seen one of those recently?

"Mrs. Speers, I'm sorry, I've got to run. My next patient is here," Justin said, and Sadie thanked him for his time and let him go. She sat still on the bench a few minutes longer, thinking through all he'd told her.

If he was telling the truth, he and his friends hadn't had anything to do with the fire. But the Buick could be a lead, if only she could figure out why it was ringing a bell. Was there some way to deduce who had driven such a car in those days? And what he'd said about Mickelson's gas station putting in a new pump was also rolling around in her mind. There was nothing suspicious about that, necessarily, but after the strange way Charlie had reacted when Sadie had mentioned the fire the other day, she couldn't help but wonder if there was more to find out about where the windfall had come from.

For now, Sadie slipped her phone into her purse and headed across the flagstones to the parking lot, mulling over the conversation with Justin. There was something just below the surface; if she could just bring it to mind, surely she'd ...

She was almost at her car when it hit her.

She knew where she'd seen a black Buick Riviera recently.

Sadie turned and rushed back into the school.

16

SADIE HAD INTENDED TO HEAD TO THE SHOP—IT WAS ALREADY
early afternoon, and she hadn't even been in yet—but as she made
the short drive through town, thinking about all she'd learned
at the high school and district office that morning, she decided
to make one stop first. Sadie called Julie to make sure things
were okay at the shop. When Julie assured her she had everything under control and she didn't need to rush back, Sadie kept
driving down Main Street past the Antique Mine. She kept going
until the thickly settled buildings of downtown Silver Peak were
behind her, and she was out on the mountain road that led toward
her house. She flipped on her blinker and pulled into Mickelson's
Auto Repair. She pulled up alongside the small market, and a
moment later Charlie came out of the garage, rubbing his hands
on a rag.

"Afternoon, Sadie," he said, and stuffed the rag into a
pocket of his overalls. "Everything okay with the gas you got
yesterday?"

"The gas is just fine." Sadie laughed. "But I wondered if I could
ask you a couple of questions."

He looked dubious.

"It's just, I was talking to a Justin Orr a little while ago. He worked here when he was a teenager, back in the 1960s."

"Oh yeah." Charlie was nodding. "I remember that kid. Tall, skinny, glasses?"

"That's right." Sadie fiddled with her car keys. "He was telling me about when he worked here, his junior year of high school and the following summer."

Charlie nodded slowly.

"The thing is, that was the same time period as the fire I was asking you about earlier, and Justin mentioned something interesting. He said that that summer, your father was able to install a second gas pump here at the station, and how unusual that was at the time."

Charlie nodded again, watching her carefully.

"I have the impression that it was quite expensive to install a pump in those days. The station must have been doing quite well."

Sadie watched his face as he registered her line of questioning.

"I guess so," he said simply.

"Do you know of any reason the station might have come into a sum of money around that time?" Sadie asked. Something in his face changed, some understanding dawned, and yet he stood still, immobile.

"My father was still running the station in those days," Charlie said. "Any business of that sort was handled by him." But Sadie could see from the look on his face that he knew more than he was saying.

"I understand," Sadie said. "And I know that you have no good reason to tell me anything, even if you did know something more. The thing is, I have reason to believe that the crash that landed Virginia Radcliff in the hospital"—Sadie gestured at the broken chassis of Virginia's car, parked to the side of the lot—"was related to what happened on that night of the schoolhouse fire all those years ago. So I'm trying my best to figure out everything I can about what might have happened that night."

"Oh yeah?" Charlie looked at the shattered hulk of Virginia's car. He was quiet for a minute. "It was a shame, what happened to her. Terrible." He seemed to be mulling something over. "You say you think that was somehow connected to the fire?"

Sadie nodded. "I think she'd figured out who set the fire, and someone really didn't want her to tell anyone."

He whistled, low and under his breath. "Someone must have wanted to keep it quiet real bad, if that's true."

"I believe this person is dangerous. And the thing is, since I've started looking into this, I've been threatened as well. So I am very interested in finding out what happened, sooner rather than later."

Charlie nodded, his eyes still on the car.

"And how do you think I might be able to help?" His tone was skeptical, but not belligerent.

"I was wondering if anyone had bought gasoline in a carry-away container in the days leading up to the fire. And I wonder if that someone paid a sum to make sure no one talked about it."

Charlie was silent for a moment. Sadie held her breath. If he'd straight-out denied it, she wasn't sure what she'd have done, but he seemed to be thinking, considering.

"If someone had done that, what are you going to do about it?" Charlie said.

"I'm going to try to stop them before they cause another accident trying to keep their secret quiet," Sadie said.

Charlie seemed to be mulling this over. And then he nodded, and said quietly, "You know, now that I think about it, I do remember selling a gallon of gasoline to someone the day before the fire."

17

WHEN SADIE FINALLY ARRIVED AT HER SHOP THAT AFTERNOON, there were several customers browsing and Jimmie Rodgers was crooning over the sound system, but Julie had things under control, just as Sadie knew she would. Sadie set her things down, said hello, and ate the sandwich she'd picked up while she spent a few moments answering e-mails and looking through receipts from the day. Julie had sold a number of items, including a vintage dress and a collectible porcelain figurine.

"Hey there, Sadie." Julie approached the desk and set a cardboard box of brass candlestick holders on the edge. "Productive morning?"

"Yes, I suppose it was, though not as productive as yours," Sadie said, looking at the next receipt in the stack. "You sold the Flying Geese quilt?"

"Those quilts have been hits. Maybe we should get some more in." Julie pulled one of the candlestick holders out of the box and placed it on top of a highboy dresser across from the desk.

Sadie nodded. "Or maybe I just need to leave the shop and let you run things more often."

Julie laughed, and Sadie laughed as well, though she was only partly kidding. Then, as Julie busied herself finding places to display all of the candlestick holders, Sadie brushed the crumbs off her hands and tossed the paper from her sandwich into the garbage. Then Sadie pulled out her notebook and recorded what she'd learned. Sadie now had a good idea who had started the schoolhouse fire all those years ago, but she couldn't yet be sure that was the same person who had run Virginia off the road. She still had so many questions about that. And she couldn't stop thinking about that school bell. At some point, the valuable silver antique had been swapped out for a cheaper cast-iron model. Knowing when, where, and how that had happened would shed a lot of light on what had happened before—and, critically—after the fire.

Sadie pulled out her phone and looked at the photos of the bell she'd taken with the camera function a few days back. She'd seen photos of the charred school bell resting among the still-smoldering ashes of the schoolhouse. Was that bell the cast-iron replacement, or the original silver bell? In Sadie's mind, it almost made more sense if the bell that had survived the fire had been made of cast-iron instead of silver all along. But that would have to mean...

Sadie checked the time. The high school had just let out for the day. She picked up the phone and placed a call, and a few minutes later, Brian Tomasso, the chemistry teacher at Silver Peak High School, picked up.

"Sadie!" Brian said. "So good to hear from you. Hey, I learned a good joke today. Want to hear it?" A tall, gangly man with a shock of curly white hair, Brian was always upbeat, even in the face of the daunting task of teaching high schoolers to care about chemical bonds and the periodic table.

"Sure." Sadie was one of the few teachers at the high school who had always relished Brian's bad science jokes. He had been trying—and mostly failing—to entertain the other teachers with them for years. Sometimes they flew right over her head, but she seemed to be one of the few who shared his corny sense of humor.

"Why can you never trust atoms?"

"I don't know," Sadie said. "Why?"

"Because they make up everything!" Brian laughed a little at his own joke, and Sadie let out a loud belly laugh.

"Hey, I'm looking forward to seeing your presentation tonight," Brian continued. Sadie stifled the anxiety that ran through her as she was reminded of the presentation she would be giving in mere hours. The school bell featured heavily into her presentation. She needed to find answers quickly.

"Thanks, Brian. And speaking of that, I actually have a quick question."

"Sure thing. You know chemists are great at solving problems because we have all the solutions."

Sadie laughed again. That was a clever one.

"I was wondering about the melting point of silver."

"Easy. Elemental, pure silver? One thousand, seven hundred sixty-three degrees."

Well, that was less useful than she'd hoped. "I guess what I'm asking is, would a fire get hot enough to melt an object made of silver?"

"That depends," Brian said. "On both the fire and the object."

"Let's say the fire was lit using an accelerant like gasoline or kerosene. And the object was a large silver school bell."

Brian let out a whistle. "I can see where you're going with this, and now I really can't wait for your presentation tonight. And I'm no fire expert, but adding gasoline to a fire definitely increases its burning temperature. Still, I would guess there's a chance the bell would survive, depending on how long the fire burned."

"And what if the bell was made from a different metal, like cast iron?"

"Iron has a much higher melting point than silver. A fire would need to be least two thousand degrees to melt that."

So there was a better chance the bell would survive unscathed if it was the cast-iron bell instead of the silver bell, but it wasn't conclusive. Sadie would need to keep digging.

"Thanks so much for your help, Brian. I appreciate it."

"I look forward to seeing you tonight at the fund-raiser," Brian said.

Sadie hung up and turned to study the shelf of reference books she kept behind the desk. She selected a book that gave a short overview of many of the major American metal workers and flipped to the section on cast-iron smelters. She found, just as she remembered, a brief overview of Garrett and Sons, a St. Louis–based family foundry that had been casting bells, horseshoes, and household objects for more than 150 years. There was a picture of the familiar script logo, as well as diagrams showing the typical proportions of a Garrett and Sons bell, which would help antique dealers distinguish an authentic Garret and Sons bell from a reproduction. The sad truth was, cast-iron items were easy to manufacture and pass off as old, so assuring authenticity of a purported antique object was paramount. But Sadie wasn't concerned with finding out whether the bell at the school was a genuine Garrett and Sons. She was interested in learning why, how, and when a cast-iron bell manufactured in St. Louis in the last 150 years had been passed off as a valuable historic silver bell that had come from England.

Sadie flipped to the section of the thick book that gave information about silver manufacturers. She paged through the entire section, but didn't find an entry for a Wilcox Company. Sadie supposed that would have been too easy. She flipped back to the beginning of the section and look at each entry, scanning for companies that specialized in church bells and the like. Most of the companies made things like tableware and jewelry, but Sadie found a few that made larger objects. Sadie read these entries carefully. They all quickly started to sound the same, and her eyes were starting to glaze over when she noticed something. One of the silversmiths, a Harwich Silver, was based in England but listed an American-based subsidiary that did mostly recovery and recasting. That company, according to this entry, was called the Wilcox Company.

Sadie tried to process what this meant. The Wilcox Company, it appeared, specialized in buying and melting down large pieces of silver and recasting them. Which meant that the unexplained entry Sadie had found in the district's financial records *could* have been…

Now it was all starting to make sense. If the troubled school district, in an effort to turn things around and avoid laying off more teachers, had started to liquidate its assets… It was possible it had sold off one of its most valuable assets, the historic school bell, and passed off a cast-iron model as the original. A large, solid piece of silver like that bell would have fetched a pretty penny. Sadie turned to her computer and quickly pulled up a Web page that tracked the history of silver pricing, and found that in the early- and mid-1960s, silver mining was declining, while demand for fabrication was increasing sharply. The silver in that bell, as a raw metal, was quite valuable. Sadie did some quick math based on the numbers on her screen and realized that the bell could very well have fetched over five thousand dollars. Which just about matched what she'd found in the district records earlier perfectly. Sadie found a currency calculator online and discovered that that in today's dollars would be enough to pay a teacher's salary for the year.

It was really hard to imagine how no one could have noticed a switch had been made for more than fifty years; silver and cast iron were very different in texture, weight, and appearance. But Sadie remembered the bits that had flaked off when she touched the bell this afternoon. It must have been coated in something to make it resemble tarnished silver more closely, probably after the fire. And, she reasoned, who would have thought to question whether this was the original bell? Sadie had seen the bell in the display case every day for decades and had never questioned that it was exactly what it was supposed to be.

The question, then, was not *how* was the old historic bell sold and replaced, or even *why*—the district's financial records showed that the profits from the sale had helped turn the district's budget deficit around; the sale might not have been ethical, but it had, in a very real sense, helped saved Silver Peak's failing schools—but *who* had done it. And thinking over the timing and what she'd learned in the past few hours about the fire—and about who would have cared enough to sell off the bell and get rid of the upkeep expenses that had been choking the school district—Sadie had a pretty good idea. It was the same person Charlie had confessed had bought gas the day before the fire, and who, Sadie knew, drove a black Buick Riviera in 1965.

Now all she needed to do was link that person to the accident last week. And, as she thought back over everything that had happened in the past week, she had an idea how to go about that.

Sadie pulled out a local yellow pages and scanned the entries for car rental agencies. A few phone calls later, she knew exactly who was behind the accident—and exactly what she needed to do at the fund-raiser that evening.

18

─────

A FEW HOURS LATER, SADIE WAS ALMOST FINISHED STYLING HER hair and getting ready for the fund-raiser when her cell phone rang. She jumped, and realized she was a little bit on edge. She hurried to the phone, and was relieved to see that it was Sara calling from her cell phone. She wasn't sure what she'd been expecting, but... well, after what had happened to Virginia once she realized who'd started the fire, Sadie wasn't taking any chances.

"Hi, hon." Sadie held the phone between her ear and her shoulder and used her hands to scoop some food into Hank's bowl. The greedy dog immediately dropped his head into the bowl and started wolfing it down.

"Hey, Grandma. I thought you might want to hear the news."

"The news?"

"Elena Garza turned Theo down."

Sadie's heart lurched. Even though she'd expected that outcome since talking to Elena, it still stung, especially since Sadie realized she had unintentionally set Theo up for failure.

"How is he taking it?" Sadie asked.

"He's moping. But that's what he's been doing for two days anyway."

"Is he around? I'd like to talk to him."

"I don't think he's going to come out of his room."

"Still, do you think you could—"

Just then, the doorbell rang, and Sadie jumped again. Goodness. She peeked out through the kitchen window and saw Edwin's silver BMW in the driveway. Of course it was Edwin, coming to pick her up for the fund-raiser. What did she think, that someone with nefarious intentions was going to ring her doorbell?

"Actually, Sara, I have to go. But could you tell Theo that I want to talk to him? I'll call later."

"I don't think it's going to do much good, but sure, I can try."

"Thank you." Sadie tried to shake off the disappointment about Theo, then set down her phone and went to the door to let in Edwin.

"Hello, Sadie. You look beautiful." Edwin stepped into the entryway, handed her a bouquet of sweet-smelling flowers, and leaned in and gave her a peck on the cheek. Sadie had put on a long skirt and an ivory blouse and paired them with her brown boots and a cameo necklace she'd inherited from her mother, and she felt professional yet feminine.

"You look quite nice yourself," she said, gesturing to his emerald-green sweater vest and brown sport coat. "And these are beautiful. I just need to grab my bag, and I'll be ready to go." Sadie led him into the kitchen, where she had her purse and the tote bag that held her laptop ready on the table. She slipped the flowers into a vase and filled it with water, then reached for her bags. Sadie had left the shop a bit early today and had spent the past few hours putting the finishing touches on her presentation. She hadn't been sure how to handle the revelations that she'd uncovered about the cause of the fire and the historic school bell. But she finally decided that the front of a crowded auditorium was not the place to make an accusation, so she'd kept the presentation itself neutral and cut back the part about the fire so she wouldn't have to say anything untrue. The early history of the schoolhouse, when it had been actively used for education, was the heart of the presentation anyway, and it would do just fine to showcase the importance of education in Silver Peak. Still, that didn't mean she didn't have plans for this evening.

"You're going to do a fantastic job tonight," Edwin said as Sadie tucked her purse under her arm. She smiled. She sure hoped so.

When they arrived at the school, the parking lot was filling quickly, and most of the cars there were not the small hatchbacks and family cars that filled this lot during school days. Edwin's BMW fit right in among the Mercedes and sports cars, and the people emerging from the cars and streaming into the school were dressed to the nines. Sadie suddenly felt dowdy, but as she took Edwin's arm and let him lead her toward the school building, she reminded herself that she was the one here with the mayor tonight. Not only was he handsome and well-respected, but he was a comforting presence, a strong arm to lean on as she thought over whom she planned to confront tonight. The person who had hurt Virginia, who had slipped that threatening note under her door, would be here tonight, Sadie was almost sure of it, and Sadie knew this would be her best chance to talk to him and try to convince him to finally admit what he'd done. She knew she should be worried—look at what had happened to Virginia, after all—but walking next to Edwin now, she felt safe. Edwin would do whatever he could to protect her, no matter who she angered; that thought gave her the courage to walk inside with her head up.

The auditorium had been transformed. Sadie could hardly believe this was the same room she'd seen earlier. Now the walls were hung with giant printouts of historic photos of Silver Peak. Round tables draped in linen were topped by vases of fresh flowers, set with delicate place settings, and dotted with dozens of tiny tea lights. At the front of the room was the stage, where the presentations would be given while guests ate. Edwin had already been intercepted by a group of town council members, so Sadie started to walk toward the stage to deposit her laptop.

"Sadie!" Sadie turned and saw Roz coming toward her, wearing a flowing, colorful print skirt and several thick, chunky bracelets. "I saved us seats at this table," Roz continued, gesturing to a round table at the side of the auditorium. "Are you all set for your presentation?"

"Just about," Sadie said, hitching up the tote bag that held her laptop. "I just need to get this set up and I guess I'll be as ready as I'll ever be."

"Why don't you go do that now and get it out of the way? I see that I need to rescue Roscoe anyway," she said, pointing to the far side of the room, where her husband, dressed in a brown suit with a bolo necktie, was gamely chatting with Pat Walkins, a third grade teacher who was known for telling long-winded stories about her ailing cat.

"I'll meet you at the table," Sadie said, and continued toward the stage. It took a few minutes to get the cords all squared away, but soon Sadie was as sure as she could be that the laptop would project onto the screen as it was supposed to. Once she had that set up, she stood at the side of the stage and looked around the room.

Sadie recognized some of the people milling about the room—Silver Peak's teachers had been given complimentary tickets to the event, and many of the small business owners in town could be counted on to support the local schools, and had been invited at a discounted rate. Sadie spotted Hector and Luz Vidal talking with principal Anne Hastings, and trigonometry teacher Julia Turner was chatting with Ramon Garza. Sadie also saw a clump of people she recognized as part of the crew Sadie referred to as the big-wigs—Samuel Bradley, Simon Riley, and Howard McNaught. Sadie watched the little group interacting for a moment. They were all dressed in well-cut suits, with shined shoes and sedate and tasteful ties. Howard even had a pocket square, and Samuel was wearing a black fedora, an accessory that signaled, even among this crowd, an impeccably dressed gentleman.

And then, suddenly, she saw Samuel Bradley quickly excuse himself, step away from the little group, look around the room swiftly, and move toward the auditorium door.

Sadie's heart stopped. Where was he going? He could be leaving the room for any number of reasons, but the surreptitious little swivel of his head, like he was making sure no one was watching him, made Sadie immediately suspicious. And the way he tugged at the brim of his hat, pulling it down just before he stepped into the hallway, made her think he was hoping to avoid being identified by somebody or something.

Well. She had hoped to talk to him tonight, but this hadn't exactly been how she'd intended things to go. Still, something told her this was her chance. He was up to something.

Sadie climbed off the stage. She should go get help—but Edwin was in the middle of a group of people chatting right now. It would take too long to pull him away. Where was Roz? Or Anne? With every second that passed, Sadie felt her opportunity to catch Samuel slip away. She looked from Edwin to the now-closed door he had vanished through. She knew she should let someone else know what was going on, but—

She glanced at the door to the hallway once more. And she made a split-second decision. There was no time to lose. She followed him.

She headed across the room, and though she was stopped by a few people who wanted to chat, she made her excuses and quickly extricated herself. She managed to slip out the door after Samuel just in time to watch him disappear around the corner. The hallway he was following led toward the main wing of the school, where the classrooms were. Sadie walked as quietly as she could; fortunately, the noise from the party spilled out over into the hallway there, so her footsteps were muffled, but she knew that as they got farther away from the party, she would have to stay back to keep from being detected.

Samuel moved faster than she would have expected for a man his age, and though she tried to stay back, where he wouldn't see her if he turned around, she had to scurry a bit to keep up. Fortunately, as she followed him around another bend in the hallway, it quickly became clear where he was headed, and she realized now that the fedora was not simply a fashion statement. After so many school shootings had hit the news, Silver Peak High School had installed security cameras in all public areas. With that hat pulled down low over his face, it would make it difficult to tell who he was if anyone ever had cause to review the footage.

Sadie peeked around a corner and watched him pull a set of keys from his pocket, unlock a classroom door, and step inside the doorway.

Sadie waited a moment, steeling herself. He was definitely up to something. There could be no good reason for him to go—

Just before he stepped inside, he looked around one last time. Sadie ducked out of the way, and hoped he hadn't seen the movement. He nodded, seemingly satisfied, and stepped inside the classroom.

She said a quick prayer for God's protection, then moved quickly to the door, pulled it open, and followed Samuel Bradley into Virginia Radcliff's classroom.

19

─────

SAMUEL LOOKED UP WHEN SADIE STEPPED INTO THE ROOM. HE was bending over the bottom drawer of Virginia's desk. Sadie could see that he had gotten it open somehow—no doubt whatever set of keys he'd managed to get his hands on contained a skeleton key for every lock in this building—and he was lifting a stack of papers out of the open drawer. It should have surprised Sadie that he'd been able to get his hands on the keys, but it didn't; he, of all people, knew the right people in town.

"What are you doing here?" he asked, anger flashing across his aged features.

"I could ask you the same thing," Sadie said, stepping into the room. She let the door fall closed behind her. He looked around the room, searching for something.

"I'm just helping clean out some old files and things," Samuel offered—a poor attempt, in Sadie's mind, at trying to fish out if she really knew what he was doing.

"Of course you are," Sadie said, nodding. "But what I don't understand is how you knew exactly where Virginia had put the evidence that proves you were behind the schoolhouse fire, and how you knew the moment she figured out she was about to go public with what she had uncovered."

"I don't know what you're talking about," Samuel said. His voice was loud, authoritative, but his eye was twitching. His pants, though finely made and well-pressed, hung off his too-thin frame, and she could see that his hands were shaking a bit.

"I think you do know. And I think it's time for you to tell the truth."

A look passed over his face—fear? Resignation? He started to say something, and then faltered. And then, "I thought I told you to stay out of it."

Sadie could see how, years back, he could have been intimidating. He was, even now, a man used to getting his way, powerful enough that people listened when he spoke and, cowed, did whatever he said. Even if his position as former superintendent didn't inspire respect, the sheer amount of money he poured into this town did. Things like that mattered in a small town like Silver Peak.

Sadie, undaunted, stepped forward into the room. "Believe me, once I realized why you did it, I actually sort of understood. The schools were failing, and the historic property was an albatross around your neck, dragging the school district down. You couldn't afford to keep the property up and pay for the teachers and expenses the current school needed. One or the other had to go. Once I saw the financial records and realized you lit that fire to save the current and future schools, it actually made a lot of sense. I understood that you saw it as the noble thing to do, and wondered if I would have had the guts to do the same thing myself."

Samuel was listening, Sadie could tell.

"What I don't understand, though, is why you tried to hurt Virginia Radcliff to keep your secret from coming out."

"I didn't—"

"I know how much power you have in this town, Samuel, and I know how bad it would look if it came out what you'd done all those years ago. But was it really worth hurting Virginia over?"

Sadie couldn't believe the words that were coming out of her mouth. She didn't know where they were coming from, and she couldn't quite believe she had the courage to say them, here, now, alone in a room with him. But right now, he didn't look like the power-hungry, sociopathic criminal she'd pictured Virginia's attacker to be. He didn't seem like a man who would stop at nothing to keep his secrets from coming out.

No, now that they were here, Samuel Bradley just looked like a scared old man. With his liver-spotted hands and shrunken frame, he almost reminded her of her father in his later years. He was trembling, and Sadie realized that he was actually afraid that someone would find out what he'd done. That this was a final act of desperation.

Samuel dumped the files in his arms into the metal wastebasket next to Virginia's desk and reached into his pocket.

"I didn't try to hurt her." His voice had risen in pitch, and it shook as he spoke. Sadie saw that he had pulled something out of his pocket—it was an antique silver lighter, the kind that stayed lit as long as the lid was open. "I didn't—" He flipped open the lid of the antique lighter and turned the flint, but the flame didn't catch. "I didn't mean for it to—"

He turned the flint again, and this time, the flame caught.

"Samuel, please be careful with that." She wasn't sure what he intended to do, but Sadie knew what he was capable of. Sadie took another step closer. "The schoolhouse fire was so long ago. The statute of limitations is surely long since past. At this point, what does it matter if people find out? Especially once they realize why you did it."

For a moment, he stood, staring at the flame in the lighter, as if mesmerized, but then he looked away. "No one can find out. After all the good things I've done in this town, after everything I've done to try to make up for that one night, the only thing anyone would remember about me would be something I did when I was young and foolish. Do you think I want that to be my legacy?"

As he spoke, he was looking at the papers in the metal trash can. Sadie realized what he was about to do. He intended to burn the evidence.

"I have copies of most of those," Sadie said, indicating the papers in the trash can. "It doesn't matter if they burn up. Virginia might have put the pieces together first, but I have enough evidence in my hands to prove it was you."

"You couldn't possibly."

"I do. I found the records that show when you sold off the silver school bell and passed off the cast-iron one as the original."

He hesitated, like he wasn't sure what to do. But then, a look of desperation passed over his face, and he bent down and dropped the lighter into the trash can with the papers. Sadie was too far away to see the papers catch, but she heard the crackle as they started to burn. Sadie's breath caught, but she saw that the fire seemed contained inside the trash can. She hoped it would burn out on its own quickly.

"I know you hoped it would be enough to save the school district," Sadie continued. "Something dramatic had to be done when it became clear the bell hadn't brought in enough. But though the answer was buried in the public records, what gave it away for me was when I found out there'd been a black Buick Riviera in the woods that night. I remembered seeing a picture of you posed in front of that car in the old yearbook."

Sadie was starting to smell the papers burning, and tiny wisps of flame began to appear over the rim of the trash can.

"And once I realized that, of course, it suddenly made sense why the sheriff, your brother-in-law, had quickly declared the fire an accident, in the face of all evidence. He'd figured out it was you too, and was trying to protect you."

"You have no way to prove any of that," he stammered.

"I can prove that you were driving a maroon rental car at the time of Virginia's accident. Maroon, just like the car that hit her. And when I called the rental agency today, they confirmed that it was returned with damage to the front left panel. Which, I'm afraid, is consistent with the damage that would have been on the vehicle that caused Virginia's accident. I think the police are going to be very interested to find the evidence that links you to Virginia's accident." Sadie watched him. He didn't say anything for a moment, his eyes fixed on the tendrils of smoke rising from the trash can.

"Was getting rid of this evidence really worth hurting a woman?"

"I wasn't trying to hurt Virginia," he snapped. "What happened to her was an accident. I wasn't trying to hurt her!" He stamped his foot, but as his foot came back down, it hit the side of the wastebasket, and suddenly, the flaming papers were tumbling out of the trash can and onto the classroom floor. "I never meant to hurt her," he said, his voice rising to a high pitch. And then, he seemed to notice for the first time what he had done. He yelped, and jumped back.

Sadie rushed forward, holding up her long skirt, to try to stamp it out. "And yet you ended up knocking her into a ravine."

He seemed frozen, gazing at the fire licking at the carpet. "I knew she'd been looking into the fire. Everyone in town knew that. And when she called last Wednesday night, I knew she'd figured it out. She told me she was calling from here, so I knew there was a good chance the evidence was here as well. So I followed her."

"You followed her." Sadie stamped her foot on the flames, glad she had worn her thick-soled boots.

"I was downtown. I saw her car pull out of the lot. I jumped in my rental and followed her. I wasn't thinking; I just wanted to follow her wherever she was going and see if I could talk some sense into her. Pay her to keep her mouth shut. I never meant to hit her car. I—the roads were slippery. I wasn't used to the car. I lost control—"

Sadie still tried to suppress the spreading fire with her feet, but she looked up at Samuel, and saw that he seemed to be lost in some sort of reverie. He could see that he'd accidentally set the carpet on fire, but he wasn't totally processing what was happening, Sadie realized. But she also realized something else.

He looked sincere. He seemed to genuinely be unsure of how he had landed Virginia's car in a ravine. And, Sadie realized, she could actually kind of see it. Samuel was very old, and clearly not totally aware of everything going on around him. His eyesight was probably bad, if his thick bifocals were any indication. He had been driving an unfamiliar car on slippery roads. If he'd been following too close, he very well might have simply lost control of the car, and ended up sending Virginia's car flying. Was it possible...

Had Samuel turned around as soon as he realized what he'd done? Had he headed straight for the nearest pay phone to call for help? The hat he was wearing could indeed be the very one from the security video.

"You sent me a threatening note."

"Why couldn't you just stop? There was no need to go digging all this up again." He was staring at something far away. "But I was never going to hurt you, and I never meant to hurt Virginia."

It didn't make what he had done any better. He had still seriously injured a woman in his quest to keep his secret hidden, to keep his social position in town secure. But if he hadn't meant to hurt her—if it really had been an accident—it did mean that she wasn't facing down a heartless criminal. She was, in reality, staring at a scared, desperate old man.

A scared and desperate old man whose pants were about to catch fire.

"Samuel!" Sadie pointed to the flames that were now spreading quickly across the carpet. Her sharp voice jolted him, and he looked down and seemed to realize what kind of danger they were in. He made a noise, somewhere between a grunt and a squeal, and jumped back. He began tapping at the edge of the flames with his shoe, but Sadie had already spotted a fire extinguisher hanging on the wall behind Virginia's desk, only a few feet behind Samuel. "Grab the fire extinguisher!"

Samuel sprang into action, and though it took him a minute to wrench the extinguisher free from the wall, he did manage to point the extinguisher at the fire and pull out the pin. But when he squeezed the handle, only a thin stream of white chemical came out. He squeezed again, aiming at the flames, which were growing every minute, quickly eating a trail across the dry industrial carpet, but the liquid inside fizzled and died.

Sadie realized that the fire, which had started out small and contained, was quickly spreading and was starting to lick at the leg of one of the wooden desks. She saw that the lighter, still open and lit, had tumbled out of the trash can and was feeding the fire. She began to cough from the smoke.

She gestured for Samuel, who was on the wrong side of the flames from the door, to come around to where she was, and he obeyed, his eyes wide, like he couldn't quite believe what he was seeing. Sadie hadn't brought her purse with her; she'd left it sitting on a chair at a table in the auditorium, so she didn't have a cell phone.

She cast her eyes around the room and spotted a phone on the wall by the door. Sadie ran to the phone and lifted the receiver, but instead of a typical dial tone, she heard the special buzz that reminded her this was an internal phone. It was designed and installed mainly so teachers could contact the front office. But these phones did, if Sadie remembered correctly, connect to the 911 emergency system. How did that work? She had to dial 9 first, she thought.

Smoke was stinging her eyes, and making her cough. They had to get out of this room. But first, she had to get help. She had to stop the fire from spreading.

Quickly she punched in 911, and just as the operator picked up, the school's fire alarm system started blaring an alarm over the loudspeakers. Samuel, Sadie saw, was standing a few feet from her, fixed in place, frozen.

"Hello, I'm calling to report a fire at Silver Peak High School," Sadie said into the phone. "I'm not sure which classroom, but it's—"

"We've already got trucks on the way," the woman said. Just then, the overhead sprinklers began spinning, and water came tumbling down from the ceiling. "The school's alarm system contacted the fire department directly. Where are you, ma'am?"

"I'm in the classroom."

"You need to get out now," the woman said. "Move to safety, please. Help is on the way."

Sadie dropped the phone and yelled for Samuel to come with her, but he didn't seem to hear her. She stepped toward him, getting wetter every moment from the surprisingly powerful sprinklers, and touched his shoulder, intending to steer him out of the classroom.

He stood, transfixed, gazing at the flame, something like horror on his face. For just the briefest moment, Sadie felt pity for him. She would bet he was reliving that night in his mind, watching the flames he'd set devour the old wooden schoolhouse. But there was no time for reverie now, they had to get out of—

Just then, the door to the classroom flew open, and Anne Hastings rushed into the room, followed by Roz, Edwin, and a few of the teachers from the school. They were all drenched.

"Sadie!" Edwin yelled. "What in the world?" He pulled her toward the door, and Roz steered Samuel away.

"The fire trucks are on their way," Anne called. Sadie nodded, and then, just before stepping out of the room, she turned and looked back at the flames. They were almost out, Sadie realized, beaten back by the relentless spray from the overhead fire sprinkler. A wave of relief coursed through her, and she sagged against Edwin as he led her to safety.

20

It was more than an hour later, and Sadie still found herself wrapped in a blanket in Anne's office, answering questions fired at her by Sheriff Slattery. Samuel Bradley was being questioned by Officer Kenmore in the assistant principal's office, down the hall. Edwin, Roz, and Anne sat in the corner of the room, listening, blankets wrapped around their own shoulders, sipping hot cocoa, taking it all in. Thankfully, fire trucks had arrived only moments after the sprinklers had doused the flames, and the firemen had declared the fire totally out before they'd left. And only the sprinklers in the wing of the school where the classroom was had gone off, so the main office was high and dry, and the fundraiser was still going on, mostly as planned, in the auditorium.

"Okay, so I understand how you figured out Samuel was our man," Sherriff Slattery said, shaking his head, like he couldn't quite believe it. They'd already been talking for the better part of the hour, and Sadie had already explained how she'd found the clues that led to the conclusion Samuel Bradley was behind the schoolhouse fire and Virginia's accident. Sheriff Slattery had listened, incredulous, but had shown a grudging sort of respect as Sadie explained how the trail of clues about the old fire had led her to the unwitting culprit behind Virginia's accident—which she now knew really had been an accident, not a deliberate act of vengeance. "But what I don't understand is what you thought you were going to do when you followed him out of the auditorium tonight."

"I wasn't really sure," Sadie admitted. "But I knew what he'd already done and I suspected he was up to no good, so I just followed my instinct and went after him."

"Why didn't you tell one of us what was happening? I would have gone with you, and I'm sure Edwin or Anne, or anybody, would have readily gone along too," Roz said.

Sadie tried to imagine exactly how Roz would have helped as she faced down Samuel Bradley, and the image made her smile. "I just didn't really think about it."

It sounded crazy, Sadie could see that now. She understood the exasperated look on Edwin's face, the way Sheriff Slattery was staring at her now. But she *hadn't* really been thinking, that was the point. She had simply acted.

"Well, in the future, I wish you would think about it a little more," Sheriff Slattery said. That was it, Sadie realized. That was all he could say, because in the end, she had caught Samuel red-handed, destroying evidence that proved his guilt. The police had their man, thanks to Sadie.

"And maybe try not to set the school on fire next time," Roz added, smirking.

Sadie laughed out loud, and Roz joined her. Now that the danger had passed, it felt good to laugh about it.

"Some people really will do anything to get out of giving a presentation," Anne said, winking at Sadie.

Though she did feel bad about the rug in that classroom, and about the hassle and panic the fire alarms had caused, she did have to admit that she was a teensy bit relieved not to have to give that presentation after all. She had offered, but given the fact that she was drenched, Anne had insisted the show would go on without her. She felt certain that saving the school from a fire would be enough to garner donations tonight.

"What I don't get," Sadie said, "is how you all knew exactly which classroom to come running into once the alarms went off."

"There's a fire control panel in the front office, by DeeDee's desk," Anne said. "When the alarm went off, it registered exactly where the problem was and sent a signal to the fire department."

Edwin let out a low whistle. "Fancy."

"We had the system installed a few years back. It wasn't cheap, but it was supposed to keep the school from burning to the ground."

"Apparently, that was a good investment," Sheriff Slattery said.

"You should make sure to tell the folks out there about that," Sadie said, gesturing toward the auditorium. "That ought to make them pull out their wallets."

Anne laughed, and she pulled the blanket from her shoulders and ran her fingers through her hair. "I probably should get back out there, now that you mention it. Are we all done here, Sheriff?"

Anne had already shown Sadie and Edwin that she had a change of clothes in her office, and as principal she felt obligated to attend the rest of the fund-raiser, even after the evening's excitement. Sadie admired her dedication and energy level. She was looking forward to climbing into bed.

Sheriff Slattery looked over his notes, and then he sighed and nodded. "I guess that's it for now. I'll let you know if I have any more questions." He closed his notebook and tucked his pen into the pocket of his shirt. "And, Sadie?"

"Yes, Sheriff?" Sadie had a feeling she knew what was coming, and she tried her best to look innocent.

"Please don't go looking for another adventure, at least for a few days."

Sadie laughed and promised that she would do her best, and then she allowed Edward to help her up and lead her back to his car. She had never been more thankful for his strong, comforting presence. Kids these days might not understand the security of trusting in a man to be there for you, to protect you and care for you, but as she leaned on Edwin and they made their way to the car together, she thanked God for the blessing this man was in her life.

Sadie awoke suddenly, and she sat up in bed, looking around. What had caused her to wake up like that? The sunlight filtering in through the closed curtains made it clear it was morning, though she felt like she'd barely slept a wink.

The phone rang. That was it! That must have been what had woken her. Sadie hopped out of bed and ran for the extension and held it to her ear.

"Sadie?" It was a man's voice, and Sadie knew she'd heard it before, though in her groggy state she couldn't place it.

"Yes?"

"It's David Radcliff. I'm sorry to call so early, I just had to tell you." Sadie glanced at the digital clock on her bureau and realized it was actually after 9:00 AM. She must have forgotten to set her alarm. She would have to scramble to get to the shop on time, and she was grateful for the phone call. "Virginia is awake!"

It took Sadie a moment to process what he'd said, and then the words sank in.

"She's awake?" Sadie felt like laughing and crying at the same time. She couldn't believe it. "How is she?"

"She's groggy and in a lot of pain, but the doctors say she is going to be just fine. And one of the first things she said after she opened her eyes was that she needed to tell you who set the fire, so we're taking that as a good sign."

Sadie smiled, and her heart warmed. Virginia was going to be just fine. What an answer to prayer. "You can tell her the police have him in custody," Sadie said. "And that she has more important things to worry about than a fifty-year-old fire at the moment."

"I did tell her." David laughed. Sadie knew the police had planned to notify David last night that they'd arrested Samuel Bradley for causing Virginia's accident, and it would be up to the Radcliff family whether or not to press charges. "But she still wanted to talk with you."

"Tell her I'll stop by to see her today."

"I'll tell her. Anyway, I should get back in there and sit with her for a while, but I thought you'd want to know. And I wanted to thank you for what you did to track down Bradley. I know it was only because of your hard work that we know who was behind all this. We still need to figure out what to do about it, obviously, but it means a lot to at least have some answers."

"I'll be praying for wisdom for you all in the coming days," Sadie said, and David thanked her. Sadie knew the crash had genuinely been an accident, that Samuel had done what he could to make it right afterward, that he was a senior citizen who had given so much to his community; on the one hand, Sadie hoped for leniency for him. At the same time, though, in an effort to hide a past crime, he'd caused a near-fatal accident and fled the scene, so she hoped there were some consequences. In any case, it was not in her hands. All she could do was pray for wisdom and that the Lord's will would be done.

"Thank you, Sadie. Thank you for all you've done."

"Please tell Virginia I can't wait to see her."

"Will do."

Sadie hung up the phone and started to get ready for her day, all traces of grogginess gone. God was good. She knew it in her heart, but she was always grateful for the reminder. As she stepped into the shower, she thanked the Lord for the good news, and though she was filled with a light heart, she couldn't quite rejoice fully.

Something was still weighing on her.

There was still one thing she needed to do.

That afternoon, when the after-school rush had started to fill Arbuckle's with the chatter of teenagers, Sadie asked Julie to cover the store one more time, and she slipped out and drove the short distance to her daughter's house. As she suspected, the lights were on inside, which meant at least one of her grandchildren was home. She rang the doorbell, and as she held her breath, she prayed for wisdom and the right words to say.

The door opened, and Theo stood in the entryway.

"Oh. Hey, Grandma." He was wearing jeans and a Broncos T-shirt, and he used one bare foot to scratch the other.

"Hi, Theo. May I come in?"

Theo looked around, like he wasn't quite sure how to answer, but then he stepped back and opened the door.

"I was just working on my homework," Theo said, and Sadie nodded and followed him to the kitchen, where a math textbook and some papers were scattered across the table. He sat down in one of the chairs, and Sadie sat down across from him. His hair flopped in front of his face, and he pushed it aside.

Sadie struggled to find the words to say what she wanted to say, and finally she simply blurted out, "I'm sorry."

Theo nodded, but he looked down at his textbook, and his hair fell in front of him again. He picked up the pencil that was lying in the spine of the book.

"I was trying to help, but I know I gave you some bad advice," Sadie continued. She thought about Edwin once again, about how good it felt to be able to count on him and lean on him. How he always came to the door to pick her up and paid for their dates and let her walk into a room first, just like a gentleman should. How he always treated her like she was worth protecting. No, she didn't actually think what she'd told Theo was wrong. But she hadn't taken into account that his world wasn't her world, and that *was* her fault. "Well, if I'm honest, I still think it was good advice, but I can see now that it was advice based on what my generation thinks and it didn't take into account that kids do things differently these days. And I'm truly sorry about that."

"I guess someone told you she said no," Theo mumbled, twirling the pencil between his fingers. He was putting on a brave face, but she could see he was hurting. Until she'd had her own child, she hadn't understood how it could possibly hurt more to watch someone else in pain than to be in pain yourself, but seeing Theo struggling now, she felt like she had lost an arm.

"Yes, I heard. And I wish I had taken the time to understand the situation better before I blurted out my thoughts and encouraged you."

Sadie's advice about romance might not have changed, either way—she still felt that there were right and wrong ways for men to treat women they were wooing—but if she'd understood that Elena was interested in Curtis Younts, she probably would have tempered her wholehearted enthusiasm for the plan.

"I wish there was something I could do to help make it better at this point," she said, and again, he simply nodded. For a moment, there was silence, the only sound the high-pitched buzz of a lawn mower somewhere down the street.

In her mind, Sadie had pictured this going differently. She'd imagined apologizing, and Theo wholeheartedly acknowledging her honesty and forgiving her on the spot. But that, too, was unrealistic, she now understood. That was looking at it through her own perspective, what would make her happy, without taking into account who Theo was and the situation she'd created. Theo was a sensitive kid, and they'd always been close, but he was also a seventeen-year-old boy. Overt displays of emotion were not in his repertoire these days. When he forgave her—if he forgave her—it would probably not look anything like the weepy hug she would have chosen.

"A bunch of kids from youth group are going to the dance together, just as friends," Theo finally said. "I may go with them."

Sadie felt something in her chest loosen. "That sounds like a wonderful idea." It wouldn't be the traditional prom night, with a corsage for his date and pictures in front of the mantel. She would miss seeing those, but this wasn't about her. And she had to admit that it would certainly be a lot less pressure, and probably a lot more fun for him. No dream date to impress. Just friends—good kids from church, she reminded herself— hanging out, going through a rite of passage together. It would probably be more fun, and no doubt safer in so many ways. And if Sara was right, this seemed more in line with how kids did things today.

"I'm not sure yet. But maybe," Theo said.

"I think it sounds like a wonderful idea," Sadie said, and then quickly continued, "not that what I think is what's important here."

Theo laughed, and then shook his head. "No, but it counts. Believe it or not, I do care what you think." Sadie knew enough to know that might be as close as she would ever come to hearing that she was forgiven, and it warmed her heart.

Theo twirled his pencil between his fingers. "There's this other girl I'm kind of thinking about asking. But I don't know yet."

Sadie tried to stop her heart from beating faster, but she couldn't. Either way, she reminded herself, it would be good. What was important was that Theo had a good time. But still, she couldn't help but hope.

"And I'm glad you didn't burn the school down last night," Theo added, a sly grin on his face.

"Hey now, I had nothing to do with setting that fire," Sadie said, laughing. "I was trying to put it out!"

"Uh-huh," Theo said, but he was smiling. "Mrs. Radcliff's class got to meet outside in the sunshine today while they were replacing the carpet. Everyone in school suddenly wished they were taking American history."

Anne had told her that they were still able to use the other classrooms that had gotten wet from the sprinklers, though it would take a few days for the carpets to dry out completely.

"If nothing else, I'm glad that my efforts encouraged an interest in our nation's history," Sadie said.

"They also made me think again how much I'd like to do what you do," Theo said, a bit sheepishly. "It was pretty cool how you figured out who set that old fire."

Sadie knew that Theo was entertaining the idea of becoming a detective someday, and though she was flattered, she also knew that hadn't ever been her own goal.

"All I do is run an antique store," Sadie said. The other stuff, the mysteries that somehow seemed to come her way—those were not something she looked for. Antiques were her passion.

"Sure, Grandma." Theo laughed again. "That's all you do."

Well, maybe it wasn't *all* she did, but being the Antique Lady was enough for Sadie Speers for now. That and Grandma. No matter how old she got, she'd never get tired of being called Grandma. She'd stood by and watched as Theo first emerged into the world, took his first steps, lost his first tooth. Now, as he stood on the cusp of adulthood, she knew the real trials and challenges were still ahead of him, but she hoped she could support him through those trials as well.

She might not be a perfect grandmother, or always know the right thing to say, but her family meant more to her than anything else in this world. And looking at Theo right now, she couldn't have been any prouder.

About the Author

CAROLE JEFFERSON IS THE PEN NAME FOR A TEAM OF WRITERS who have come together to create the series Mysteries of Silver Peak. *Wildfire* was written by Elizabeth Adams, who lives in New York City with her husband and two young daughters. When she's not writing, she is cleaning up after two devious cats and trying to find time to read mysteries.

A Lode of Secrets

"GRANDMA, I HEARD YOU WERE GOING TO BE ON A TV SHOW!" Sadie's granddaughter Sara said, as she rushed into the Antique Mine.

"I'm not actually going to be on TV, Sara. Have you heard of *American Treasure Chest*? I'm the historical consultant for a documentary television series they're putting together."

Sadie's best friend Roz clapped her hands together. "Still, it's so exciting, Sadie. Roscoe and I love that show." She turned to Sara. "They go behind the scenes to recreate unsolved mysteries from America's past."

"Right now," Sadie explained, "they're working on a six-part series on mines around the country, and one of those six just happens to be right here in Silver Peak."

Sara's eyes brightened. "So does that mean you're a consultant?"

"For starters, I've spent the past few weeks corresponding with the director to answer his questions, researching details of the story, and ensuring the script is as accurate as possible."

"Though not everyone was thrilled with the fact that Abigail and Raymond's story is being told," Roz added.

Sara gave Sadie a puzzled look. She was clearly intrigued—and perhaps as star struck at the thought of a television crew in town as Roz, but she waited to see what her grandmother had to say.

"Well, Priscilla Hewitt told me she didn't want to be involved in the documentary, even though it centers on her mother's story," Sadie explained. "She believes that there are some secrets from history that should stay that way."

"Are you going to be there during the filming?" Sara asked, leaning against the counter.

Sadie went back to sorting through the perfume bottles. "Well, I'll be providing the majority of the props and costumes for the reenactments, and they've asked me to help them be sure the historical clips woven into the document are accurate." Sadie pointed to the stack of boxes she'd lined up by the back door, ready to be loaded into her Chevy Tahoe. "I've got carbide lamps, a miner's lunch pail, folding candlesticks the miners used, and other blasting-related items. The costumes are already up at the mine."

"Where did you get all of this?" Sara asked.

"A lot of it comes from here"—she motioned around her shop—"but other items I was able to borrow from Ol' Sam at the American Mining Museum. Greg and Evelyn Winston, the mine owners, offered some things as well."

Greg and Evelyn Winston, along with their fifteen-year-old son, Craig, lived near the Silver Peak Mine where they ran tours of the silver mine that had been in the family for three generations.

Sadie picked up an antique perfume bottle that she had recently purchased at an estate sale. "I just had another thought. This will be a perfect addition to Abigail's dressing table."

"And who exactly was Abigail?" Sara asked, picking up one of the bottles.

"You remember that skeleton Greg Winston found up in the mines a few weeks back?" Sadie began.

"Of course she does. Everyone in town knows about the skeleton Greg found. And now the police claim that the victim had been murdered," Roz leaned in and lowered her voice, as if she were divulging a tantalizing secret. "It was tragic love story. A vanishing fiancé presumed dead by the hands of Abigail Chaplin's brother, though no one really knows the truth about what happened up in the mines that fatal night."

Sadie laughed at her friend's flair for the dramatic. "And since it happened over half a century ago, no one probably ever will know."

"What *do* you know?" Sara asked.

Sadie glanced at her friend, wondering how much of the story needed to be repeated in front of her granddaughter.

"Grandma." Sara rolled her eyes and let out a huff of frustration. "It's not like I'm a kid anymore. And if everyone in town knows the story, I'll hear all of it anyway."

Sadie weighed her granddaughter's logic. "I supposed you're right. But no one knows for sure who Greg discovered up in the mines. The crime lab is trying to identify the body, but most people assume it's Raymond Butler."

"And who's he?" Sara sounded impatient.

"Back in the mid 1950s, a young woman who lived right here in Silver Peak, Abigail Chaplin, fell in love with Raymond, a handsome stranger, the story goes, who waltzed into Silver Peak and swept her off her feet."

"How romantic," Sara said.

"So it would seem. But Abigail's family was wealthy and her father and brother in particular were convinced that Raymond was simply after her money."

"Was he?"

"No one knows for sure. Supposedly Raymond and Abigail's brother Philip had a big argument right in the center of town at the library where Abigail volunteered." Sadie could remember the old library building, now replaced by a modern glass-and-steel structure that she privately thought looked out of place with the rest of Silver Peak.

"What happened?"

"Words were flung back and forth at each other," Sadie continued, "along with a few punches. After the fight was over, Philip threatened Raymond that he would kill him if he didn't stay away from his sister."

"And did he?" Sara asked.

"No. Because Abigail's family was against the marriage—and Raymond was afraid for his life—he tried to convince her to elope with him. But before they did, Raymond disappeared."

"What happened to him?"

"That's the problem," Roz cut in, "no one knows for sure, but it was rumored that Philip made good on his threat, killed Raymond, and hid his body up in the mines."

Sara's eyes widened. "What happened to Philip?'

"Philip was taken in and questioned by the authorities, but even though there were witnesses to their fight in town, they weren't able to tie him to Raymond's disappearance. Nor did they have a body," Sadie said. "And without a body, it was impossible to prove there'd even been a murder."

"How about Abigail?" Sara's phone buzzed beside her on the counter, but in a rare display of indifference, she ignored it. "What happened to her?"

"Her parents sent her to Europe for a few months to stay with a relative, hoping it would get her mind off the incident. She eventually returned to help out the family when her father became very ill. Philip died a few months later in a car crash on his way back to Silver Peak from Denver. Her father died right after that."

"What a sad story." Sara shook her head. "What do you think happened to Raymond?"

"I wish I knew." Sadie glanced at her watch. "But for now, I need to get going. I'm supposed to meet the television crew up at the mines in less than an hour. If the two of you wouldn't mind helping me finish loading up my car with the props, I'd be grateful. Julie's on her way right now to watch the store while I'm gone."

Sara tapped her fingers against the counter. "Grandma…"

"What's up?"

"Would it be okay if I came along with you?"

Sadie set the box she'd picked up back on the counter. "To the mine?"

Sadie studied her granddaughter, wondering where her motivation to 'hang out' with her grandmother had come from. "Did the story intrigue you that much, or does your wanting to help out have more to do with the fact that there will be television crews and cameras?"

Sara gave her grandmother a mischievous grin. "This would be...educational."

"Educational, huh?" Sadie laughed.

"I'm serious." Sara drummed her fingers against the counter, then glanced at her reflection in the dark screen of her cell phone and tucked a strand of hair behind her ear. "And if they happen to need an extra, then I'll be available."

"So now the truth comes out." Sadie laughed. "What about your mother? The mine isn't the safest place."

"I asked her before I left the house. She said if it was okay with you, it was okay with her."

"You're sure?" Sadie asked.

Sara nodded, her eyes wide with excitement. "When she told me what you were doing, I hoped they might need some extras. It would be fun."

Sadie made her decision. "They've hired a small number of actors for the main parts, but I understand they're looking for some extras, especially for the town shots. And I could always use an assistant. Call your mom and let her know I said you could come, then let's load up the car. We've got a documentary to shoot."

Greg Winston, owner of the South Ridge Mine, walked up to the house as Sadie arrived with Sara.

"Good morning, Greg."

"Hey, Sadie. Ready for the big day?"

"All the props are here, and just about organized, so yes. I believe so."

Greg leaned against the railing at the top of the stairs. "I was kind of surprised when I heard you were going to be involved in this project, knowing how busy you are in your store."

"I think it'll be a lot of fun. Is the documentary crew here yet?" she asked, brushing the dust from her hands.

Greg's gaze slid to his watch. "They're going to be late, actually," Greg said, as Sara stepped out onto the porch. "They called and said they'd had a flat tire twenty miles out of Denver. But there's no reason why I can't start the two of you off with a tour of the mine and a little history. How's that sound?"

"Sara?" Sadie asked her granddaughter. "What do you think?"

Sadie caught a glimpse of disappointment in Sara's eyes flash before she shot them both a smile. "Sounds great to me."

Sadie chuckled inwardly. Apparently, touring an old mine didn't rank quite as high as hanging out with a film crew.

Fifteen minutes later, with all of the props and costumes tucked away in the house for safekeeping, Sadie ducked into the narrow, rock passageway that led into the mine, careful to watch her step as she crossed the cart rails running along the horizontal shaft. She shivered behind Greg and Sara, wondering if her chill was as much from the sharp drop in temperature or the thought of what had happened in this very mine a half a century ago.

She'd taken this tour—run by Greg and his employees—but this time she was looking at it from an entirely different light. She could imagine Raymond and Abigail meeting outside these mines, with the Rocky Mountains in the background as they declared their love to each other, and tried to decide what they should do. Until the fatal moment when something had happened to change everything.

"Watch your step, ladies." Greg stopped in an open section of the cavern that was filled with old mining equipment and rubbed his hands together. "Our tunnels are lit by solar panels, but it's still pretty dark in here. Especially when it comes to filming. The crew is bringing in extra lighting, though, which they've assured me will solve that problem."

"It sure is cold in here." Sara brushed up against Sadie.

"True, but you won't find a better air conditioner system. And in the winter, believe it or not, this will seem warm compared to outside." Greg's enthusiasm came through in his voice. "This is the section where we normally do our tours. We also have a place outside down the hill where people can pan for gold."

"Anyone ever find anything?" Sara asked.

"We've had a few small finds over the years." Greg stopped in the middle of a small cavern where there was more space to move around. "Back in the late 1800s, there weren't the big blasts like you might imagine. Instead, they would hand drill in a spiral fashion to bring down the rocks." Greg showed them an example in the wall. "There are tales of men finding deposits of silver the size of a grapefruit. Boys as young as seven earned seventy cents a day as powder monkeys to carry the dynamite into the mine, which, let me tell you, was good money back then."

"Sounds dangerous," Sara said.

"It was. And it was just as dangerous for the miners," Greg continued. "Most miners back then died before they were thirty-five from breathing in the granite dust, which is like glass on the lungs."

"That's awful!" Sara said.

"You don't have to worry about that today. We do regular oxygen checks to ensure they're safe, so you don't need to worry about anything other than watching your step and your head. That and stay out of the tunnels marked with the warning signs. Those areas of the mines aren't safe." Greg hit the beam above him with his fist. "Right here, though, it's solid as a rock."

Greg rushed on with his speech, clearly in his element. "At the height of the silver rush, over a hundred years ago, two brothers arrived from Europe and staked their claim in this very spot. Silver Peak became a boomtown over night, driven by mines like this and the others dotting the area. They built up the town with large, Victorian-style houses, shops for commerce, and even the opera house where the educated brought music and plays to the stage during the long winter months. Silver Peak put itself on the map. Before long, people from all over came to jump on the bandwagon, certain they too would find their fortune. And some of them did. Others, unfortunately—most in fact—ended up leaving with nothing. Which is why—"

The lights above them flickered. Greg paused. Seconds later, Sara screamed next to Sadie as the tunnel plunged into darkness.